Total

Single title

Crude Oil
Beg Me
Down and Dirty
Interlude
Intermission
Four Play
Game On
Swingtime
Party of Three
All Jacked Up
Top or Bottom
Rodeo Heat
Night Heat
Cupid's Shaft
Trouble in Cowboy Boots

Strike Force
Unconditional Surrender
Lock and Load

The Sentinels
The Edge of Morning
Night Moves
Dark Stranger
Animal Instinct
Mated
Silent Hunters

Cat's Eyes
Pretty Kitty
On the Prowl

Corporate Heat
Where Danger Hides
Double Deception
Masquerade

Erector Set
Erected
Hammered
Nailed

Antholgies
Night of the Senses: Carnal Caresses
Christmas Goes Camo: Melting the Ice
Treble: Trouble at the Treble T
Subspace: Head Games
Bound to the Billionaire: Made for Him
Three's a Charm: Double Entry

Collections
Heatwave: Summer Spice
Feral: Black Cat Fever
Clandestine Classics: Northanger Abbey

Strike Force

ADVANCE TO THE REAR

DESIREE HOLT

Advance to the Rear
ISBN # 978-1-78686-390-4
©Copyright Desire Holt 2019
Cover Art by Cherith Vaughan ©Copyright February 2019
Interior text design by Claire Siemaszkiewicz
Totally Bound Publishing

ADVANCE TO THE REAR

Dedication

First and foremost, to Joe Trainor, my favorite deputy, whose knowledge and plotting skills are invaluable as always. To Nikki Strathmann, his significant other, for the use of her name and her knowledge as a nurse. To Margie Hager, beta reader extraordinary and total best friend. And to Maria Connor, the very best VA an author could have, as well as the perfect friend.

Prologue

Marc Blanchard took another swallow of his beer and wondered just how much it would cost to cab or Uber back to Slade's ranch. He supposed he could call Teo, Slade's foreman, but he hated to put someone out just because he had turned into the most antisocial person on the planet. Maybe he could just find a corner to hide in until the party started to break up. See if one of the guys could haul his ass back to the ranch.

Maybe not. It looked like everyone was into this party except him. Slade was all into an intense conversation with a hot woman and seemed oblivious to anything around him. Beau Williams, their Delta Force team's sniper, was being his usual hot-guy self with some people near the bar. And Trey, well, Trey was surfing the crowd, not spending too much time with anyone.

Every square foot of space in the living room, family room and kitchen seemed to be taken up by people who didn't look at all like they'd be moving any time soon.

Fuck.

He should have just been his usual douchebag self, dug in and told Slade he wasn't going to the party unless ordered to. He knew Slade — all the team — was worried about him. Hell, he was worried about himself, too, but he didn't know what to do about it. He'd crawled into a dark place to escape the destructive memories that he lived with and he couldn't seem to free himself of it. The only place he could block them out was on a mission, but hell, they couldn't do that three hundred and sixty-five days without a break.

He dumped his empty bottle in the trashcan next to the bar and plucked a full one from the big cooler by the patio door. He stood for a moment in the open doorway, scanned the patio and, seeing no one, headed for a bench in the far corner. He sat with his back to the house, blocking out light and sound and wrapping himself in the familiar cloak of misery.

He took a swallow of beer and stared at the thick trees in the back yard. Maybe he could hang himself from one of them.

Okay, asshole, enough with the self-pity.

Jesus. He was getting so he couldn't even stand himself. If he could just bleach that picture of Ria, high on cocaine and tumbling naked in bed with their next-door neighbor, maybe he could find a way to get on with his life. But it seemed the image was burned into his brain.

Everyone had told him to back away from her. Slade Donovan, his team leader, was always right on the money. Too fucking bad he hadn't listened to him. It certainly showed how bad his judgment sucked. As devastating as the marriage had been, the divorce hadn't been any better. She had tracked him down between missions and caused scenes so outrageous and embarrassing he'd finally had to have her arrested.

Thank the lord he had a tough attorney who had taken care of everything so he didn't even have to go to court.

But since then he just hadn't been able to pull himself out of that hole he crawled into between missions. Which again made him question why the hell he had allowed himself to be talked into coming to this party. Did his teammates think sticking him in a social situation would be some kind of miraculous cure? Or did they worry that if they left him alone he might think suicide wasn't a bad choice?

He sighed and tried to figure out the best way to slide out of tonight's situation without putting up with a whole raft of shit from his teammates. A strange noise coming out of the darkness pierced the edge of his consciousness. At first, he thought it was an animal, like maybe a cat, that had gotten itself up a tree or something. But then he realized it was the sound of someone crying. *What the hell?*

Setting his beer bottle on a nearby table, he stepped off the patio and headed into the little copse. He hadn't gone five steps before he nearly tripped over a female sitting on the ground, leaning against a tree. And doing her best to contain the sobs that were shaking her body.

Oh, fucking swell. Just what he needed.

But all the misery he'd suffered hadn't wiped away his sense of decency so, sighing, he crouched beside her.

"Is there something I can help you with?"

He tried to get a good look at her, but the lights didn't reach this far and tonight there wasn't a damned star in the sky. All he could make out was long blonde hair covering her head like a shroud because she was bent over, her face buried in her hands. For all he knew, she could be someone's kid out here having a meltdown.

"Hello?" He touched her arm, just a brush of his fingertips. "Can I do anything for you?"

She just shook her head, her body continuing to shudder with her quiet sobbing.

Well, there was no damned way he was just walking off and leaving her.

Come on, asshole. Figure out what to do.

Being as gentle as possible, he pried her hands away from her face and brushed the smooth thickness of her hair back. When she raised her face to him, he felt like an elephant had kicked him in the stomach. Her eyes might have been swollen from crying and her cheek stained with rivers of tears, but this was no kid. This was a woman with such simple, classical beauty that it stunned him. It was hard to make out details, but he didn't miss the thick lashes that sparkled with her tears, or the full, sensuous lips.

"Come on," he urged. "Let's get you off this ground. I think we can find a better place for you to sit."

She resisted at first, then gave in to the pressure of his hands helping her to rise. When she was standing he realized she was taller than he'd thought, only a couple of inches shorter than he was, and slender. Something about her attitude gave her the appearance of being much smaller

"I don't want to go back inside." The words were little more than a whisper.

"Yeah? Well, guess what? Neither do I. But let's go sit on that bench over there. We'll be out of everyone's glide path."

What the hell am I doing? The last thing I need to do is to help a woman falling apart. I can hardly help myself.

Cursing himself under his breath, he guided her over to the bench and sat them both down so they faced away from the house. When she lifted her hands to her face again and started to lean forward, he brushed back the thick curtain of silken hair that obscured her face. Then he tucked the tip of a finger beneath her chin and tilted it upward.

Shit!

Big mistake. Huge mistake.

There was enough ambient light that he could see the high cheekbones, full lips and slightly pointed chin. But what slayed him were the eyes, a stormy gray that were filled with so much misery that his cold, hardened heart turned over. The pain radiating from her was so visceral he could feel it.

He paused. "Um, not trying to stick my nose in your business, but maybe if you share what's causing you so much misery, it will help."

She looked at him as if he was crazy. Then she sighed, one that seemed to come from deep inside her.

Whatever this was, he'd figure out what to say to get her through the next few minutes. He'd bet his misery won over hers.

"I killed my fiancé."

Her tone was soft, faint, but the words went through him like a rifle shot. How was that possible? She was so small, and nothing about her shrieked *killer.* He took a breath to gather his thoughts together and make sure whatever he said did not come out in an accusing voice.

"I hear you, but somehow I don't think that's right. I can't see you deliberately taking someone's life. So what really happened?"

Again she was silent and the moment stretched out. He wanted to repeat the question, even as a chaotic tumble of thoughts bounced around in his brain.

Then she sighed. "He was so sick and I couldn't save him."

Okay, it was official. She won the 'lowest point in life' contest. He felt like the biggest piece of shit. The pain edging her words was so sharp that for a moment he forgot to breathe.

Well, asshole, don't just sit there.

He dug around in what was left of his brain for some kind of appropriate remark. Something that would not make him look any stupider that he felt.

"I'm sure you've had a lot of people tell you that's probably not true."

Teas rolled down her cheeks, more poignant because she made no sound at all, just shook her head.

"No, they didn't? I can't believe that."

She grabbed his free hand and squeezed it so hard he was sure she left fingerprints on the skin.

"It doesn't matter." She said the words in a toneless voice. "Nothing matters."

He had let himself become such a hot mess that he'd lost all his people skills. This was going to be a real challenge.

I'm not a human being anymore.

He wanted to shoot the words at her, but instead he pulled out his clean handkerchief and blotted her cheeks.

"I'm a totally neutral person, right? So how about telling me why you think it's your fault? I'll bet I can give you an objective opinion." Assuming he even knew what that was any more.

She sat there for so long he began to wonder if she'd changed her mind and just clammed up.

"He came down with a terrible disease." She recited the words without inflection. "I was his nurse, taking care of him. And he died."

Okay, so he didn't know what to say. He lifted the hand digging furrows in his and held it between two of his.

"I'm sure there's a lot more to it than that. But you don't have to tell me anything you don't feel comfortable with." He paused. "Except your name. How about that?"

More silence.

"Nikki. Cynthia Nicole Alvarez, but everyone calls me Nikki."

"A perfect name for you. Hi, Nikki Alvarez. I'm Marc Blanchard."

She looked at him and a hint of a smile lifted up the corners of her mouth, "Hi, Marc Blanchard. I'll bet you're kicking yourself for coming to rescue me in my puddle of tears instead of partying inside."

"No, not in the least." He shook his head. "I'm not much of a party animal anymore."

She lifted a delicate eyebrow. "Anymore? Is there a story there?"

Oh, yeah. There's a big story. But I sure don't want to talk about it tonight.

"A long one and not for tonight. So, are you friends of the people throwing this party?"

She shook her head. "Some of my friends threatened me with bodily harm if I didn't show up at least for a little while."

He snorted. "We sure have that in common."

She studied his face. "You, too?"

"Uh-huh. It was easier to come along with them than spend an hour arguing. Listen, I'd ask you to go get a cup of coffee with me except I don't have any wheels."

She frowned. "Then how did you get here?"

"Slade Donovan drove. He's our team leader. We're visiting him at his ranch for a few days. But he reconnected with someone at the party and I have no idea what the other two guys are doing."

"Team leader?"

"Uh, yeah." *Shit.* He wasn't supposed to just broadcast his Delta Force situation to the world. "We're in the Army together."

"Oh."

Nikki drew in her eyebrows and nibbled on her lower lip. Marc had to clench his jaw because, for the first time since his life had gone down the toilet, he had the desire to kiss someone. He wanted to lick that plump little lip with his tongue.

For fuck's sake.

"Don't worry about it," he said at last. "It was just an idea. You don't know who the hell I am, anyway, so it's probably a bad idea."

More nibbles on the lip. *Holy shit.*

"Um, I have a car here. I came by myself because I didn't know if I'd want to stay. Like I said, my friends bullied me into it."

"Yeah?" He chuckled. And hell, how long was it since the last time he'd laughed? "Like I said, me, too."

Again she almost smiled.

"Aren't we just the big party animals." She paused and did that thing with her lip again. "Um, I don't usually do this, but, um, I feel like I can trust you. Weird, huh? Maybe it's because you're military and the military is such a big presence here in San Antonio. But if you're serious about that cup of coffee, that sounds nice. And I could take you home afterward."

"Nikki." He chuffed a laugh. "It's a forty-five-minute drive from here."

She lifted her shoulders in a delicate shrug. "I have no place to go or to be."

From somewhere he found a smile, so foreign to him he wondered if his lips would crack. He had to be crazy for doing this. This woman was carrying a huge emotional burden and he was so fucked-up he couldn't handle his own feelings, forget about someone else's.

But she looked so sad, so bruised, he couldn't just get up and walk away from her. Besides, where the hell would he go? He was trapped at this party. If Trey and Beau hooked up with some females, Teo would have to haul ass to the city to fetch him.

She shifted a tiny bit so there was no contact between their bodies.

"It's okay," she assured him. "I tend to drive everyone away these days anyway. I didn't mean to dump all this on you."

Good going, asshole. Very smooth.

"It's not that," he began.

She waved a hand in the air. "No problem. And you don't need to assure me it's not me because I know it is. All is good."

But that was a big fat lie and he knew it. Did he have the stones to pull his head out of his ass and think of someone else for a change? He reached for her hand, closing his fingers around it when she tried to pull it away.

"But coming from me it's I promise it's not a lie. You have no idea what a fucked-up mess I am." *And isn't that just* the truth.

"It's okay," she repeated. "Besides, there's no way you could be a bigger hot mess than me."

He laughed, a soft sound and so foreign to him at first he wasn't sure what it was. "Maybe we should go get that coffee and compare."

"As long as we don't have to go through the house."

"No problem." He pulled out his cell phone and typed a text to Trey.

Getting a ride home. All is good.

He showed the text to Nikki. "If you're still up for it?" he asked. He really ought to tell her to run as fast as she could in the other direction.

"Yes. I am."

Marc's phone dinged with the reply from Trey.

R U OK?

Yes. Don't worry. Not suicidal.

Nikki stared at him. "Why did you write that?"

"Long story. One I don't talk about."

"Not even over coffee?" she asked.

"We'll see." But he knew he wasn't about to dump his shit all over her. He didn't want her to know just how much of an idiot he was.

His phone dinged again.

Call if you need me.

Nikki glanced up at him, a questioning look in her eyes. "They must really be worried about you."

"Yeah. Stupid stuff on my part." He shoved the phone back into his pocket. "I'm ready to leave if you are."

"If you're sure."

"I am. Yes." And strange to say, he was. He took her hand and pulled her to her feet. "Lead on to your chariot."

They circled around the house through the back yard and out to the street. About three blocks from the house, she stopped beside a silver hatchback.

"It's pretty plain vanilla." Her voice held an apologetic tone.

"I like plain vanilla," he assured her. "You always know what you're getting."

The words hit him like a punch to the solar plexus as he realized the truth of them. He *did* like plain vanilla. Ria, the fancy sundae with many flavors, had tempted him with her exotic makeup. But now he wondered if their marriage had lasted any longer, would he have gotten tired of her? A guy couldn't depend on exotic, a lesson he learned the hard way. For the first time since that gut-wrenching day he'd discovered the truth about his wife, the bands around his chest loosened.

Oh, he wasn't fooling himself that meeting an emotionally anguished Nikki Alvarez was a sudden cure. He had been broken for so long he wasn't even sure he was fixable. But he told himself to pull his frayed edges together and think about somebody but himself for a change. After all, the worst thing he'd done was make a bad choice, a massive case of rampant stupidity. He was nowhere ready to take all that out into the light and give it a hard look. Maybe, though, he could put it aside for a couple of hours and help someone else. He had to admit, with great reluctance, that a person losing someone they loved to death and feeling they were to blame was a lot worse than feeling sorry for himself because he'd married a promiscuous drug-addicted tramp. At least for this moment, he was looking forward instead of backward.

He opened the door on the passenger side. "It's your city, so you'd better drive. Is there some place not very fancy that you can get a real cup of coffee?"

"I know just the place."

She hesitated a second before opening her door, and he wondered if she'd had a change of heart. Then she climbed in and motioned him to do the same. As he settled himself in the seat, he closed his eyes for a moment to gather his wits about him. This was just coffee. With someone who needed a person to talk to. And he sure knew that so much of the time a stranger was better than a friend.

He was just so out of practice. Hell, he hardly even talked to his teammates any more. Maybe this was a step forward for him, too.

Don't fuck this up.

Chapter One

One thing you can say about Niger, Marc Blanchard thought, *it's fucking hot. And full of sand, with a wind that blows it everywhere.* He gave thanks regularly that they didn't have to wear full battle rattle every day. It was bad enough that it got into every fold of the clothing he was wearing for this op. And his ears. And his teeth. And worst of all, his jockey shorts. He'd decided there weren't too many things worse than constant sand in his crotch. He almost longed for the mountains of Afghanistan. Of course, there he was always freezing his balls off.

It figured they'd be sent here at the height of summer, when on an average day a person could be boiled alive by the temperature. Even the heavy rains couldn't cool it off, so sometimes the guys were hot, and sometimes hot and wet. *Wonderful.* Of course, he never complained. Neither did any of the other three men on his Delta Force team. They just accepted their assignments, prepped for them and did the deed. They were in the furnace-like climate of Niger to do what Delta force did best—rescue hostages.

Niger had in recent months become a hotbed of activity. According to the briefing they'd received, the group's current leader, Adnan Abu Walid-Sahrawi, had broken from an established al-Qaeda group and pledged allegiance to ISIS and its leader, Abu Bakr al-Baghdadi. A spate of kidnappings had occurred, with hostages taken. The country of origin would then demand ransom, which most of the time was paid.

Welcome to Agadez, Marc thought, climbing into the body of a produce delivery truck. Once upon a time, caravans had delivered gold and salt to this town in the desert. Now it was a major trading post for arms, drugs and the most widely traded commodity—humans.

Now two of them, American humanitarian aid workers, had been captured. If this followed the established pattern, a ransom demand would arrive shortly. Of course, there was no guarantee that if it was paid, the workers would be released unharmed. And in this situation, unharmed was an amorphous figure of speech. Uncle Sam had said, *'Go get them and bring them home. Period.'* Which was why Marc's Delta force team, led by Slade Donovan, was enjoying the furnace-like climate of this landlocked North African country, bouncing along in a battered fruit truck at least twenty years old on roads mostly made of dirt.

On the surface, the mission sounded simple. Get to Agadez, hide while they scoped out the situation, find out where ISIS was holding the aid workers captive and rescue them. *Right. Just another day at the office for this Delta Force team.*

But they also had a secondary mission, one not so easy to complete. DHS had learned of a camp in northern Mexico that trained terrorists in everything from ways to kill to how to make bombs. Word had come down that this particular ISIS group was smuggling terrorists into the States over the Mexican border from that camp. That they'd painted a target on a spot somewhere in Texas and a team would shortly be sneaking in to accomplish the assignment. *Well, Texas is a fucking big state, so good luck with that.*

While they'd been waiting to complete their mission, Slade had questioned Ibrahim, their local contact, about it. The man had told him he'd heard rumors about it. He also cautioned that ISIS had a tendency to brag about things, considering themselves invincible. But he wasn't sure if the person supposedly spearheading it was still here or had moved on. Or even if it was just a figment of someone's imagination.

Ibrahim had his best to get them a name or names, or any piece of information but had come up empty. *'No one is saying a word,'* he'd told the team. *'Not surprising, my friend. They are too afraid someone will find out and kill them and their families.'*

Crap. That wasn't what the brass would want to hear.

Okay, Blanchard. Put that aside for the moment. It's on Slade's list, anyway. Concentrate on this mission.

Earlier tonight, an hour after full dark, an MH-60 M Black Hawk helicopter—flown by a Night Stalker, a member of SOAR—Special Operations Aviation Regiment—had dropped them in a carefully selected place outside of Agadez. Ibrahim had met them in this battered produce delivery truck and now was taking them to a house on the outskirts of the city.

They were hidden in the back of the truck, behind the boxes used to deliver vegetables and fruit from the community gardens. Ibrahim's job had proved a boon to Special Forces and others who needed insertion into the area. In a country deprived of enough food to feed most people three meals a day, no one questioned or disturbed the delivery of produce to families unable to get to the marketplace. The aroma of the fruits and vegetables was overpowering and the bed of the truck harder than concrete, but none of them complained. They'd been in worse situations before.

There wasn't a lot of room for four big men behind the produce, but they were used to adapting. Somehow they managed to fit themselves in along with their gear and their weapons. Marc, Slade and Trey each carried the favored Colt M4 carbine. Beau, their sniper, cradled his own personal choice, the Heckler and Koch MP5. Driving through the streets of Agadez, Marc knew they could be stopped at any time for any reason. Or no reason at all. Even with the produce as camouflage, some irrational radical could order Ibrahim to offload the truck to check it all out. So they sat with their fingers close to the triggers, waiting.

Sequestered in the confines of the cargo body of the truck, they saw nothing on the trip, could only feel the constant jolting as the truck passed over uneven roads. Every so often they stopped, and Marc knew the others, like him, would be prepared to do whatever was required to keep the mission going. But fuck it all, it would be nice if it didn't all go to hell before they got to Ibrahim's.

The truck came to an abrupt stop and Marc figured they'd reached their destination. The rear doors of the cargo area opened and Ibrahim moved enough cartons of produce that they could get to the tailgate and jump down. Marc knew the others had to be as glad as he was to get out of this enclosed space filled with the cloying, lingering aroma of the cargo it carried each day.

They were in a courtyard of some kind, surrounded by walls of the mud bricks he knew were used to construct every building in Agadez. It was pitch dark, not even a star in the sky. For a very brief moment, Marc relived another starless night and the woman he'd met who'd been falling apart piece by piece. Then he shut down everything in his mind except this mission.

The walls surrounding the courtyard were solid clay, no peep holes or anything. He had a feeling there was another house on either side. When they'd looked at photos of the city during the briefing, they'd seen a rabbit warren of clay houses jammed together, built in a circle with the giant tower of a mosque at dead center. Everything except the mosque was the dead, dull tan of the clay used in building.

Ibrahim stacked the produce back in the truck then hustled them into the house with their guns and their gear. The place was threadbare and sparsely furnished. The dust of the area seemed to have settled everywhere, yet no one appeared to notice. Marc would bet a month's combat pay that the bulk of the wealth, such as it was, resided with the core of the ISIS leadership.

A woman he assumed was Ibrahim's wife bowed to them as Ibrahim shoved and pushed them into a room at the back of the house. It was small and quite empty.

"My cousin used to live with us." Ibrahim spoke the words in a short, clipped sentence.

Marc could guess that whatever had happened to that cousin wasn't good.

Slade thanked the man for his hospitality and the four of them sat on the dirt floor, legs stretched out and weapons cradled in their laps.

"You will have some tea," Ibrahim said, bowing. "And food."

They all had their ration kits in the packs they carried, but Marc knew it would be an insult to Ibrahim to refuse his offering. Whatever it consisted of. When he looked at Slade, the team leader dipped his head a fraction.

There was a lot of whispering in another room between Ibrahim and his wife. Then Ibrahim poked his head back into the room. "Food coming soon."

Marc looked over at Slade, and spoke while barely moving his lips. "We need a sitrep. Where the hostages are being held. How many guards there are."

"Ibrahim's not going to discuss it while his wife is in the room. I'm going to remind him time's fleeting and we need details right now. As in yesterday."

They all sat very still, looking relaxed but ready to act at any moment if the need arose. Five minutes passed. Ten. Then Ibrahim scuttled back into the room, followed by his wife, her head down. She carried a metal tray holding four bowls of something. Still with eyes averted, she distributed them to the members of the team.

"Rice with sauce," Ibrahim told them. "It's good. Eat, eat."

They accepted the food, but as soon as the woman had left the room, Slade motioned Ibrahim to come closer.

"Thanks for this, but time is critical. We need to know where the workers are being held and to scope out the situation. Plan what we have to do."

Ibrahim nodded and bowed twice.

"Please eat while everyone goes to bed. Then talk."

They ate in silence and, if previous missions had told Marc anything, each running through in his head what they knew so far. The United States was building a very expensive drone base just outside Agadez. In fact, the military had sent a Predator drone to survey the area, so they had a fixed image of the terrorist camp just beyond the city limits. Agadez had morphed from being a caravan nexus to being a hub for smuggling people out of the country.

Hostages taken in Niger were usually transported through the desert and across the border to Mali, where terrorism was more prevalent and hostage imprisonment easier to control. From the drone recordings and Ibrahim's feedback, they knew the hostages were still here, but the window of opportunity to free them was closing.

By the time they'd all finished their servings, Ibrahim was back in the room. He sat in the middle of the floor and motioned the team to gather around him.

"We are here." He drew a diagram in the sand of the floor. "And the hostages are here." More diagrams. "Just as the pictures on the drone showed you."

Slade studied the layout. "Which building are the hostages in?"

"Right here." Ibrahim pointed with his stick. "These members of ISIS have confiscated these four houses. They did some restructuring for their purposes, creating interconnecting passages so they could sneak people in and out. This works in our favor."

Marc knew exactly what 'confiscated' meant. He wondered how many people had been killed when those members of ISIS had grabbed the houses for themselves.

"How many tangoes?" Beau asked.

Ibrahim sighed. "That is where the problem is. There are at least a dozen. They will not all be in the room with the hostages."

"Can you guess how many in that room?" Slade asked.

"No more than two."

"Then it's the others we need to deal with. Ibrahim, we need a distraction to cover our entrance into the house and also draw as many of them as possible out through the front. And we need to time it."

Ibrahim nodded. "I can arrange that." He explained what he could do then sketched out the best place for it. "Will that work?"

"Yes." Slade nodded. "Can you also get a transport vehicle besides the produce truck?"

The other man nodded again. "My cousin has a van. It is pretty beat up, but…" He shrugged. "It runs."

"That's all we need. It has to get us out of town and to the extraction point. Will he give you trouble if you ask to borrow it?"

"No. He uses my truck sometimes. We help each other." His face turned hard as stone. "And we don't ask each other any questions."

Marc wondered what had prompted Ibrahim and his cousin to do whatever they did in their own war with ISIS. They had to know discovery was always imminent and the results wouldn't be pretty.

As if he'd read his mind, Ibrahim turned to look at him. "We have paid dearly because of ISIS. Any little thing we can do to help in the fight against them is an honor."

Marc could see Slade knew better than to ask anything else. Ibrahim's face was stone cold but there was a wealth of misery in his eyes.

Slade looked at each member of the team. "Okay, here's the plan. We'll stay here at Ibrahim's until it's full dark, then head to the house on foot. We'll have one chance to do this, so let's not fuck it up."

Marc knew the plan was chancy, but so was everything else they did. Besides, it wasn't like they had a choice.

"When do you want me to call for extraction? What's our zero hour?"

As the comms man on the team, it was his responsibility to maintain communication with the brass at the Forward Operating Base and to let them know when they needed the pickup.

"Tell them our target time for extraction is twenty-two hundred. We'll confirm one hour before."

"Is that enough time for the Night Stalker to get here?" Marc asked.

"Yes. But remember. Every bit of this is split-second timing and things can go wrong at any point in this op."

Beau gave a short laugh. "Just like all our missions, yeah?"

"That's right." He allowed himself a tiny chuckle. "Nothing new here, right?" He looked back at the diagram. "Let's go over this once more."

By the time they looked at it and discussed it six ways from Sunday, each man had the diagram etched in his brain. Marc knew how important that was. Once the op began, there would be no margin for error. They couldn't control outside activities, which had fucked up their planning more than once. But knowing every detail allowed them to adjust for those circumstances.

Ibrahim brought them tea and rice shortly after dawn. After that they took turns napping, knowing they needed to be fully alert for the night ahead. By the time it was full dark again, they were more than ready. Marc had radioed the extraction information and Ibrahim's cousin had agreed to provide a distraction, something that would draw the attention of the terrorists away from their little compound.

Ibrahim was gone for an hour while he worked out the details with his cousin. When he returned, he was driving a sorry-looking panel van. Marc didn't care, nor did the others, as long as it got them to where they were going.

Then it was time.

Ibrahim had provided all the members of the team with boubous, the long, flowing robes many of the men wore, and geles, headdresses with ends that could be wrapped around the face so only the eyes showed. Beneath them they wore their desert fatigues and all their gear. But their weapons were arranged beneath the voluminous fabric for quick access and execution. It was crucial that they blended in with other men heading home at that hour, but mission critical that their weapons be instantly ready.

Worried about being out in the open, they took their time snaking between houses and along the streets. Blending in with others on foot, they made their way to the destination. Marc thought it was a good thing they'd spent so much time memorizing the route because every damn fucking house looked like every other. While the others took their places behind the building, Beau climbed to the flat roof of a house across from them, stretched out and sighted his rifle, which was fitted with a suppressor. Marc had seen him like that so many times he could imagine it now. The planned diversion should draw at least one of the terrorists outside and Beau could pick him off, and anyone who followed him.

They passed by the rear of the target house, not wanting to risk the terrorists spotting them before things got hot and hairy. Trey paused only a moment to press a small amount of Semtex against the rear door. They stood in darkness, waiting for their signal to move. Marc checked his watch, then began silently counting down in his head, just as he knew the others were.

Bang!

The explosion two streets over erupted in the night air. At the same moment, Slade detonated the small amount of Semtex on the back door and blew it open, the sound barely seconds behind it. Then they were in the rear room of the house, a room as barren as the one at Ibrahim's. The two hostages, a man and a woman, huddled together in a corner, looking both terrified and bewildered. Both appeared disheveled and each of them sported bruises on their arms and their faces.

Bile rose in Marc's throat, as it always did when he saw how human beings had been unnecessarily abused. Once out of here and back at the FOB, they'd get proper attention. Right now, though, the only focus was getting the fuck out of here.

This was always the hairiest part. They had scant seconds to pull it off. Slade held up a finger to his lips to signal silence, then mouthed "*US Army.*" He and Marc pulled the hostages out through the back door, silent as ghosts. Trey had his gun out, ready to hit anyone who came through the door from the front of the house, and Beau was set to take his shots from his position on the roof. In seconds, they were all out in the alley behind the house where Ibrahim, good as his word, now waited in his cousin's van. Seconds later, they were all inside. Down the narrow street and around the corner. They stopped only long enough for Ibrahim to get out and melt away. If he was caught driving them, he and his family would be annihilated.

Then Slade took over and they headed hell for leather out of town.

The hostages sat silent and petrified in the middle seat, sandwiched between Trey and Marc. They clung to each other as if that contact was their only salvation.

"I know you can't figure out what's happening," Trey said, his voice soothing. "All you have to know is you are with American soldiers and in less than thirty minutes we'll all be out of here."

Still neither of them spoke. Marc could imagine the treatment they'd suffered, the way their captors had terrorized them. But at least they weren't screaming and trying to run away from the team, or doing anything else to hinder their departure. Beyond a cursory examination to make sure the two were mobile and didn't need to be carried, the team had not questioned them.

"Still all clear back here," Beau said from the third seat. He was on his knees, his rifle pointing out of the window of the rear hatch door.

Marc knew he had one order to execute. If anyone came up behind them, shoot and keep shooting. Marc kept checking his watch, counting down to when the Night Stalker would be there. So far so good. They were out in the desert now, the driving slow going through the sand.

They were almost at the extraction point when Beau hollered back to them.

"Enemy vehicle on the horizon. Right on our tail."

The MH-60 M Black Hawk zoomed in and hovered just past the van, skillfully handled by its Night Stalker pilot. Marc helped hustle the aid workers out of the van and into the chopper, handing them up to the two men crouched in the open doorway. Sand kicked up everywhere from the rotors, even getting into their eyes and teeth.

Beau was the last one in, crouched in the open doorway, positioned with his gun. Just as they lifted off, the four-wheel drive vehicle made it to the outskirts of Agadez and came plowing through the sand. The man riding in the rear began firing the vehicle-mounted machine gun while two others climbed out and started firing assault weapons at the chopper.

The pilot banked to the left, away from the line of fire, even as Beau fired steadily at the men below. Then they were out of range, rising higher until the desert was far below them.

Beau tumbled back into the cabin and Marc moved out of his way. Trey, their team medic as well as Beau's spotter, was checking over the aid workers, giving them a cursory look to see if they needed medical attention at once. There were no seats in the cabin of the helo, so they sat on the floor, still looking traumatized but otherwise unharmed.

Marc sat back, leaning against the metal of the cabin wall, coming down from the adrenaline high he found himself on after every mission. Usually he just switched off, separating himself mentally from the team, and made his mind a blank. Today his mind was doing its own thing, with pictures of a petite doe-eyed blonde nurse flashing one after the other like a continuous slide show.

The feeling was so weird. He couldn't remember the last time he'd had pleasant images of a female running through his brain. Usually he tried to blank everything out, not leave himself vulnerable to the soul-scorching image of Ria, high as a kite, naked, sprawled beneath their neighbor as he pounded into her.

Today, he didn't think he could call it up even if he tried.

Instead there was Nikki, with her gentle touch and her soft voice and the anguish always lurking in her eyes. He had seen her twice more before the team had left Texas for this mission. Teo had given him the keys to the ranch truck. Slade was camped out with his lady, Beau had found himself a woman to hang with and Trey was…off doing something. *Thank god for that.* There was no one to question him and Teo swore his lip was zipped.

His mind drifted back to that last night in Nikki's apartment.

Although he'd spent two nights with her, they had not had sex. As a matter of fact, they'd both seemed to shy away from it, as if taking that step would bring them into a relationship neither of them was sure they were ready for. Talking consumed all their time together. She'd told him all about her fiancé and, in the predawn hours one morning, he'd finally blurted out the details of his disastrous marriage. They had both dumped their personal hell on the table and neither had run screaming into the dawning day.

But then…

He'd leaned back against the arm of the couch, a beer bottle loosely held in the fingers of one hand. He'd been awed at the easy way they were able to talk to each other. For the first time since the disastrous blowup of his marriage he was able to speak about it in detail and see where he should have paid more attention.

Nikki just made talking so easy. No pressure. No censure. No criticism.

He couldn't believe he'd had two overnights with a woman and sex hadn't even come into the picture. Not that he didn't find her attractive. On the contrary, the curves of her body begged for his hands to trace their lines. Her mouth, so soft and full, had *kiss me* written all over them. But he was so damn out of practice. The only partner he'd had in two years was his right hand, and that couldn't be called sex even on its best day.

But sitting on the couch with her next to him, knees drawn up and hands clasped around them, he'd wanted nothing more than to run his hands over her and see if she felt as soft as she looked. Tasted as good as she smelled, the soft scent of jasmine she wore so incredibly tempting.

Before he'd realized what he was doing, he'd set his empty bottle on the side table, reached out and taken one of her hands. At first, she'd started to tug her hand away, but then, for whatever reason, she'd stopped and linked her fingers with his. Heat unlike anything he'd felt in a very long time had zapped his body, making his nerve endings sizzle and his cock jump to attention. *Yes, jump.*

Down, boy!

'*This is nice,*' he'd said at last. '*Just sitting here like this with you.*'

'*Yes. It is.*'

She'd wet her bottom lip with the tip of her tongue, and it had been all he could do to restrain himself. Where the hell had all this come from? Up until this week, a five-star beauty queen could have danced naked in front of him and it wouldn't have elicited a physical response.

Of course, five-star beauty queens didn't do it for him. Not anymore, anyway.

He'd debated with himself whether to make a move, afraid he'd destroy the fragile relationship they seemed to be building. *Would I even know what to do after all this time?*

He'd given a tentative tug on her hand. If she'd pulled her hand away, he'd stick to conversation. But if she'd leaned toward him…

She'd moved, shifting her body so she was now leaning into him in the curve of one arm. God, she'd felt so good against him. Placing two fingers beneath her chin, he'd tilted her face up to him.

'Fair warning,' he'd told her. *'I'm going to kiss you, Now's the time to tell me to get lost if that's not what you want.'*

Although conflicting emotions had swirled in the smoky gray of her eyes, she hadn't moved away. He'd lowered his mouth to hers, brushing against the velvet surface. The surge of electricity that had powered through him had consumed his body. When he'd stroked her lips with his tongue, a soft moan had drifted from her throat. Encouraged, he'd pressed his tongue harder until she'd opened for him and he could slide inside.

Holy fucking shit!

This kiss had electrified him more than full-out sex with other women. He'd probed, licked, teased, and her small tongue had answered. He'd taken it slow, not wanting to spook her, holding her head in place so he could plunder her mouth at will.

When he'd lifted his head at last, looking into her eyes to read her expression, he'd been stunned at the heat flaring there.

'Nikki?'

'I-I know. I was sure I'd never respond to anyone ever again in my life.'

'I have to touch you, but understand at any moment you can tell me to stop and I will.'

She'd run that sexy pink tongue over her bottom lip again and once more his cock had sent him an urgent message.

Pressing his mouth to hers again, he'd slid a tentative hand down her back, easing it beneath the soft material of her sweater. He'd caressed her satiny skin just beneath her bra, half-lost in the kiss, half on edge waiting for her to push him away. When she hadn't, he'd moved his hand to cradle one breast in his palm and...*holy shit!* Her nipple had been rock-hard, poking at the silky fabric.

He'd lifted his mouth from hers and slid his lips along the line of her jaw to just beneath her ear. Nibbling the lobe, he'd pinched the pebbled tip of one breast, heat rushing through him as she'd gasped and arched to press more fully against his touch.

He'd fumbled slightly as he unhooked her bra and loosened it. A tiny sound had escaped her mouth and he'd paused, wondering if he'd gone too far. But then she'd nipped his jaw and licked the spot where her teeth had been and need had flooded him. He'd palmed the bare flesh of her firm breasts, squeezing it and stroking the tip with his thumb.

Unable to help himself, he'd tugged up her sweater to give him better access and taken the tip of her breast in his mouth. When he'd sucked it hard, Nikki had moaned and arched into his touch. Emboldened, he'd slipped his hand down over her warm abdomen and flipped open the button on her jeans, then slid down the zipper. Still holding her against him with his other arm, he'd eased his hand low between her thighs until he'd reached her sex and the silky fabric covering it. Pushing the fabric aside, he'd moved his idle finger between the swollen lips, aroused even more to feel how wet she was.

'If you want me to stop, tell me now.' He'd almost growled the words.

'No.' Her breath had been a soft whisper as she'd hummed the word.

'No what?' He'd had to be sure.

'No, don't stop. Please.'

He'd strummed her clit with the tip of his finger, holding her against him. Her soft little moans had aroused him to the point where the press of his shaft against his fly had been almost painful. The more he'd stroked, the wetter she'd become. He'd slipped two fingers inside her and she'd clamped down on them at once, riding them with short, jerky movements.

He'd captured her mouth again and pinched one nipple at the same time. Hard. She'd gripped him with her inner walls, pushed down on his fingers and come apart. Her inner muscles had clenched and released, her body had strained against his, and he'd captured her moans with his mouth.

The spasms had subsided, but Marc had kept his fingers inside the heat of her sex, stroking them in and out, until she'd gone limp in his arms. Marc had eased his fingers from her body and very deliberately licked each one until he'd swallowed every drop of her delicious cream.

Limp then, she'd relaxed against him in the cradle of his arms, pressing her face to his chest. Marc had stroked her back, sprinkling gentle kisses on her face, wondering if he should say something or let her take the lead. He'd had plenty of sex in his life but there had been something almost mystical about this, even if his own needs had been shoved into the closet.

At last she'd stirred and with a deep sigh had pushed away from him. Marc hadn't wanted to let her go, but he hadn't wanted to hold her against her will either. *Is she sorry? Does she regret this? Does she want me to leave right away?*

She'd looked up at him, her eyes still slumberous. Her lips had curved in a tentative smile.

'I, uh, haven't done anything like this in a long time.'

He'd chuffed a short laugh. *'Me neither.'* He'd stroked her cheek. *'But I'm not sorry. Are you?'* He'd held his breath, waiting for her answer.

She'd shaken her head. *'No. Not even a little.'* She'd nibbled her lower lip, a gesture that made him even harder, if that was possible. *'I'm sure it's obvious but in case it's not, you might as well know now I haven't been with…a lot of men. Before Jon, there were only a couple. Then I was with him for a long time. I can't imagine what you must think.'*

'I think you're a woman who is passionate and giving and that passion's been buried for a long time. And' —he'd held up a hand as she opened her mouth— *'I think I'm a lucky bastard that I'm the one you choose to let your guard down with.'*

'I haven't —'

He'd shaken his head. *'Not done. I don't want just some quickie on the couch with you, Nikki.'* He'd blown out a breath. *'Jesus. I haven't had honest to god sex for so long I'm not sure I remember how to do it.'*

She'd giggled. *'Me, neither.'*

'But I want to. With you.' He'd hesitated. *'If you want to, that is.'*

This time she'd laughed for real. *'Look at us. You'd think we were too horny teenagers trying to act like adults. And you got nothing out of this tonight. I got all the pleasure.'*

'Making you feel good was enough pleasure for me. Besides, I don't have any condoms with me. I stopped carrying them the day I got divorced.'

'Well, I don't have any, either. Haven't kept them for a long time.'

He'd shaken his head. *'This will never do. Listen, tomorrow I have to leave again for another mission. But when I get back, we're going to see where this goes. For real. Okay?'*

He'd held his breath when she'd just sat there for a moment. Then she'd nodded.

'Okay,' she'd told him in a soft voice. *'I'd like that.'*

Marc swallowed a smile as the scene replayed in his head. For the first time since he'd crawled into his black hole, he was actually looking forward to the company of a woman. He'd check with Slade and see when they were up next. Maybe Nikki could get some time off and they could get away somewhere. Someplace isolated and secluded, where it would just be the two of them and a chance to see if what they had was the beginning of something good.

God, how he'd wanted to bury himself in her wet heat. Feel her clench around his cock rather than his fingers. But maybe the lack of condoms had been a good thing. They'd gone from zero to sixty with no warm-up. They both needed to make sure this was not a mistake.

He wasn't yet ready to look into the future by any means, but one day at a time? Better than he'd been in a long time.

He just hoped no loose ends from their mission came back to bite them all in the ass.

Chapter Two

Nikki Alvarez tossed her empty coffee cup into the trash and headed to her locker to retrieve her purse. Today had seemed endless, an unusual situation for her. Usually she immersed herself one hundred percent in her patients and their care. ICU was demanding, allowing her to hold on to her sanity and make it from one day to the next. She had tried not to fidget during the change-of-shift report, but she wanted to get home, shower and try to get her collective shit together. She couldn't remember the last time she'd been in a hurry to leave work. At least here she had the security of the familiar and the sense of Jon's continued presence. At home there was only emptiness and the eternal sense of tremendous loss.

But now, for the first time in more than a year, she actually had something to look forward to. Okay, so it was a text, then maybe a call. But she hadn't even had those in what seemed forever, except from her sister, who kept trying to pull her out of her year-long depression. She had shut everyone else out of her life.

No one had been able to understand her guilt and she was tired of trying to explain it. And too often she wondered why they didn't agree with her.

Marc was the first person she'd opened up to. Somehow the whole story had come tumbling out. Jon's illness, which he'd blown off twice as the flu. The night he'd coughed up blood and she'd insisted on taking him to the emergency room. The awful diagnosis of lung cancer, too advanced at that point for surgery. The chemo and radiation that he'd finally insisted on stopping, telling her the pain wasn't worth it.

All those months when she'd continued to work her shifts in ICU and spend the rest of her time in his hospital room. Blaming herself for not insisting he go to the doctor before it became acute. The agony of having watched him die a little at a time, finally only kept alive by drugs and an IV to hydrate him. And the night he'd gone to sleep and never woken up. Every time she remembered it, her heart ached so badly she wanted to cut it out of her body.

For so very long, he'd been the only man in her thoughts, even though he had been gone for more than a year now. Did she feel guilty? Of course, but now that guilt had shifted to a different level. She had met a man who could pull her out of her depression because of his own situation. He didn't rant at her or tell her to get a life. He sympathized and empathized and understood what being in a dark place was like.

Lately, in moments when she was alone, she pulled out the memories of the three nights they'd spent together and analyzed every detail. That first night, the one when they'd met, when he'd practically tripped over her at the Huttons' party, she'd been such an abysmal mess she wondered why he hadn't just run off as fast as he could. There she'd sat, huddled against that tree, blubbering all over herself. He'd been so nice, even gentle with her. She'd figured he'd take a look at what a disaster she was and head back inside, leaving her to her troubles. But he had been sensitive and caring, and had listened for hours while she'd vented all her grief and the blame she shouldered.

When he'd told her the details of his own story, she'd realized she wasn't the only one in a very dark place. She could not imagine having gone through what he had. *What an absolute piece of trash his ex-wife was. He deserves someone so much better. Could that someone be me?* It shocked her that the thought even rattled around in her brain. She was barely beginning to heal herself.

She was so out of practice in this kind of situation. Three years with Jon that included the long stretch of his illness, followed by a year of mourning she hadn't been able to snap herself out of. She'd been so grateful for Marc that night.

She was stunned she'd even connected with the man. In the year since Jon had died, she'd had no interest in even talking to other men. Instead she'd wrapped herself in her misery and guilt, preferring that to taking a chance on another relationship that she didn't feel she deserved. Or, in fact, even had anything left to give to one. But some little spark had flared.

When he'd asked in a very tentative voice if he could see her again while he was on leave, she'd shocked herself at the speed with which she'd said yes. She'd had no idea what they would do or what would happen. From then until the next time they were together, she'd spent much of her time battling a bad case of nerves.

How amazing that the two of them had clicked the way they had. She figured it was the blending of two shattered souls seeking comfort from maybe the one other person who could understand where they were in their life.

They'd spent two more nights together, one of them turning into more intense hours of learning about each other. Talking until the sun came up about anything and everything. Telling each other things they'd kept bottled up forever. Hours that had created an invisible bond, fragile but still there.

But then that last night together. *Wow!* One minute they'd been talking, the next she'd been cuddled against him and he was kissing the life out of her and using his clever hands to give her one of the best organs she'd ever had. She was still embarrassed when she thought about how fast he'd been able to make her come. And how unselfish he was. They'd been like unprepared kids, neither of them with condoms, and he had refused to let her return the favor and use her hands and mouth on him.

'I want the real thing,' he'd told her. *'I can wait.'*

They'd fallen asleep on the couch, her body nestled into the curve of his shoulder, clothes still askew and his arm wrapped around her so one hand could cup her breast. There had been a few awkward moments in the morning, but then Marc had gotten a call on his cell that his leave had been cut short by a couple of days. Nikki had had to work so Teo had driven up from the ranch to fetch him. They'd been scheduled wheels up that afternoon.

Since then she'd parsed and analyzed every moment they were together until she could have written it as a script for a movie. There was something about Marc, about the situation, that reached into her and pulled her out of the darkness she'd chosen to stay in for so long. She tried not to get too excited about it. *Maybe,* she thought, *it was just two wounded souls finding a place to dump the pain they lived with.* Besides, he was a warrior, dedicated to serving his country. When he had finally told her he was with Delta Force, even she realized what a commitment that was. Maybe grasping that all of this might prevent them from looking at something long-term was what made things easier for her.

But, lord! That one little bit of erotic playtime had her body still humming with need. *Okay, then.* Whatever this turned out to be, she'd just enjoy their time together then try taking the rest of her life one day at a time.

'*I don't know when I'll be able to call you,*' he'd said as he waited for his ride. '*We'll be in mission protocol for most of the time and I don't have any way to communicate. Not until we're between missions.*'

'*It's okay,*' she'd assured him. '*I understand. Please don't worry about it.*'

She wanted him to take pleasant memories of her into battle, not the sounds of a nagging shrew. Deep down, she wasn't even sure she'd hear from him again, anyway. Still, she couldn't seem to stop him from invading her dreams every night, remembering the feel of his tall, lean, muscular body, the thick strands of his hair the color of ripe tobacco and the look of heat in eyes that reminded her of warm whiskey. She guessed if all she had were dreams she'd find a way to make do with them.

Briefing for mission. Out of contact. Take care.

She'd stared at it for ten minutes. Was she supposed to answer him? When he'd left her that last time they'd made no promises at all. She'd hoped that maybe...possibly...

Then this morning another text, one that caused her heart to do tiny flips.

Mission accomplished. Can I call tonight?

She'd hugged the phone to her breast for ten minutes before answering him. She'd felt like a teenager, and wasn't that just too ridiculous? She'd reminded herself she was a grown woman, albeit one who had shut herself off from everything but work. Jon's death had taken all the pleasure out of life for her. So how was it possible she'd had such a hot episode with Marc Blanchard the other night? And was looking forward to a stupid phone call like a teenager?

For one moment, she'd felt a stab of disloyalty to Jon and had even considered texting Marc and telling him not to contact her anymore. But then she could almost hear her sister's voice in her mind, telling her it was time to get on with her life. Could she do this? So many emotions had swirled inside her. Then she'd swallowed and typed a message.

Yes. Home at eight o'clock.

She was working the seven-to-seven shift, three days on and four days off, and had wanted to give herself plenty of time to get home and be ready.

Ready? For a phone call? He wouldn't even be able to see her. She must be losing it. Truly.

And what if he's only calling to say hello and how are you and that's it?

Really? After the intimate moment we shared?

Have a little faith, Nikki.

She walked into her apartment at a quarter to eight, just enough time for her to shower and change.

Shower? Change? Good lord. This was a phone call, nothing more.

But what if he wanted to FaceTime?

Ohmigod. I'm driving myself crazy.

Nevertheless, she dumped her scrubs in the hamper, showered and changed into shorts and a tee, and pulled her hair back in a ponytail. She seldom wore makeup and Marc had commented he liked her without it. *Okay, then.* She got a glass of iced water and settled herself in the armchair in the living room. She was ready, phone in one hand, water in the other.

When her phone buzzed at her, vibrating in her hand, she nearly dropped the water. Setting the glass down on the end table, she punched the Answer button on the phone.

"Hello?"

"Nikki?" His voice was just as deep and rugged as she remembered.

"It's me." *Wow. Brilliant comeback, Nikki.* "I mean, yes, and hi."

His laugh had a low, rough, sexy sound to it that sent a shiver through her body.

"I, uh, called to let you know…" He paused, a note of uncertainty creeping into his tone. "I mean, we're back from our mission, and…" Another pause.

Okay, I can do this.

"Are you coming back to San Antonio?"

"Yeah, we are." Another pause. "Listen, Nikki, I—"

"If you just wanted to let me know you won't be seeing me, I understand." She said the words so fast they ran together, but if he was calling to say he wouldn't be seeing her anymore, then she wanted it out there now. Then she wanted to kick herself. If he didn't want to see her, why had he even called? Fear and excitement did a rapid tango in her bloodstream.

"What? Wait. No. Where did that come from?"

Nikki cleared her throat. "I don't—I mean—I just—"
Damn! Okay, open mouth, insert foot.

"I, uh, wanted to see what your schedule is and ask if we could get together again." Another pause. "I thought about you a lot while I was gone."

Excitement surged through her and she struggled to maintain her composure. *Don't scare him away,* she told herself.

"I'm working the seven-to-seven shift," she told him. "I work three days on and four days off. Does that work? When are you due back?"

"Tomorrow, as a matter of fact. Are you at the beginning of your three days or the end?"

"The beginning." *Damn!* "But two more days and I'll be off for a week. What did you have in mind?"

There was a long silence and for a minute she wondered if he was about to think better of this whole thing.

"I want to ask you something," he began in a slow voice. "If you think I'm out of line, just let me know and it's all good. Really."

What on earth? She couldn't imagine what kind of question needed such a setup.

"Um, okay. Sure. What's up?"

"Like I said, feel free to say no, but—"

She was seized with an urge to reach through the phone and shake him. *Enough already.*

"Marc, whatever it is, just say it. No problem. Really."

"It's not bad," he said in a rapid voice. "I mean, I hope not. I— Oh, hell. I'm so out of practice I forgot how to do this kind of thing."

"*What* kind of thing?" She did her best to keep the exasperation out of her voice.

"I had an idea," he said, "and I ran it past Slade, since he knows the area. I wanted someplace to take you without a lot of people around. You know, no crowds. A place where we could be alone and talk and—" His voice dropped. "—anything else that comes to mind. So how much notice do you have to give when you ask for time off at work?"

What on earth?

"Depends. Usually a month to six weeks, but—"

"Damn!"

"If you let me finish, please. The way I'm set up, I work, let's say, Sunday, Monday and Tuesday, then I'm off until the following Thursday, Friday and Saturday. So I have a week off in between. Would that work? What are the dates you're looking at?"

"The dates are gonna work out just fine. I thought maybe a change of scenery would do both of us good. A new place with no memories for you, a change of environment for me. And we could, uh, see where this goes."

A week alone with Marc to explore this thing between them? For a moment her mouth went dry while other parts of her body were suddenly damp and needy.

"Okay." She swallowed. "Sounds interesting. So what did Slade suggest?"

"He's got a friend who owns a little cottage not too far from San Antonio," he explained. "Their married kids use it now and then, but no one's asked for it for the next couple of months. It's on a small lake that only has a couple of other houses on it." He chuckled. "It comes with a rowboat. When's the last time you were in one of those?"

"Well, um, never, as a matter of fact."

"Good. A new experience." He paused. "There are some interesting restaurants within a half hour of the place, and some other spots we can go exploring if we want. So, uh, what do you think?"

She didn't want to think. If she did, she might say no.

"Yes." She blew out a breath. "I say yes."

"Whew." He chuckled. "I was holding my breath the whole time. Okay, listen. I've got to run here, but I'll be back tomorrow. I guess I'll go to Slade's and call you from there."

Before her brain caught up with her mouth she said, "Why don't you just come here?"

"But you said you'll be working," he pointed out.

"No problem. I'm off by seven at night and if you drive me to work you can have a car during the day." She laughed. "Although you'd have to get up at six to do it."

"No sweat. That's almost like sleeping in. You're sure this is okay with you?"

"Yes, it's fine. More than fine. Where do you land?"

Did I really say that? Holy shit. Yes, this is me, going from zero to ninety in the blink of an eye.

"We're flying commercial. Couldn't hitch a ride this time, and we're stuck with a later flight, so we land in San Antonio at seven-thirty tomorrow."

"Perfect." Yes, her mouth was still running away with her. "I'll pick you up. Text me your flight info."

There was a second's worth of empty air before he spoke again.

"I just want you to know," he told her in a low voice, "if this doesn't work for you, I'm okay with that. I just had the idea that getting away someplace where nobody can bother us would be great to see where this is going." Another pause, then in a low voice, "Whatever this happens to be."

Was he having second thoughts? No, he would have thought it through before making this call. She knew that much after the intense hours they'd spent together. She was sure he was just as confused by the whole thing as she was. Neither of them looking for a relationship — in fact, running away from one — but then, bam! Out of the blue, connecting with another person. She felt pretty sure his nerves were jumping here as much as hers.

And wasn't that just a hoot. The macho Delta Force soldier, not afraid of the most dangerous situations, fumbling his way through what was happening between them. But of course, she wasn't much better.

"Nikki?" Marc's voice pierced her fog. "You still there? You didn't hang up, did you? Because if — "

"What? Oh. No, no, no. That sounds like a great idea. Really. Great." And there she was, babbling like an idiot again.

Shut up, Nikki.

"Good. Whew." A soft chuckle eased through the connection.

"I can pick you up at the airport. No problem."

"Great." His voice softened again. "I'm looking forward to this."

"Me, too."

After he disconnected she sat there with the phone hugged to her chest, smiling and a tad nervous. Was she making a big mistake here? She was just so stunned to meet someone in a place as dark as hers and finally see a little light shining in her world. Hopefully that light wouldn't go out while they tried to figure the details of their very new situation.

* * * *

Jamal Baqri punched the button to disconnect the call on the burner phone in his hand and did his best to keep from swearing. The people who were supposed to facilitate this for him seemed to be hanging him out to dry. How did careful plans get fucked up so easily and quickly and turn to such shit? Six months ago, this had all looked so good, so well put together. The plans so carefully constructed. The target set, the arrangements made.

But now, he decided, Allah must be punishing them for something.

Two weeks ago, he and three others had left the training camp in Mexico after six months of intensive preparation. They had then been given their assignment—take out a specific target in San Antonio, Texas. A job that would kill a lot of people. They had contacts for the materials they needed and the date and location of their target. They had then been connected with a coyote to take them across the border. And that was where it turned to shit.

They had just about made it across some rancher's land headed toward a two-lane highway for pickup when a ranch hand, out late, had spotted them and shot at them.

Two shots. *Blam! Blam!*

Jamal had thought for a moment they had escaped unscathed, but then he'd heard a groan and a string of curse words. He'd turned to see that Malik Kouli, at the end of their single file, had taken a bullet in his leg.

'Help me,' he'd hissed at the others. *'Those assholes are on horseback. We need to get him in the van and get the fuck out of here.'*

They'd dragged him the last few yards to the road, where the driver hired by the coyote had swooped them up into a van. But now they had a big problem. Malik, groaning and sweating in the rear seat, needed medical help. *Now.*

"That got me nowhere," he told the driver. "I want you to contact the man who sent you to pick us up."

"If he refused your request, I doubt he will pay attention to mine."

"Do it anyway. And get us the fuck out of here."

As they hauled ass down the highway, the driver made a call to the person arranging all this.

"It is not my fault he got shot," he said into the phone for the third time. "He needs medical attention." He paused. "But I was told to take them to the apartment that is waiting for them."

An apartment in San Antonio, Jamal knew, where they would begin to build the bombs. He wanted to smash something when he heard the driver asking where to take them instead. Then he hung up the phone.

"What did he say?" Jamal asked. "The contact. We need help for Malik. Right now. Right this minute."

"He said he will call me back."

"Call you back? *That's* what he said? *Telhas Teeze.*" *Son of a bitch.*

The driver lifted one shoulder. "I just do what I am told. I do not make the decisions."

"Well, you'd fucking well better make one soon. If my friend dies because of this, you're next."

"He will call," the drive said in a hasty voice. "He will call. Soon."

"And tell you where to take us? When will he do that?" *Ya eben al shar-moo-ta. Son of a bitch.* "I told you. I have to get my friend inside someplace and tend to his wound." Jamal hauled in a breath and reached for calm. "He is badly hurt. If I don't take care of him, he might die. I don't think that would look very good to whoever takes your report."

"He will call back in good time," the driver repeated again, although he didn't sound quite so positive.

Jamal wanted to reach over and snap his neck, except the man was behind the wheel, driving. Waiting for whoever that was to call back didn't satisfy him at all. They had a deadline to meet and Malik needed medical attention.

"I will tell you again, my friend could be dead in good time," Jamal protested. "Plus, we have a deadline to meet. I am not prepared to meet Allah because someone is too busy to call back."

"Perhaps if you had not managed to make a mess of things, there would not be a problem."

"A mess of things? Did you think we planned for one of us to get shot? Well?"

The other man ignored him and just kept driving.

"We are still on the same road," Jamal commented. "Will this take us to where we need to go?"

"We will be fine," the driver told him, although by now his voice had a little edge to it.

Jamal couldn't exactly blame him. The man was stuck with four strangers, one of them with a bullet in his leg, a sudden change of plans and no new directions. Jamal was getting pissed off himself. But sitting there wringing his hands didn't help.

He took off the long-sleeved shirt he was wearing, leaving him just in a T-shirt, and wrapped the cloth around Malik's thigh, hoping to slow the bleeding. He had to figure out a way to remove the bullet that was still in Malik's leg. None of them had any medical training and he didn't want to make matters worse.

Malik's skin felt feverish and he continued to moan softly. The other two men, occupying the bench seat in back, just sat quietly. Neither of them had spoken since the van had picked them up, even though one of them was a brother to the wounded man.

At the moment, Jamal wished fervently they had never left Syria. Surely Allah would have tasks for them to perform in their own country? He should never have listened to the man who'd recruited him and told him he would do the greatest service to Allah in the United States.

They drove on in a silence punctuated only by Malik's soft moans. Five minutes later, the phone rang again. The driver held a brief conversation with the person on the other end then hung up.

"We have an alternate site for you," he told Jamal. "Just until your friend is better."

"Better?" Jamal wanted to scream. "How can he get better when I have nothing to treat him with? And why can't we just go to the apartment that is ready for us? We have a deadline."

He was not liking this one bit. Everything had turned to shit and they had no control over anything. This was not what they had been promised. Not even close.

"Too many people around," the driver explained. "If someone sees your friend, there could be a problem."

"Maybe if our crossing had been worked out better, my friend would not have gotten shot. Did you think of that?"

The driver shrugged. "I only do what I am told."

Scant minutes later, they reached an intersection with some civilization in it. Too small, Jamal thought, to consider calling a town. It had a gas station, café, a couple of nondescript buildings and — wonder of wonders — a convenience store.

"Wait here," the driver told him, climbed out and headed for the store. During the ten minutes he was inside, Jamal kept looking nervously around. The other two men on his little team didn't look any more comfortable than he did. Praise Allah, he thought, not too many people were at this little intersection so there was hardly anyone to stare at them.

He was just about ready to go inside the store and see what was taking so fucking long when out came the driver, at last, carrying a filled plastic bag. He handed it to Jamal.

"This will help you treat his wound."

Jamal looked through it and found bandages of different sizes, alcohol, antibiotic ointment, surgical gloves and scissors. It also contained a large bottle of aspirin and one of liquor.

"He needs medicine," Jamal protested. "Not just aspirin. Antibiotics, and not in a cream. And we do not use liquor."

"If you want to knock him out from the pain, you do. I will see what I can do about anything else. Meanwhile, this is what you've got. Make it work."

The driver put the van in gear and pulled away from the curb. In a few minutes, he turned onto a very narrow road with trees thick on both sides, heading away from the country road they'd been on.

"Where are you taking us?" Jamal wanted to know.

"You will see. It is a place where we sometimes take people to hide out. It is fully stocked with food and you will be comfortable there."

"I don't care about comfort except for my friend," Jamal protested. "I came here on a mission and I want to complete it."

"Yes, yes, yes. In good time."

Jamal wondered what this idiot considered 'good time'.

The road curved suddenly and now he could see they were at a lake. *A lake?* The land was overgrown with high grass and natural shrubbery, shielding everything from view and giving plenty of privacy from the road. They could just see the water sparkling in the sun between the leaves of the trees. Just when he was wondering if there were even any houses in this godforsaken spot, the road forked. They turned to the right and, after another quarter of a mile, pulled into a clearing and parked next to a house. No, not a house. A small cottage. One story, made of weathered wood, it had a porch in front and faced the lake. If he was on a vacation. it might be tempting, but that was not the case. He was on a mission and everything had gotten fucked up.

"We are here," the driver said, and heaved himself out of the van.

With the help of Farid and Kasim, he maneuvered Malik out and into the house. Although there was a couch in the living room, he insisted they put Malik in one of the two bedrooms. He placed the bag from the store on the nightstand. As soon as the driver left, he would go to work on his friend.

"Is there any food here?" he demanded. "A refrigerator with ice? A stove."

"Of course, of course. Look here."

The man—whose name he still did not know—led him into the kitchen. The refrigerator wasn't large, but it had plenty of fresh food and the icemaker was full. At one corner of the room was a pantry closet, small but also well stocked.

"When was this done?" Jamal asked. "It's only been a couple of hours since you picked us up and plans had to be changed."

The other man shrugged. "He had someone take care of it. That's all I know. He has a friend who arranged it all."

"All of that is good, but what about a car? You cannot leave us out in the middle of noplace without some kind of transportation."

The man just shook his head. "I am told it will be taken care of. Soon. Wait a moment."

He hurried back out to the car and Jamal worried he'd leave with too many questions unanswered. But in a moment he was back with a large hard plastic case and three cell phones that he handed to Jamal.

"There is one number programmed into each of them. The same number. I am told alternate plans are being worked on and you should call that number every day at noon for an update. Alternate the phones, so you do not use one on successive days. Do you understand?"

Jamal glared at the man. "Do I look stupid to you? Of course I understand. What's in the case?"

Jamal felt a little better when the man opened it to show him the handguns and ammunition.

"We hope you will not need this, but just in case. There are only four cottages on this lake and three of them are unoccupied at the moment."

Jamal wasn't sure if that was good or bad. In case of an emergency, it would have been nice to have an alternative to the driver who would not even give them his name.

"What about other arms? AK-47s? And the materials we need for our assignment in the city? Which, by the way, is coming up very soon. We have trained for this for a very long time."

The man gave one sharp nod. "I am assured all will be handled."

Jamal wanted to smack the man. *All will be handled?* There were too many loose ends dangling here.

"And that's it?"

Jamal had not heard Farid Kouli, Malik's brother, come up behind him, but he stood there now, glaring at the driver.

"My brother is badly injured," Farid said. "He could die if not properly attended to. And you just plan to walk off and leave us? No car? No other information?"

"I can only follow orders," the driver said. "Our people know of your brother's situation."

"The man needs a doctor," Jamal insisted.

"Yes, yes," the driver soothed. "I will bring one."

"When?" he pushed.

"Soon. Soon."

But Jamal got the feeling that if Malik died, the other man couldn't care less. None of his business.

"Tell me again why you are not taking us to San Antonio?"

The man hesitated. "We have to make sure you can arrive with little attention."

In other words, not dragging a man with a bullet hole in his leg.

"I want to know when you will be back," Jamal insisted.

"I will call you tomorrow with arrangements. And now I must go."

He all but ran from the cottage and, in seconds, they heard the motor crank. The car pulled away, leaving Jamal with the three men, one with a bad leg wound, no transportation and no idea of what would happen next.

He was doing his best to hold on to his temper and also tamp down the fear that everything had fallen apart. It was just so fucked-up. He had been assured ISIS planned well for everything, but this sure didn't look like it. The contact they'd been given to use once they arrived in town was apparently unavailable at the moment. They had no transportation and, even if they did, no idea how to get anywhere.

They had none of the explosive supplies they needed to build the bombs. None of the maps and information they'd been promised. He supposed he was damn lucky the place had satellite, so they had an internet connection. But here they were, alone in a foreign country with no credentials and no way to get anywhere. Were they supposed to just stay here and wait?

Great. Just fucking great.

He clapped his hand on Farid's shoulder. "I promise Malik will pull through this. Let's go take care of him right now."

He only hoped he was not lying through his teeth.

Chapter Three

Traffic was a bummer on the main streets and the interstate when Nikki left work. She kept her eye on the time and cursed every driver under her breath as she headed for the airport. She'd texted Marc when she walked out of the hospital so he'd have her message when he deplaned, that she'd pick him up at the Arrivals area.

It was twenty to eight when she drove into the airport and headed to the pickup spot. The cars in front of her seemed to be inching along as if they had no place else to go and she had to stop herself from pounding the steering wheel with impatience. She spotted Marc standing out on the covered sidewalk, duffel by his side, scanning the cars for her. She honked her horn and he looked over and waved.

In seconds he had tossed his bag into the back seat and climbed into the front. As they pulled out onto the exit road, he reached over and squeezed her thigh.

"I've been thinking about you. A lot."

"Me, too." A tiny laugh bubbled out. "Of you, I mean. I don't think of myself. That is…" Oh, crap. She was babbling like an idiot.

"It's okay. I know what you mean." He turned to look at her and grinned. "And I'm glad."

He stretched out his legs as much as he could. His six-foot-four frame didn't fit easily into her small hatchback.

"I think that seat moves back a little," she told him.

"Don't worry. I've folded myself into tighter places before." He reached over and squeezed her thigh again. "I think this is the first time I've looked forward to downtime in two years."

She slid a quick glance at him. "I'm glad. I mean, not that you never looked forward to it, but that you did this time." Then, before she could put her foot any further in her mouth, she said, "Tell me about this place you've found for us."

"I'll do better than that. I've got a couple of pictures Slade texted me. I'll show them to you as soon as we get to your place. I think—I *hope*—you'll like it. We didn't really get into a lot of specifics, but I'm not one for noisy, busy places or being around a lot of people. At least, not anymore."

"Neither am I. And speaking of noisy, busy places, I had a feeling you wouldn't want to go out for dinner tonight. Not after just coming in off a mission and wanting to unwind. But I don't really know what you like to eat."

"I'm easy to please." He slid a grin at her. "Cross my heart."

Heat flashed over her at the implied double meaning of what he said.

"Well, anyway, we had pizza both nights you were at my place last time so I thought we'd try Mexican food for tonight. There's a great little restaurant down the street from my apartment and they deliver."

"Sounds good to me."

It was dark now, so when they reached her apartment, she flicked on lamps in the living room then dropped her keys on the little table in the foyer. Marc stood there with his duffel, obviously waiting for her to tell him where to put his things.

Holy shit. What was the matter with her? She was acting like a nervous virgin. *Talk about being out of practice.*

"This way," she told him and led him to her bedroom with its en suite bath. "I, uh, wasn't quite sure what you'd need, so I made room in a drawer for you and some space in the closet. And there's room on the vanity in the bathroom for whatever stuff you want to put there."

She pulled out an empty drawer then stood there, clasping her hands.

My god, am I seventeen again?

"It's fine, Nikki." Marc dropped his duffel and moved over to her, placing his warm hands on her shoulders. "Don't worry about anything. It will all be okay. I'm glad you're as out of practice as I am, so I don't feel like an idiot and a fool."

She let herself relax and even managed a smile. "Okay. Um, would you like to shower?"

The slow grin he gave her was positively lethal to her hormones. Heat flashed through her and the pulse between her thighs pounded like a drum out of control. She gave him a glance that was part teasing, part shyness.

Marc looked at her, hunger flaring in his dark eyes. "Can I ask you to join me?"

She gazed over at him, stunned, while hot and cold flushes took turns in her body. "I, uh, already showered. When I came home. Uh, that is…"

Great. I sound like an idiot.

Marc reached for her hands, his touch electric. She looked at him, aware that the hunger and desire they'd flirted with last time had roared up full steam. They seemed to have gone from zero to sixty in a heartbeat. She swallowed hard and her pulse skittered, and suddenly she felt as if the room was too small to contain them.

He studied her with a mixture of emotions swirling in his eyes. Then he shook his head.

"My bad. I'm sorry, Nikki. I'm really out of practice with this. I had plans to do all this the right way, to make this very special for you. But damn! It seems as if it's all I've been able to think about since last time. The hunger in me has been building up all this time and I can't seem to get it under control. Don't be upset with me, okay? I'll shower then we'll do this the right way."

She stepped up and put her palms on his cheeks, looking hard into his eyes. There was something zipping between them she'd never thought to find again. This connection. This…whatever it was.

Tell him. It's time to move forward.

Her lips curved in a hint of a smile. "I've been hungry for this, too. More than I ever thought possible." She let out a slow breath. "I'd love to take a shower with you."

"You sure? Because—"

She touched her fingers to his lips. "I'm sure. Positive."

"Come on, then." He walked backward toward the bathroom, tugging her with him. "I really, really need a shower." He brushed his mouth against hers, setting off tiny ripples of need in her body. "Bad. I might need you to wash *my* body." His eyes bored into hers. "You should know I've been thinking about this while I was gone. A lot. About what it will be like with us."

"Me, too," she whispered.

"I don't want to wait anymore. There won't be any ghosts in the room with us, Nikki. All I've been able to think about is you and this."

Before she could think of anything else to say, she found herself in the bathroom with him. She watched, fascinated, as he stripped off his camo pants, T-shirt and dark green boxer briefs. His lean body was all hard, corded muscle, with a dusting of black hair on his chest, his thighs and his forearms. Not to mention the nest of it surrounding a cock that made her mouth water. Long and thick, it stood out from his body, the head a dark purple, a tiny bead of fluid winking at her from the opening on the soft dark purple skin.

She reached into the shower and turned on the water, then, while it heated, pulled two thick towels from the linen closet.

"Only one of us is shower-ready." Marc's deep voice washed over her like a coating of warm molasses.

"Oh, um… Yeah, right."

She started to pull her T-shirt over her head but he moved her hands away.

"I'll do it."

He fisted the bottom hem of her top and drew it slowly up her body, pausing for a moment at her breasts before pushing it higher and finally up over her head. He raked his gaze over her, stopping at the sight of her in a lacy pink bra. He cupped her breasts in his palms, taking a moment to give her nipples a light pinch. They hardened and throbbed at once, a thread of heat shot straight to her core and she squeezed her thighs together.

Marc had his gaze locked with hers as he unfastened the bra and tossed it aside. He stroked his fingers along the slope of her shoulders, then lightly down her arms and across to her midriff. Trailing the tip of one finger between her breasts, he reached the hollow at her neck where her pulse now pounded furiously in anticipation of what was to come.

Moving his finger again, he pressed it just beneath her chin to tilt her head upward and molded his lips to hers. The kiss was tentative at first, gentle, a light back and forth movement of his mouth. But then he increased the pressure and gently insinuated his tongue inside. Heat instantly blasted through her as she swept her own tongue against his in a dance that sent messages throughout her body.

She was so lost in the kiss, in the heat of it, that she barely realized he had unsnapped her jeans and pushed them down past her hips. Only when his thumbs stroked her skin, pushing at the lace edge of her bikini panties, did she realize he was onto the next part of this strip show.

His lips were still fused to hers, his tongue still dancing inside her mouth, as he eased his hands inside her panties. Cupping the cheeks of her ass, he gave them a possessive squeeze. She pressed herself against his naked body, swallowing a gasp as she came into closer contact with his hard, thick cock. She tried to slip a hand between them so she could wrap her fingers around it, but he stopped her.

"Not yet. This is my playtime."

She groaned, already so turned on she was sure it wouldn't take much to make her come.

Marc dropped to his knees, pushing her jeans and panties down as he did and maneuvering them from her body. She shivered when he ran the tip of one finger the length of her slit. But then he eased her lips apart and followed the same path with his tongue. She had to grip his shoulders to steady herself, shaking as he licked and tasted, blowing little puffs of air on the damp curls of her mound.

Nikki rocked forward, thrusting herself toward his mouth, but he held her in place so movement was difficult. She'd been so primed for him that mere seconds had her in a state of readiness.

His low, rough laugh vibrated against her skin.

"In a hurry, are we?"

"Mmmm." She dug her fingertips into his shoulders. "Been a long wait."

"For me, too. That's why I want to enjoy every single second of it." He rose to his feet. "Shower's ready and I can't wait to get to it."

"Me, too," she whispered.

He tugged her into the shower with him. For one brief moment, his features were cast in the look of tortured emotion he'd worn when she first met him. Then, as if swept aside by a broom, it was gone. He poured some of her body wash into the palm of his hand and worked it into a lather.

"I thought about you every minute I wasn't focused on the mission," he told her. "It was a nice change to have thoughts of you filling my brain instead of all the dark thoughts about Ria."

"I'm glad," she told him.

"Not half as much as I am."

He began to smooth the foam of the body wash over her shoulders and worked his way down her arms. His palms against her skin sent more shivers through her and the pulse in her core was now beating a demanding tattoo.

"Thinking of you—of us—kept me going during the missions."

He coasted his hands along her collarbone then palmed her breasts. His thumbs flicked at her nipples, the touch sending electricity straight to the center of her sex.

"I—I'm glad." Her ability to think and form words was rapidly disappearing.

"Me, too. Do you know I love touching your skin?"

"I like touching yours, too." She moved his hands aside so she could stroke the hard plane of his chest, taking a moment to ruffle the soft hair there and use her fingers to outline his muscular torso.

He braceleted her wrists with his fingers. "Uh-uh. This is my show this time."

He went back to spreading the silky foam of the body wash on her skin, skimming over her breasts again before sliding over her abdomen and down to her pussy. Nudging her legs apart, he soaped the inside of her thighs, crouching to lather her legs from her thighs to her ankles then all the way up to the crease of her thigh and hip. When he cupped her pussy with his palm and traced her slit with his finger, she couldn't help the little groan that escaped her mouth. She tried to urge him to slide his finger in deep—more than one finger—and rocked against his palm to force some friction on her clit, but he was way ahead of her, anticipating her and pulling his hand away.

"I've thought about this every spare minute while we were gone. Dreamed about it. I'm not rushing anything, so just enjoy it, darlin'."

Nikki closed her eyes and leaned against the shower wall while he stroked and caressed and teased every inch of her body. He danced his fingers through her hot slit, pausing to tease her hot little button, rubbing it until she wanted to impale herself on him. So many sensations rioted through her, not the least of which was the thrill of actually making love with this man. She just wished he'd hurry the process and get to the main event because she wanted him inside her *now*.

When he'd covered every inch of her front with strokes more sensuous than she'd have believed him capable of, he turned her around so she faced the shower wall.

He kissed one shoulder and put his lips close to her ear.

"Brace yourself with your hands, feet apart, and close your eyes."

Seconds later she felt the touch of his fingers smoothing the creamy body wash over her back, moving in slow sweeps down to her waist then back up again. He paused to brush her hair aside and nibble at her neck, just enough to feel the electric current that crackled from the tips of his fingers and sizzled her nerve endings. She drew in a deep breath and let it out slowly, reveling in the erotic feel of his touch, when he cupped one cheek of her ass and gave a gentle squeeze. Then he moved his hand to the other one, and before she could enjoy the feel of it, he slid his fingers into the hot crevice that separated them and stroked its length.

Little tremors raced over her skin and she clenched her muscles, trying to hold him in place.

He gave that low, rough laugh again that went straight to the center of her sex. He pressed gently with his finger, just barely touching her opening.

"I think you like when I touch you here. I'll have to remember that." He paused. "For later."

Later? What's he going to do now? She wanted him so badly after minimal foreplay that she wanted to scream. She could not recall another man affecting her that way, even her fiancé, whom she'd loved beyond anything. What would happen when this man was inside her at last?

He turned her to face him again, rinsed his hands in the shower spray and cupped her cheeks.

"I want to do so many things with you I don't know where to start," he murmured, then took her mouth in a kiss that singed her down to her toes. He traced his tongue over every inch of the inner surface, sliding it over her own tongue while he held her head in place.

Not that she would have moved. He tasted so good, so utterly male. For a frozen moment, she wondered if everything was so heightened because she hadn't had anything like this in so long. But in the next second, she realized she hadn't had anything like this ever, not even with Jon. What they'd had was excellent, but maybe a person had to go through fire, like she and Marc had, to get to something like this. She wrapped her arms around him and held him tight to her. The water spraying down on them couldn't even begin to cool the heat blazing from them.

Nikki coasted her hands down his body, stopping when she reached his thick, hard cock, hot where it pressed against her. She wrapped her fingers around it and began to slide her fingers up and down its length.

Marc grabbed her wrist and held her hand still.

"I want that." His voice was thick with need, his lips still touching hers. "But I want the first time I come with you to be inside you." Then he grinned. "But that doesn't mean *you* have to wait. I've been dying for a taste of you and I can't wait any longer."

He knelt on the tile, nudged her thighs apart and pressed open the lips of her pussy. One slow lick of his tongue nearly sent her over the edge. She gripped his shoulders to steady herself as he lapped her tender flesh, now adding light strokes to her clit until she was ready to scream.

"Please," she begged.

In response he banded one arm around her hips to hold her steady and slipped two fingers into her hot sex. She clenched down on them at once, rocking hard as he set up a steady in-and-out rhythm. She closed her eyes, letting the delicious sensations wash over her. As ready as she was, it took only seconds before a climax roared through her, the walls of her pussy clamping down on Marc's fingers. He pressed hard on her clit with his thumb and held her in place as spasms shook her and the walls of her sex convulsed over and over.

By the time the tremors had subsided she was weak, her legs trembling with the effort to remain upright.

"I didn't get to wash you," she pointed out as she tried to settle her racing pulse.

"I'm saving that for next time." He grinned. "I don't want it to be hurried and right now I'm in a big hurry."

He managed to keep her upright while he soaped his body then rinsed both of them off. Finished, he dried them both, then lifted her and carried her into the bedroom where he yanked the covers back on the bed with one quick pull and laid her down. In seconds he had opened his duffel and found the condoms he was looking for, dumping them on the nightstand. Then he was kneeling over her, the hunger blazing fiercely in his eyes.

Nikki looked at him, read the same craving and want and need in them and realized that between the last time they'd been together and now, something had moved this situation light-years ahead. They had a connection that she was sure stunned him as much as it did her. They'd been looking for a way out of their pain and here they were on the verge of something astounding.

"Yes, we are," he told her, as if she'd spoken the words aloud.

He grabbed one of the condoms and rolled it on with hands that she noticed were shaking the slightest bit. At his urging, she bent her legs and planted her feet on the bed, opening wide for him. He nudged her opening with the head of his cock, just that simple contact igniting the heat in her body again. With his gaze locked with hers, he eased himself into her. He was hot and hard and thick, and stretched her inner walls to capacity.

"Jesus!" he breathed. "This is so fucking perfect."

It mightn't have been the most romantic statement, but to Nikki it was better than anything he could have said.

"It is," she whispered, not moving her gaze from him.

"Get ready for a hard ride," he told her. "I've been dreaming about this the whole time we were gone."

He more than kept his promise. Slow at first, his thickness dragging against the walls of her sex, each friction setting more nerves on fire. Then easing into speed, not rushing, although she could tell he was holding back. In and out, thrust and retreat, her slickness easing his path. She tried to be aware, to memorize each sense and feel of him, but as he increased his movement, she became too lost in sensation.

She wound her legs around his waist and locked her ankles at the small of his back, holding them together more tightly, allowing him to push into her even more. He increased his movements again and her orgasm began to rise from deep inside her. He still had not broken his gaze, locked with hers, and it was just she and Marc, looking deep into each other as the climax grabbed them. She could feel the pulsing of his cock as he came, feel her own body so tight around him.

She didn't even know at what point they stopped, only that they had crested a peak together and tumbled wildly down the other side. They lay there, panting, bodies slick with sweat again, hearts pounding. But Nikki was filled with a pleasure she'd never known before, a completeness. She wanted to find the words to tell him, but when she looked into his eyes, she could tell he knew.

"Yes." Just the one word, but it was enough.

He eased himself from her body, pinching the edge of the condom to hold it tight, and made a quick trip to dispose of it in her bathroom. Then he was back, sliding into bed beside her and spooning around her.

"We need to think about dinner," she murmured, although at the moment she wasn't sure how she'd be able to move.

"Later," he said. "For now, just this."

She smiled, thinking how nice *just this* was.

Chapter Four

Sunlight was slanting in through the louvers on the windows when Marc roused himself and blinked. A sweet lethargy gripped his body, as if he'd spent the night in pleasurably exhausting exercise. Which, as a matter of fact, he had, in Nikki's king-sized bed, losing himself in her enticing, exciting body. It all felt so new to him. So arousing. As if hot sex had been invented just for the two of them and they were bound together with an emotional cord. And it was better than he ever could have imagined.

It certainly seemed that way to Marc. Nothing in his life had prepared him for the way he felt. For the first time since that nightmare with Ria, he had focused only on the woman he was with, giving her pleasure and receiving it. The scent of her skin was still on him, sweet and fragrant, mixed with the erotic tang of her juices. He was sure he could spend forever in bed with her and never tire of it.

But it was more than that. It was as if they'd both been set free after a long imprisonment, their ghosts exorcised, and they wanted to gorge themselves on each other. Well, they'd certainly done that and more. He couldn't remember the last time he'd felt both so lethargic and so fulfilled and energized at once.

Next to him, Nikki shifted and curled into his body, pressing back against him. His cock, which had awakened aroused and with new purpose, was hard as a rock in seconds just from the contact.

"Somebody's in a good mood," she teased, her voice still soft with sleep even as she pushed back against him.

"If it were up to him, we'd never get out of bed today." He gently bit the rim of her ear. "But we have places to go and things to do."

He was looking forward to being out in the middle of noplace with her, where no one could bother them and he could see if this thing that had hit him—both of them—so unexpectedly was real or not. A vacation cottage on a nearly deserted lake seemed like just the thing.

For one hot minute she trapped his cock in the crevice between the cheeks of her ass, then with a laugh tossed the covers back and climbed out of bed. The little minx swung her hips in a provocative manner as she headed for the bathroom.

Marc chuckled. He realized he'd laughed more with her than he had since the disaster with Ria. In fact, he couldn't remember feeling this kind of joy at all until Nikki came into his life.

"If we had time I'd make you pay for that right now," he teased. "I'll just have to think up more ways to get my revenge."

"Promises, promises," she teased as she walked away.

Desiree Holt

In a minute he heard the shower running. He was tempted to join her but decided to wait until they got to the cottage. Then they could take their time. He picked up his kit and headed for the guest bathroom, anxious to get going. There was always the chance that if they hung around her place too long one of them would get a call to disrupt their plans, most likely Nikki. He didn't want anything to disturb this little vacation. This was a chance for them to see that out of their dual pain, they'd found something real and could move forward with it. He was both skeptical and nervous, but looking forward to this getaway with anticipation.

He had just finished zipping everything into his duffel when she came out of the bathroom, wrapped in a towel. Her long, shiny blonde hair was pulled up into a high ponytail and there wasn't a speck of makeup on her face.

"I decided to go with a naked face." She brushed a hand over her cheeks. "We won't be any place where I'd need it, right? Think you can stand it?"

He cupped her face and brushed his lips against hers.

"You could stay naked all over as far as I'm concerned." His thumbs stroked her cheeks. "You don't need to wear makeup for me—or clothes, for that matter."

She grinned, a wicked glint in her eyes. "I'll have to see what I can do about that."

It made his heart swell to see her so happy and playful. They'd both been in such a bad place when they'd met at the party—the one he hadn't wanted to attend. He thought it a minor miracle that they could both now smile and tease each other. He was pinning a lot of hopes on this week in an isolated lake cottage. Hope that whatever this was between the two of them

74

would grow into something he'd given up thinking he'd ever find.

"You look totally lost in thought." Nikki poked him in the ribs. "No thinking allowed. Not until after this week. Remember? Give me a second to get dressed and throw my stuff into a bag and I'm good to go."

He grinned when she came out of her bedroom wearing denim shorts and a T-shirt that said, *Nurse. The first person you see after saying Hold my beer and watch this.* He'd bought it for her because he wanted to lighten her mood, make her smile and laugh again.

"Glad you're wearing that." He reached out and pulled her toward him. "I wanted to bring a little humor into your life."

Even her smile was serious. "You do, Marc. More than you know. And thank you for that."

He meant the kiss to be just a light brush of lips, but before he knew it they were plastered together, tangling tongues. He forced himself to break it off and take a step back.

"Let's save that until we get to the lake or we'll never get out of here. I've got big plans for us there." He hadn't felt this kind of excitement and anticipation in a long time.

They decided not to stop in a restaurant for breakfast. Instead, on their way to shop for groceries, they grabbed breakfast sandwiches and coffee at a drive-through and headed to Lookout Lake. They followed State Highway 16 out of San Antonio, watching as the heavily populated road slowly gave way to agricultural land. Ranchland. Cattle grazing peacefully.

"I love driving around in the Hill Country." Nikki inhaled deeply and let her breath out slowly. "It makes me relax."

Marc couldn't help the low laugh that rumbled out of him. "I've got some ways to relax you, too."

She gave his thigh a soft punch. "You have hidden talents."

"And I plan to use every one of them this week."

Just thinking about seven days alone with her made Marc's cock harden.

Please don't let me fuck this up.

Slade had sent Marc an email with the directions and a map, and he'd forwarded it to Nikki. She pulled it up now as they got closer to the little town of Lookout Lake.

"There." She pointed through the windshield. "That flashing light there? That's the intersection we want."

"I wouldn't exactly call this a town," Marc commented.

"There are lots of places like this in Texas. If a train ran through here, they'd call them whistle stops. Basically an intersection with a few amenities. See?" She pointed again. "There's a convenience store, a gas station, a couple of shops. Even a little restaurant."

"That must be the place Slade told me about, with the cinnamon buns that people kill for. Maybe we can get some tomorrow morning for breakfast."

"Yum." She rubbed her tummy.

Marc's cock twitched. Of course, everything she did made his cock sit up and beg. He did his best to send it a stern message.

"It's like a foreign country to a city boy like me," he told her. "What do they do for the rest of their shopping and entertainment?"

"Well, it took us less than thirty minutes to get here from San Antonio, and Bandera is just a ways farther down the road." She giggled. "Afraid you might get bored, city boy?"

He reached over and gave her thigh a gentle squeeze.

"I'll never get bored with you." He trailed his fingers along the inside of her legs and slid between the fabric of her shorts and her barely there panties. *Jesus!* He'd better be careful. His cock was already straining at his fly.

Nikki squeezed his hand, effectively trapping it before she lifted it and moved it away.

"Pay attention to driving," she teased. "By the way, I didn't ask you, but how long will you be around? The big San Antonio Rodeo starts in a couple of days and I'd love it if we could go together."

"Rodeo? Sounds great! I think we'll be in the area, but I'll check with Slade when we get back. Right now, the most important thing on my calendar is this week with you away from everyone."

"Sounds good. Okay, here is where you make the left-hand turn. Go about a quarter of a mile and you'll see a narrow little road. Oh, look, Marc." She sat up straighter. "You can see the lake from here."

He saw the water almost the same time she did.

"This isn't much of a road," he remarked as he turned right. "It's mostly dirt. And you can hardly see it from all the overgrown grass and shrubs."

"Didn't you say Slade told you it wasn't very big? And that there were only a couple of cottages on it?"

"Yeah, that's right. And here we are."

He pulled off the road and parked right next to a typical small cottage perched on the water's edge. A small stairway led up to the front door and a porch that wrapped around the place. Marc hauled their gear out of the car, climbed the couple of steps to the porch and unlocked the door.

"Oh!" Nikki stood in the middle of the cottage and looked around. "Marc, this is so very cute."

Cute wasn't in his vocabulary, but it really was a decent place. A living room led from front to back, taking up half of the space. The other half was allocated to two bedrooms, a bathroom and a tiny kitchen. Compared to some of the places he'd stayed, it was paradise. He found Nikki standing on the back porch staring out at the lake and looking more relaxed than he ever remembered seeing her.

This was a damn good idea. Thank you, Slade.

She turned around to face him, grinning. "This was a great idea."

"And we're just getting started."

She looked at the little dock and frowned. "I thought you said there was a rowboat with this pace. I was thinking maybe we could go out on the water."

"That's what Slade told me, but I don't see it. It was supposed to be tied up at the little dock at the water's edge." He was a little baffled, also. "Maybe it's at one of the other cottages, although I believe they are individually owned."

"Let's put the food away and go for a little walk. Can we?" She pointed to the water. "I want to see what the rest of the lake looks like. It's not that big, so it won't take that long and we can look for the rowboat."

"Sure." He pulled her tight to his body for a quick but hard kiss. "We can do some sightseeing around the lake. Then I can do some sightseeing around your body."

"You did a lot of checking out my body last night," she teased. "Shouldn't that hold you for a while?"

"Maybe just a little while." He winked. Then he sobered and reached for her hand. "I thought about you so much these last weeks. God's truth, this whole thing hit me like an elephant. I never thought I'd trust or want a woman again. But you've opened my eyes, Nikki. Made me hope that this is different. That it's real. That's why I wanted us to have this week. We both come from a bad place and I want to make sure we're not fooling ourselves."

She studied his face, looking hard into his eyes.

"Me, too. So. Ready to take that little walk and check out the area? "

"Yeah. Let's see what the landscape looks like around here." He grinned at her. "Then we can come back and check out each other."

He made sure to lock both the cottage and the car before they left, then took Nikki's hand and they headed down the path obviously created by years of traffic over the natural grass growth. He didn't think anyone was here today, though, because the only sounds to break the silence were those of birds flitting here and there, and a wild animal or two diving through the bushes.

Marc loved the feel of Nikki's hand in his, soft yet strong against his palm. He was content to walk with her in silence, just enjoying her presence, happy that they didn't need to fill the silence with words. The day was warm without being hot, the sun was bright in the sky and a soft breeze ruffled the surface of the little lake.

Can life be better?

They made a short turn in the so-called road and stopped short as they came face-to-face with another cottage. This one looked to be closed up even tighter than the one they were using. There was no car parked in the space next to it and all the window shades were pulled down. Even though it gave the appearance of being deserted, every one of Marc's senses went on high alert.

He tightened his clasp on Nikki's hand and tugged her to a stop.

"Just hold a second," he told her in a low voice. "I want to scope this out."

She looked up at him. "Scope what? It's deserted, right?"

"So it seems. I just want to make sure."

"Is this the Delta Force soldier coming out?" she whispered.

"I can never quite put him away," he told her.

He started to walk around the cabin, trying to shake the feeling skipping along his spine, but he didn't see anything and Nikki was tugging on his hand.

"Look." She pointed to the dock for this cabin. "There's a rowboat there. See? Maybe whoever rented this cottage last borrowed it and left it tied up here. Why don't we take it out? We can always return it to this dock." She batted her eyes at him in an exaggerated gesture. "Please? For me?"

He laughed, a dry chuckle.

"Okay. If there was anyone here, it seems they've gone. There's no sign of life here." He tugged her toward the water. "Come on. We'll go for a little ride. Remember, though, I haven't rowed a boat in years."

"Oh, I'm convinced a big strong soldier like you won't have a problem."

She squeezed his upper arm with her slender fingers, sending a shot of lightning straight to his cock.

Jesus, Blanchard. Get your shit together.

"I'll do my best."

Seconds later they were both in the boat, gliding away from the docks. Muscle memory worked for him and soon he was rowing in a smooth rhythm, pushing them through the mostly unruffled waters of Lookout Lake. Slade had been right about two things. The lake wasn't that big and there were only four cottages, well spaced apart. And as far as he could tell, the only one being used was the one he and Nikki were in.

She reached out and dipped the fingers of one hand in the water, trailing them to make little ripples. "It really is like being alone in our own special world. It's so peaceful and beautiful out here."

He nodded. "I'm glad we're here this week. Another month or so, I'm guessing these other places will be occupied every week."

She closed her eyes and tilted her face up to the sun. He couldn't take his eyes away from her. Her thick blonde hair was pulled back in a high ponytail, emphasizing her expressive eyes, her delicate cheekbones and the soft curve of her chin. He reminded himself to be sure and take plenty of pictures of her this week, so when he was sitting in the icy air of the Hindu Kush Mountains or the broiling heat of the desert, he could pull his phone out and remember he had something great waiting for him at home.

At least he hoped that she'd be waiting. He could hardly believe the connection they had, or how much he was coming to trust their feelings for each other. This week was going to be a milestone for them in many ways.

They spoke very little as he rowed them around the lake, as if by mutual consent they had agreed that conversation wasn't always necessary. He braced the oars in the water for a moment, holding the boat in place and just letting the feeling of peace wash over him. He was pretty sure he hadn't ever felt comfortable enough with a woman before this to enjoy just being with her. And this was the perfect environment to savor every moment.

A small fished leaped from the water about three feet from Nikki's hand, making them both jump.

"Wow!" She sat up straighter, shaking the water from her hands. "Neat!"

"It is." He grinned at her. "Reminds me there are supposed to be poles in the cabin. We can go fishing."

"Yeah?" She leaned back. "You big on that?"

He shrugged. "It can be fun. But first…" He looked at her and was seized with a desire to lick her all over. "Let's go back to shore and see about working off some calories from breakfast."

Nikki laughed. "Do you have an exercise plan in mind?"

Marc grinned and winked. "I do. And we need to get to it."

"I guess we should return the boat to where we got it?"

He shrugged. "Probably. At least until I can ask Slade about it."

He slid the boat easily into place at the little dock, tied it to the post and helped Nikki out. They were just leaving the dock when the door to the cottage opened and two men walked out onto the porch. At once all of Marc's senses went on high alert. He was back in Afghanistan and Iraq and Niger, his gun trained on men who looked just like this.

Get over it. This is Texas and you can't paint everyone with the same brush.

He gave himself a mental shake and told himself there was nothing threatening about their posture. They were of average height, olive-skinned with curly dark hair and at least a three-day growth of beard, and their clothing was wrinkled, as if they'd been wearing it for a long time. He'd have thought nothing of it except the information they'd received was that he and Nikki would be the only ones occupying a cottage this week. He slid his hand into his pocket where he'd stashed his Glock 19 before they set out on this walk.

Come on, soldier. You're at a little lake in Texas, not the Hindu Kush Mountains in Afghanistan.

But it didn't hurt to be prepared.

"Uh, sorry about the boat." He forced a smile. "We were told there was one that came with the cottage where we're staying but it wasn't there. When we saw this one we thought it was tied up here by mistake. I apologize."

"No problem," the taller one said. "Take it to your place if you like. We aren't much for boating."

"Thanks. We might use it again."

"So you are staying out here, also?" the other man asked.

"A week's vacation," Marc told him. "A friend lent the place to us."

"Ah." He nodded. "Like us." He eyed Nikki. "You are a nurse?"

"Yes." She slid her hand into Marc's. "When I'm not on vacation. Trying to leave it all behind for a week."

Marc tugged her with him back toward the boat. "If you need a nurse, there's a good clinic about four miles down the highway."

"Thank you." This from the first man. "Well, enjoy your vacation."

"You, too."

Marc helped Nikki into the boat and shoved off from the dock. He said nothing until they had rowed past the curve in the lake and the other cottage was out of sight.

"Did those men make you nervous?" Nikki asked.

A corner of his mouth kicked up in a semi-grin. "Everyone makes me nervous. Occupational hazard." He rowed in silence for a moment. "These guys seemed okay but with everything going on in the world today, and no warning they'd be here, I just want confirmation that they pass muster."

"Are you going to call Slade?"

He nodded. "It never hurts to make sure of something. That's how people stay alive. Let me make that call." He dug out his cell out of his pocket and pressed the speed dial number he had for his lieutenant. "Hey, Slade. Got a question for you."

He described what had just happened and the two men who had looked anything but friendly.

"I'm probably just being itchy because of Niger and the knowledge of the training camp just across the border in Mexico."

"Never hurts to be careful. I'm pretty sure the guy that owns the place where you're staying also knows the owners of the other cottage," Slade told him. "Let me give them a call. It will only take me a few minutes."

"Thanks. Appreciate it."

"Slade's checking," he told Nikki as he hung up.

He rowed slowly wile they waited. Less than three minutes later, his phone rang.

"Here's what I've got," Slade told hm. "The Hustons, who own the place where those guys are staying, assured me it's all good. The word is some relatives of a good friend of theirs managed to smuggle them out of their village in the Middle East then into this country. He asked if they could hang out at the cottage for couple of weeks while they find them more permanent digs."

"And you believe him?" Marc asked. "You're comfortable with that explanation?"

"You know me. I'm the world's biggest cynic, but at the moment I have no reason not to trust this guy. He said he had no idea anyone would be using the cottage you're in. They were counting on the isolation, I think. Like I said, no one usually uses them this time of year."

Marc rubbed his jaw. "Okay, just checking. We were a little startled, is all. Also the rowboat was tied up at their dock. Did they move it?"

"Probably. With so few cottages on the lake, people tend to share things. Why?"

"We didn't see anyone there when we walked along the shore so Nikki and I borrowed it. They seemed okay when we returned it. In fact, they told us to bring it back here. I just… You know me. I get these weird feelings."

Probably more than most people.

"The Hustons don't think there's a problem," Slade told him, "but it never hurts to be alert. Just keep an eye on things and call if you need to."

"Will do."

"On the other hand, if you guys have changed your minds about staying there, I'll understand. I know you wanted privacy."

"Let's see how it goes. Thanks for checking and I'll let you know."

"One more thing. Keep this to yourself. That rumor we were chasing in Agadez about Mexico and a Texas target?"

"Yeah?"

"Well, it's still floating around. If it gets legs, we may have to cut this leave short."

Marc wanted to ask if there wasn't another team they could send, but he knew better than that. It had showed up on their list first, so they were *it*.

"Okay. Let's hope."

He disconnected and repeated everything to Nikki, except the part about their leave possibly being cut short. "So, what do you think?"

"Like you told Slade, let's see how it goes. We read and see all the time about people fleeing for their lives. I'm sure it takes them a long time if and when they get here to stop looking over their shoulders. Let's give it until tomorrow, at least."

"Okay." Marc nodded. "Sounds good."

A few minutes later they had pulled into the dock at their cottage. Marc leaped out first, tied the boat to a post and helped Nikki out to the dock. In seconds they were inside, and he reached out, pulling her body close to his. God, she was firm and soft at the same time, supple, molding herself to him. And just like that he tucked the question of their neighbors into the back of his mind. The softness of her breasts against his chest was so erotic his cock immediately sprang to life with a painful erection. He wondered if one week alone with Nikki would be enough to take the edge off his need. His desire. He wanted to wrap himself around her and stay that way forever.

She slid her palms up his chest wall and wrapped her arms around his neck as he cupped the cheeks of her ass and squeezed them. Now that he'd had a taste of her, he couldn't seem to get enough. This was different from what he'd felt for his ex-wife. That had been almost like a drug, invading his system. This had a solid feeling to it, filled with emotions he'd never experienced before.

He dipped his head and pressed his mouth to hers, loving the softness of her lips, the sweet taste of her lips, the erotic glide of her tongue over his. He sucked it hard, gently scraping the surface with his teeth, the sexy little moans drifting from her mouth making his blood pump faster.

Still cupping her ass, he lifted her so she had to wrap her legs around his waist to steady herself, and carried her over to the bed. Instead of placing her on her feet, he tumbled them both to the mattress, taking a moment to divest them both of their shoes. Taking her mouth again in a hungry kiss, he popped the button on her shorts and slide down the zipper. He pushed both them and her panties to the middle of her thighs and slipped his hands between her legs, finding the slickness of her wet heat.

And oh, god, she was most definitely wet. And hot. He barely rubbed his finger over her clit before she moaned into his mouth. His fingers slid easily into her sex, stretching her slick walls, slippery with her hot liquid. With her shorts and panties preventing her from spreading open her legs, the pressure of his fingers increased and enhanced the rhythmic in and out glide.

Even as she clenched her thighs around his wrist and nibbled at his tongue, she reached down and found the snap on his jeans. He groaned as she slid the zipper down, easing it gently over the hard thickness of his cock. As it sprang free, she wrapped her slim fingers around it and squeezed. Marc thought his eyeballs would pop out.

He broke the kiss, panting.

"Easy, sugar. He is so ready to come out and play. I don't want it to be over before it hardly starts."

"He's always ready," she teased, but the look in her eyes was way beyond teasing.

"It's what you do to me, Nikki. Every damn time. Do you have a magic wand?"

She looked at him and actually giggled. "No, I think you're the one with the magic wand, right?"

He locked his gaze with hers. "Damn straight."

He eased his hand from between her thighs and slid it up toward her neck, taking her T-shirt with him. At her breasts he took a moment to mold his fingers around first one mound, then the other before pushing her bra up and away.

Nikki tugged on his T-shirt. "Fair is fair." Her voice was husky. "Take it off. Now."

He grinned. "Yes, ma'am. Happy to oblige."

He shifted enough that he could yank the shirt off over his head and toss it to the floor. When she scraped her fingernails over his hard nipples, he felt it clear to his balls. He pinched her dusky rose pebbled tips, tugging them then bending his head to take a little nip at each one. At the same time, he never stopped stroking his fingers in and out of her very wet heat, teasing her clit over and over with his thumb.

Her pulse beat at the hollow of her neck and the glaze of passion in her eyes. She arched into him, pushing against his fingers and riding them. He felt the flutter in her inner walls, the tightening and clamping down. Her breathing became more erratic. All signs that she was close.

He took one nipple into his mouth and bit down on it and she came like a maniac, screaming and riding his hand like a bucking mare. He loved the fact that she had finally let go of her reserve with him, that she threw off all her restraint and let the orgasm overtake her. He didn't think he'd ever seen anything more beautiful, except when she came with his cock inside her.

She was still trembling with aftershocks, mini-convulsions, when he grabbed a condom from the nightstand where he'd stashed the box and rolled it on. Sliding his hands beneath the cheeks of her ass, he lifted her to him, placed the tip of his shaft at her opening and in one thrust was inside her.

Holy fucking shit!

From the very first time he was inside her, he'd had this incredible feeling, almost magical, as if together they were one person. He'd never had that with anyone before and after the disaster of his marriage had never expected it. But with Nikki, he had this connection, as if he'd been searching for home and had finally found it. Her hot flesh gripped his shaft, squeezing it, the little residual tremors from her orgasm rippling against his length.

"Look at me, sweet girl."

She opened her eyes and the emotion there nearly undid him.

"Keep looking at me," he told her.

Then he began to move, a steady rhythm, slower at first then faster, watching her for signals. Holding himself back until she began to climb the spiral again. His back muscles and balls tightened and he gritted his teeth as he watched her for the signals he now knew so well.

Nikki wrapped her legs around him and pulled him tight to her body, intensifying every thrust and retreat. Yes! There it was! The spasms in her inner muscles that grew harder and stronger, tightening around his cock.

He didn't even have to ask. He knew when she was ready. He drove in hard, once, twice, and they exploded together, gripped by the intensity of the orgasm.

Marc held her in his arms, bodies locked together, while the tremors faded, the spasms subsided and he emptied himself into her welcoming heat. He held her in his grasp for a long time, feeling the beat of her heart against his chest and the soft breeze of her breath against his skin. Then he eased himself from her, went to dispose of the condom and sat beside her on the bed. He stroked her cheek with his fingers, loving the feel of her.

"I never thought I'd find this," he said at last. "Tell me I'm not dreaming."

She smiled, and it went right to the center of him. "If you are, I'm right there with you."

He lifted her hand and kissed her fingers. "Did I wear you out, or are you good to go for a swim?"

"I think the water will do us both good." She grabbed his hand and pulled herself to a sitting position. "Too bad we can't go skinny dipping."

"We can use our imaginations." He winked, and as she slid off the bed he smacked her naked ass. "I know mine's already at full throttle."

Chapter Five

Jamal stood at the window looking out at the lake, blue water unbroken by anyone disturbing its surface. The couple who had taken the boat out yesterday must be occupied with other things, because he had not seen them since then. He was edgy and irritable, two things that he couldn't afford because they wrecked his concentration. He also needed to remain calm for the others on his team. It was up to him to set a good example.

But the circumstances would try anyone's patience. Today was their third day in this cottage or cabin or whatever they called it, and the strain was so thick as to be almost visible. Jamal could feel the threads binding them together fraying. They had a task they'd committed to in the name of Allah and there would be great retribution if they failed. The fire that burned within them all to complete this mission was scorching them inside and out, adding to the high level of tension gripping them.

Each day at noon they called the number programmed into the phone as instructed, but all they'd gotten was a disembodied voice telling them to stay put. That new plans were being devised.

Stay put?

New plans are being devised?

What plans?

And what about our assignment? This was time-specific, with no wiggle room. They could not even complete the first part because they had no supplies here, and no way to get them. *How has this happened?* Contingencies were supposed to be provided for, yet the four of them had just been dropped off like damaged merchandise.

They might all die out here, especially Malik. The bullet wound in his leg needed more attention than they could give it. All they had were the rudimentary supplies their driver had picked up for them at the convenience store. That in no way replaced real medical care. But of course, it wasn't as if they could march into an emergency room or even a walk-in clinic and get their wounded man treated.

And just where in the hell was this cottage located, anyway? He had no idea how far they were from San Antonio. Close enough to get the local television stations, but that could mean anything. There was a satellite dish on the roof so it could be anywhere up to two hundred miles. The little crossroads that masqueraded as a town offered nothing except the convenience store and gas station, and a restaurant that apparently catered to people traveling in the area. But they couldn't set foot in either of them, even if they had transportation. He was pretty damn sure they'd stick out like sore thumbs.

They were stuck inside since the couple had moved in down the path yesterday. They didn't want to expose themselves to strangers and prick someone's curiosity, no matter how innocuous they seemed, so they hid in the cottage.

This is just fucked. There was no other word for it.

Malik had been restless for the past several hours, falling in and out of consciousness. Farid cleaned his wound frequently as best he could. Now he gave his friend four acetaminophen at a time, but it wasn't doing more than taking the edge off the pain. It was clear that more than stopgap measures were needed.

"I cleaned the wound and put more antibiotic ointment on it." Farid had come up to stand beside him. "I also changed the bandage wrapped around it, but that's like trying to stop a river with a teacup. He is getting worse." He shook his head. "He is very hot, too. Jamal, we cannot go on this way. If we do not get the bullet out soon, massive infection could set in."

As if to underscore the point, a low moan rumbled from Malik's throat again, from the other room where the man was lying in bed.

Jamal nodded, silently agreeing with him. It was a desperate situation. They had not left the cabin since their arrival, when they'd been unceremoniously dumped here. So what if they had plenty of food and water? They were in an unacceptable situation. They had a mission that was temporarily derailed through no fault of their own and it had to get back on track. Malik had certainly not intended to get shot. It was just damn bad luck. But they had been assured their contacts here would handle whatever came up. That was proving to be a lie.

These men here looked to him for solutions, so he'd better find one in a hurry. He was, after all, the one who had talked them all into this and the acknowledged leader of their little group. If one of them died of neglect, it would seriously damage his leadership. He turned back into the room, considering whether he should have yet another cup of coffee.

Kasim pointed to the cell phone sitting on a table beside the couch. "You should call that number again. Now. Tell them that we cannot go on like this. And the date for the event is almost upon us."

"You think we should disobey the order?" Jamal scowled at him, although he'd been thinking the same thing himself.

"I think we are in a fucking mess." Farid slammed his hand on the small kitchen table. "That's what I think. And the situation has changed, so orders be damned. We're stranded out here with my brother who is badly wounded and no way to help him. No way to get anywhere, dumped like a load of trash. We spent weeks training in that camp in Mexico, learning what we had to do, getting our instructions drilled into us. Despite what the contact here said, if we don't get this job done, we might as well find some hole to hide in. It's your responsibility, Jamal. Step up to it."

The others looked at him, then toward the bedroom where Malik lay, still moaning. No one wanted to abandon him. The four of them shared a bond that none wanted to break.

"I say we call the number on the phone now," Kasim ventured. "If we can't get any help from that source, we will have to make another plan."

"Exactly what kind of plan?" Jamal snapped. "Are you thinking you can do better than me?"

"No, no, no." Farid held up his hands and looked from one to the other. "It will do us no good at all to fight among ourselves. We must figure out how to get medical attention for Malik and create an alternate plan to help us carry out our assignment."

Kasim cleared his throat. "That couple that took out the boat. The woman is a nurse. It said so on the stupid shirt she wore. Perhaps she could help us."

Jamal glared at him. "And exactly how do you propose we do that? Knock on their door and say we have a friend with a bullet in his leg? Can you fix it? Are you insane?"

Kasim spread his hands. "But I — "

"First, they would be obliged to call the police at once. Second, I don't like the looks of that man. I have seen it in many American military. He would kill us without blinking. Of course, then Malik dying and the rest of us being eliminated would not matter a bit."

Thick silence fell like a shroud over them. Then Malik moaned again.

"Jamal, we have to do something," Farid insisted. "We must make a plan how to accomplish this. It can be done."

The three uninjured men looked at each other. At last Jamal nodded. They were running out of options.

"If it is so, then let us be sure our that plan is good and tight. We cannot afford any more disasters. I think I might have an idea but we will have to be very smart and very cautious."

* * * *

They had spent a very lazy day doing very little. The situation was perfect, Marc thought, for exactly that.

They'd had breakfast late, then gone for a long walk around the other side of the lake where they found the other two cottages closed up as Slade had said. In the afternoon they'd indulged in what he called lazy, erotic sex, then taken a nap. The sun was already beginning to set by the time they decided they were hungry enough to eat again.

"Why don't we just order in," Marc suggested. "I'll bet I can find at least one place around here that delivers. I don't want you to have to cook."

"We brought enough food for a month," she teased. "And it's nice having someone to cook for. Why don't you crack open a beer and hang out on the porch while I get things going here?"

"Yeah? You sure that's all I need to do?"

He slid his fingers into the silky strands of her hair, tilted her head back and pressed his mouth to hers. Her lips were so soft and tasted faintly of the iced tea she'd been drinking. He drew the tip of his tongue across them in a gentle lick before tracing the seam and urging her to open. The inside tasted even more delicious, but then he was pretty sure he could say that about every part of her body.

When he lifted his mouth from hers at last, she looked at him with heavy-lidded eyes.

"If you want any dinner tonight, you'd better save that for later."

"Maybe I'll just eat you instead," he teased.

A delicate blush suffused her face. "Um, okay. That would work, too."

He loved the fact that despite the intense intimacy they now shared, he could still make her blush. The more time he spent with her, the more he wondered how he could ever have fallen for Ria. That whole chapter of his life was a nightmare from the past that Nikki had helped him deal with. What they were building together was deep and solid.

Now he gave her a light tap on the butt.

"Get cracking here. I'm thinking after dinner we can take a little dip in the lake. Slade says the water is great here, not freezing, and the bottom is very sandy."

She grinned. "I'll get right on it."

He enjoyed sitting on the porch with her after they'd cleared the dishes, just rocking back in forth in the old-fashioned swing that hung from the porch ceiling. They had both decided not to drink any more than the one beer with their meal.

"I want to enjoy everything later to its fullest," he whispered in her ear.

Her lips curved in a shyly seductive smile. "That works for me."

When he kept glancing to the right, she sat up a little straighter and try to see what he was looking at.

"Just wondering if our neighbors ever come outside that cottage. And if not, why not."

"They were out on the porch yesterday," she reminded him.

"Yeah, but I think that was just to check us out."

"Didn't Slade say they'd managed to get out of one of the countries in the middle of a war?"

He nodded. "But still…"

"Maybe they only feel safe inside while they're waiting for whatever comes next."

He shrugged. "You could be right. I think tomorrow I might ask Slade to check them out a little further, though. Meanwhile…" He moved off the swing and tugged Nikki with him. "The moon's just coming up. How about a little night swimming?"

"Are you sure it's safe in there?" She inclined her head toward the lake.

"Yup. I checked it on Google, just to be sure."

She laughed. "I can hardly believe it's even recognized by them, but okay. I trust you."

He wanted to tell her not to bother putting on a bathing suit, because he planned to take it off at the earliest opportunity, but damn! She sure looked good in just that little bit of nothing. Then he reminded himself how much fun it would be to strip it from her.

They grabbed towels from the bathroom which they dropped on the narrow strip of sand bordering the lake. Marc started forward then noticed Nikki was still standing in one spot.

He grinned. "Coming in, chicken?"

She wrapped her arms around herself and gave him a skeptical look. "You first, you big, bad Delta Force soldier. Let's see if you freeze to death."

He laughed and started into the water. "Come on, it's warm. Here. I'll show you."

Marc had expected the water in the small lake to be warm. After all, they were almost as far south as one could get in the United States. But when he waded into it from the tiny strip of beach that fronted the cabin, the shock of it hit him right away. He was lucky he didn't freeze his balls off.

He reached out a hand for Nikki and turned when he realized she wasn't right beside him. She was standing at the water's edge, clearly outlined in the moonlight, arms wrapped around herself, laughing at him.

"Come on in, chicken. It'll wake you up."

She shook her head. "It's almost time to go to sleep. Whose idea was this, anyway?"

He grinned. "I think it was yours. And I have things on the agenda before we hit the hay for the night." He motioned to her. "Come on. I promise I'll warm you up."

He was grateful for the fact that the cottage they were staying in was nestled in a curve of the lake, so none of the other cottages could see it, or them. He especially didn't want the men in the next cottage over watching them. Slade's friend might have vouched for them, but he still had an uneasy feeling, Maybe it was his overdeveloped sense of caution, but he wasn't yet ready to give them a clean slate. He'd talk to Nikki about it in the morning and see if she was up for finding an alternate place.

Of course, finding one as isolated and beautiful as this might not be that easy.

He studied her now as she inched her way slowly into the moonlit lake, the tiny ripples lapping softly against her body. The sight of her made his cock so hard that even the low temperature of the water and the little breeze couldn't make it behave. He had never met a woman who made him so hard, so fast, all the time, and had the rest of the package to go with it. A woman he could spend hours talking to and never run out of things to say. A woman who let him bare his soul and offered comfort and peace. He hoped he did the same for her, as she unburdened her own soul to him.

One thing he was sure of. This vacation had only just begun, but he knew he wanted more — a lot more — with her. His marriage had been a stupid fluke. *This* was what real relationships were made of, something he'd thought he would never have. He mentally crossed his fingers that he wasn't jumping to conclusions.

Nikki made her way through the water until she was standing next to him. Despite the fact she was still hugging herself against the chill, he could see the rounded curve of her breasts that the bikini top barely covered. Her nipples peaked in the cool, the points pushing against the thin material. He moved her arms out of the way and cupped her breasts, his thumbs brushing against the hard tips.

She inhaled softly, then looked to either side of where they stood.

"No one can see us," he assured her. "We're in our own little private world here."

He stepped a little farther out until he was waist-high in the water, holding Nikki firmly against him.

"Put your legs around me," he told her. "Come on."

She wrapped her legs around his waist, moonlight gleaming in her eyes.

"I thought we were supposed to be swimming," she teased.

"There's swimming and then there's swimming. Come on, tighter. Yes. Like that."

He could feel the press of her sex against him, the touch of her making his cock flex. He shifted her so he was perfectly aligned with her sweet pussy. And oh, god, was it sweet. He could still taste the flavor of her in his mouth. Cupping the nicely rounded cheeks of her ass, he pressed her body to his and *shit!* He nearly lost it right then. He'd have thought after a couple of days of immersing himself in her, he'd have some control, but he wondered if that would ever happen. What he felt for Nikki was a potent combination of lust and some emotion he was afraid to identify.

Holding her against him, he rocked her back and forth so the lips of her sex were rubbing against his shaft. The thin, tiny bikini panties might as well have not been there at all. He was glad of the cool temperature of the water or he'd be two steps from embarrassing himself.

He palmed the curve of her ass, giving her firm flesh a light squeeze, and despite his best intentions rubbing her in slow movements against his body. *Oh, sweet Jesus.* Had anything ever felt this good in his life?

He nibbled her jaw, traced a line along the slender column of her neck and licked the shell of her ear. His blood was racing and he wondered just when he had become this sex maniac.

No, not sex maniac. Just a man besotted by a woman with every fiber of his being.

"I really wanted to swim," he murmured, "but if we don't get into the cottage so I can be inside you in the next five minutes, I'll really embarrass myself."

Nikki tightened her legs around his waist, pulling her body even more tightly against his. Then she tucked her head into the curve of his should and whispered, "I've...I've never had sex in water."

His heart nearly thumped out of his chest at the images her words had cascading through his brain.

"I hate to kill that very erotic idea, but condoms are considerably less effective in the water."

With her head still tucked into his neck she said, "I have an IUD."

Every muscle in his body clenched as he realized what that meant. Naked skin to naked skin. *Holy god!*

"Be absolutely sure," he told her. "Because I'll tell you, once I'm ungloved inside you, I'll never want to go back to using a condom."

He felt the slight tremble in her body, a strong indication that this was a very big step for her. Her sexual experiences had been limited to a couple of short-term boyfriends and her long-time fiancé. However intimate she had been with the man she had planned to marry, he didn't want the details. This was brand-new for both of them. He wanted them to make their own memories. He held his breath waiting for her answer.

She lifted her head and looked directly into his eyes.

"I'm sure. If I wasn't, I never would have mentioned it."

Standing in the water, facing her, he managed to pull his bathing trunks down far enough to free his cock. Nikki undid all the ties on her bikini bathing suit and giggled while Marc tied them to one wrist. Then he just stood there, studying her in the moonlight, a naked goddess so tempting he almost came just from looking at her. Thank god for the cool feel of the water.

Sliding his hands up, he cupped her breasts, squeezing their fullness and rasping his thumbs over her nipples as they peaked to hardness. He pinched them lightly, then a little harder. She sucked in her breath and arched into his touch.

Marc bent his head and took one beaded tip into his mouth, even as one hand coasted down the curve of her body and over to her pussy. With the edge of one finger, he lightly stroked between the lips, brushing the swollen bud of her clit. Back and forth, pinching a little now and then and tugging on the swollen flesh. Nikki moaned and threw her head back, bowing backward to push herself harder into his touch.

When he eased two fingers inside her, testing how ready she was, the moan became louder and her breathing accelerated. She had been gripping his arms to hold herself steady but now she dipped a hand below the surface to find his cock and wrap her fingers around it.

Oh, sweet Jesus.

He pressed himself against her, easing his fingers from her hot pussy and cupping her cheeks to take her mouth in a hot, hungry kiss. He licked the soft tissue inside and glided his tongue over her smaller, more delicate one.

She squeezed his shaft in a steady rhythm, driving him close to the point of no return.

"Slide your legs around me like you did before." He could hear how ragged his breath was.

"Okay."

As soon as she did, he guided his cock to her opening and eased it slowly inside, gasping at the hot feel of her naked flesh. He had to grit his teeth to take it slowly. When she squeezed him with her inner muscles, it was all he could do to control himself. With her legs wrapped around him and his arms bracing her, he set up a steady movement of thrust and retreat. The drag of her inner muscles against his swollen shaft, the hot, intense feel of her despite the cool water, were driving him crazy.

Taking her mouth in a hard, demanding kiss, he increased the rhythm, the light slap of the water against their skin like some kind of erotic music. Nikki moaned into his mouth and he drove harder and faster. Mouth still fused to hers, he rocked them both in the water, hard, faster. He made it last as long as he could, but when he felt that first tiny quiver in her inner walls, he increased his pace, before giving one hard, final thrust and taking them both over the edge together.

Her muscles squeezed him in a steady rhythm as his cock pulsed and throbbed, spurting into her, the sensation so intense he thought he might lose his mind. Nikki clung to him for dear life, her naked breasts pressed hard against his chest, the nipples like tiny points of flame.

When he couldn't stand there with her any longer, he eased himself out of her tight clasp, lowered her legs and held her against him for a long moment until he felt steady enough to move. Then he pulled up his trunks, lifted her and carried her naked out of the water. He set her on her feet and wrapped one of the towels around her then stripped off his trunks and knotted a towel at his waist.

He took a moment to scan the area to make sure no one had been watching before he picked her up to carry her inside.

Nikki was cuddled against him, arms around his neck, head resting on his shoulder. He was sure he could hold her like this forever. It was for damn sure the image he'd keep in his mind when he was huddled down with the other members of his team stalking an enemy.

He couldn't believe that his cock was already stirring with desire, but he wanted her to know this was about more than sex. *Been there, done that, worn the scars.* This was about an emotional connection and building a foundation, something he'd been sure would never happen in his lifetime.

When he was sure they were both completely dry, he carried her into the bedroom.

"I can walk, you know." Her voice was tinged with laughter.

"Maybe I just like carrying you," he teased. "Okay, bedtime."

He placed her on the bed and slid in beside her, adjusting her so he spooned around her body. He loved the feel of her softness against his hard muscles, her silky hair brushing against him. The way her breast fit perfectly in his hand when he cupped it.

He made a quick mental note to remind himself to call Slade in the morning. Then he pressed her body more tightly to his, so his now thoroughly aroused cocked nestled in the crevasse of her buttocks. God. She made him insatiable.

"I thought you were sleepy?" There was a hint of laughter in her voice.

"Apparently not that sleepy." He kissed the shell of her ear. "But if you are, you can just relax and I'll do all the work."

Then he forgot about anyone and anything except the woman in his arms.

Chapter Six

"Are you sure you understand what I told you?" Jamal looked at Kasim and Farid, assessing them. "It's very important that you do this right."

"Do you think we are stupid?" Farid growled. "You treat us as if we are twelve. This is for my brother. Do you think I would be careless?"

Jamal drew in a deep breath and let it out slowly. It would do no good to antagonize these men. He needed them to be at the top of their game, wherever that was. To execute this without a hitch or they would all be in big trouble.

"I apologize. We just do not have any room for error."

"The error has already happened," Kasim spat at him. "From the moment Malik was shot, this has been a disaster. Why did you not force the driver to take us to whoever we are reporting to in the city? The person who put this together? You are supposed to be the team leader."

Allah, please give me strength.

"Malik getting shot was unforeseen," he reminded them. "And I do have a plan, since the person we were supposed to rendezvous with seems to be ignoring us."

"Good." Farid nearly spat the word. "Because things are very bad right now. If we do not get Malik help soon his entire body could become infected — then what would we do?"

"And we need a car," Kasim reminded him. "We cannot stay here indefinitely. Do you know where we were supposed to be taken before Kasim got shot?"

"In San Antonio. I need the address so we can put the equipment together. The man in charge there is supposed to have it for us."

"But we can't do anything unless we know where that is," Farid raged. "You must remind the idiot you call of that."

"Enough!" Jamal held up his hands. "I have a plan. It involves getting Malik attended to and procuring transportation for us. Then we will force the issue."

"Then let us hear it." Kasim glared at hm. "I am tired of being cooped up in this godforsaken place, shut off from the outside world for all intents and purposes."

"So sit and I will tell you." He glanced in the bedroom. "But first we must change Malik's dressing and give him some aspirin. Then you must pay very careful attention because absolutely everything has to be done just right."

* * * *

Nikki stood on the porch drinking her morning coffee, looking out at the lake. The picture was so peaceful, the sun just rising and reflected in the waters that showed barely a ripple. A few ducks bobbed and dipped out in the middle, two of them fluttering their wings and disturbing the otherwise mostly tranquil surface.

She felt blissful, her body sated and relaxed in only the way stupendous sex could do. She would not have expected Marc to be a gentle lover as well as an intense one, but it seemed he ran the gamut. She couldn't ever remember feeling so completely satisfied and that said a lot, because Jon also had been an accomplished lover.

But there was something about the connection she and Marc had developed, the way they'd come to know each other's bodies so intimately in such a short time. She had to keep pinching herself to make sure she wasn't dreaming.

"That looks like some serious thinking going on."

His voice still had that sexy, husky, early morning growl to it, a sound that reverberated through all her important parts. How could it be that after enjoying almost nonstop sex, she still wanted him with a fierce desire?

If this is a dream, please don't let it end any time soon.

She turned to look at him, deliciously sleep-rumpled, the scruff of beard only adding to the erotic image. His lips curved in one of his slow smiles that pressed every one of her hot buttons.

"Up early, aren't you?" He grinned. "I guess I didn't wear you out as much as I thought. I'll have to work on that."

Heat flashed over her body in a wave of warmth and the pulse in her sex throbbed with low, insistent need.

I'm becoming an addict. As much as I loved Jon, it was never like this with him.

For one second she was hit with a feeling of disloyalty and thought about telling Marc they should leave. Then she gave herself a mental kick. She had loved Jon with every fiber of her being. Done everything she could for him. Shut herself away in a closet filled with recriminations after his death, convinced she deserved the punishment of isolation. Until, that is, Marc had come along with his own demons and they'd managed to help each other to begin the healing process.

She smiled at him over the rim of the cup.

"I think that's probably a very good idea. But since we'll probably need all our strength, how about we run up to the store and get some of those sweet rolls Slade said they were famous for?"

"You go ahead. I'm going to take a quick shower then see what I can pull together for breakfast to go with the rolls." He winked. "Speaking of needing strength."

She widened her eyes. "And you cook, too? I think I hit the jackpot here."

He slid his fingers through her hair and turned her face toward him. "You have no idea."

Then he proceeded to kiss the life out of her, lightly running his tongue over her lips before thrusting it into her mouth and thoroughly licking the inside. By the time he lifted his mouth from hers, she could hardly remember her own name. Then he gave her a gentle swat on her butt.

"Better go get those rolls. Don't want to waste any time."

"Rolls?" She looked at him through a haze. "Time?"

He laughed, that low, husky sound that made every part of her body do a hula dance.

"Yes. Hurry, because there's more where that came from."

She watched as he headed toward the bathroom and the shower, mesmerized by the flex of muscles in his very fine ass and the sheer beauty of his sculpted body. Then she kicked herself into gear. Shoving her cell phone in her pocket, she grabbed her purse and keys then headed out of the front door.

She had just walked around to the driver's side of the car and was unlocking the door when a strong arm reached around her and a hand closed over her mouth and nose, pinching her nostrils. She tried to scream but no sound would come out. Kicking back was futile. Her attacker was much stronger than she was, and he lifted her from the ground so her feet were flailing. Then something pinched the nerves in her neck and blackness surrounded her.

* * * *

Jamal stared at the two men who carried Nikki into their cottage. Her head hung back limply over an arm.

"I hope you did not do her any damage. We need her to be able to do her work."

"Just put her to sleep enough to get her here," Kasim assured him as he placed the woman in an armchair.

"You had no trouble getting away with her car? That is our transportation now."

"What if the man with her reports it stolen?" Farid stuck out his chin. "What if *she* does?"

"The woman will be no problem. Trust me." Because he'd make sure of that. "And you were supposed to take care of the man, so why are you both here?" He glared at Farid. "One of you was supposed to stay and make sure her boyfriend could not come after us. Can you not follow simple instructions? No wonder we are in this fucking mess."

Farid stared back. "We wanted to make sure we got away cleanly. Getting the nurse for my brother was my priority. Now I will go back and take care of the man."

"You had better." Jamal gave a derisive snort. "We cannot afford for one more thing to go wrong. We must get out of here with no problem, and we must be sure Malik is taken care of."

"I know that as well as you."

"You be very careful," Jamal warned. "That man did not look like an ordinary citizen. If we are going to have a dead body, I would prefer it not be yours."

"As would I. Or my brother's. Be assured I can take care of this. I am going right now." He pulled his gun from the small of his back, checked it and returned it to its place. Then, glaring at Jamal, he slipped outside and headed for the other cottage.

Jamal turned to look at the woman in the chair, who was just coming back to consciousness. She was a little thin for his taste, but he did have a fetish for long blonde hair. Perhaps he could focus on that, find time to enjoy her after she performed the task he needed her for. If Farid managed to succeed in eliminating the woman's partner, he would have plenty of time to pleasure himself.

The woman blinked stared at him and opened her mouth as if to scream. In a moment he was in front of the chair, his hand closed around her throat.

"I would hate to kill you when we need your services so badly. Do not scream, and you have a better chance to live."

She stared at him for a long moment, fear flickering in her eyes, but then she nodded and he removed his hand.

"Better. Much better."

"W-What do you want with me?"

He pointed toward the bedroom where Malik, lying on the bed, was visible. "My friend has a bullet in his leg. I need you to remove it."

"Me?" Her jaw dropped. "I'm not a doctor. I'm a nurse. And not a surgical one, either."

Jamal shrugged. "A nurse is a nurse. I have seen them in crisis situations find a way to do anything. So you will find a way to do this."

"And if I don't?"

His smile was anything but humorous. "Then I will be finished with you long before I intended."

"My boyfriend—"

"Will not be a factor. He is being taken care of as we speak."

He watched as both fear and anger flitted across her face.

"I don't believe you."

Jamal shrugged again. "No matter. Either fix my friend or I will shoot you now."

Her hands tightened into fists. He wasn't sure if it was from anger or fear and, truthfully, he didn't care. Just as long as she got the job done. He watched the play of emotions on her face and knew the exact moment she'd made her choice.

"Fine. Let me look at your friend and I'll see what I can do."

At that moment a cell phone rang, the sound coming from the pocket of her shorts.

"That's my boyfriend." She pulled out the phone "If I don't answer, he'll know something's wrong."

"Something is wrong." Jamal snapped his fingers. "Give me the phone. Now!"

She jumped but handed it over. He dropped it on the floor and ground it beneath his heel.

"There. No more phone problems. Come."

She pulled back from him. "When he can't reach me, he'll come looking for me."

The man's smile held no humor. "Then he will be very sorry. Now let us look at my friend's wound."

Closing his fingers around her arm, he led her into the bedroom where Malik lay moaning on the bed. She unwrapped the bandage on his leg with gentle care, and the look on her face told him her assessment wouldn't be good.

"He needs to be in a hospital. Right now."

Jamal shook his head. "Not possible."

"But—"

"Just not possible." He said the words in a harsh, firm tone. "You have to fix him here. We have bandages and some medicine, but the bullet has to come out."

She looked as if she was again ready to argue with him, then gave a short nod. Maybe she figured if she fixed his friend, she could talk her way out of here. Fat chance. He couldn't leave any loose ends.

"Okay. Fine. Do you have protective gloves?"

He pointed to the box on the dresser. "You'll find what you need in there."

She shook her head, then lifted the box and put it on the bed.

"I need a bowl of hot water, towels and a screwdriver or something like it."

He stared at her as if she'd lost her mind.

"A screwdriver?"

She looked at him, impatient. "To dig out the bullet. Do you have any liquor?"

"Liquor? Are you planning to get drunk before you do this?" He yanked his gun from the small of his back. "Perhaps you are not the right person for this after all."

She held up her hands. "Please. I'm not stupid. But this is going to hurt your friend, and alcohol will ease that pain."

Jamal studied her for a long moment, then put his gun away and nodded to Kasim. "That bottle the idiot gave us will come in handy after all. Get it."

"If you show me where things are, I can—"

"Kasim will get it."

It seemed only moments had passed before they were all gathered around the bed, everything the nurse had asked for on the bedside table. The nurse washed Malik's leg with great care, while Kasim held the man's head and dribbled alcohol into his mouth. Then, with everything ready, she took the screwdriver and carefully probed the area of the wound.

At her first touch Malik let out an unholy scream. Kasim gave him more alcohol but it didn't seem to do much. The deeper she probed, the more he screamed.

"Are you sure you know what you're doing?" Kasim growled.

"Yes," she snapped back. "This really should be done under anesthesia."

"Since we don't have that luxury, just get it over with as fast as possible."

When Malik's shouts faded, Jamal realized the man had passed out. *Good. Better for him that way.*

"Jamal, you need to call that number in the phones," Malik whispered. "They cannot just keep us out here like this. We have to get to San Antonio. We have a job to do. One we trained for. We made those…packages…for six months to get them just right.

The rodeo starts in just a few days. It is our assignment from Allah. How do we know they even got the right pipes — "

"Shut up, you fool," Jamal hissed, clamping his hand over Kasim's mouth. "You think she can't hear us?"

"She's concentrating on Malik. She won't know what we're talking about, anyway. But regardless of this, he needs a doctor. They would just as soon let us die out here. Why does Allah not take care of us, when we are on an errand for his glory?"

"Did you not hear me say shut up?" Jamal hissed. "I will call when we are done."

He glanced at the nurse, who was bent over the injured leg, working the screwdriver into the bullet hole. She seemed to not be paying attention to them or listening to them. Still, Jamal did not want to take chances, although what did it matter? He'd probably have to kill her when this was done.

The wound was oozing blood, which she periodically stopped to mop with the sterile gauze. Jamal watched her closely, breathing a sigh of relief when at last the bullet popped out into her hand and she dropped it into an ashtray.

"It's out," she told him in a soft voice. "I'll pack the wound as best I can, but he really needs — "

"A doctor is not possible. Fix him up the best you can. With the bullet out, he should be much better off." He glared at her. "At least he'd better be."

Her fair skin turned even paler but he had to give her credit. She didn't flinch. He watched her rinse the wound with alcohol and clean the area around it, then apply the antibiotic ointment and finally wrap a gauze bandage tightly around it. The last thing she did was pick up one of the bed pillows and prop it beneath his leg.

"You should keep that leg elevated. Slows the bleeding."

He nodded, then watched her clean everything up. Killing her would not be a pleasure for him. Thinking of killing reminded him that he had not yet heard the sound of a shot from the other cottage, nor had Farid returned.

"Where the fuck is Farid?" he asked, verbalizing his thoughts. "How the fucking long does it takes to kill one lone man?"

"Should I go check?" Kasim asked.

"No!" Jamal snapped. "No one goes out there and makes themselves a target. Let me think. I need to think."

"I'll just look outside for a minute," Kasim insisted. "That crappy so-called road curves a little here, so no one can see me."

"Be careful. You don't know what's going on at that other cottage, or where the fuck Farid is."

Kasim pulled aside the curtains over the one window on the far wall, trying to see outside, when a sharp *crack!* echoed in the air. He dropped the curtains and jumped back.

"That sound had better be Farid shooting the man from the cottage," he ground out.

"What if it's not? What if the man got the drop on Farid?"

"I don't even consider that." Jamal shook his head. "But if he is not here in one minute, we are getting the fuck out of here."

"And what about Malik? And the woman?"

Jamal felt the burn of his ulcer. "Get everyone into the car. Now. We are running out of time. The rodeo starts in a couple of days and we haven't even made it to San Antonio yet."

The nurse was standing by the bed when Jamal stalked into the room. She opened her mouth to say something when he punched her in the jaw with enough force to knock her out. He caught her as she folded and lifted her in his arms.

"What are you doing?" Kasim stood in the doorway, a panicked look on his face.

"Getting the hell out of here. If Farid is still alive, we will pick him up on the way out. If he's dead, we need to get away from here before we are shot, also. Put the woman in the car and tie her hands and gag her."

"Better we should kill her and leave her here."

"Idiot! What if we need a hostage?"

"But—"

"Just shut up and do as I say."

He took a moment to toss everything they might need into the satchel the driver had given them. Then he lifted Malik over his shoulder, trying his best to shut out the man's screams of pain, and carried him out to the car. He had a tremendous sense of urgency, aware that if things had gone to shit they had little more than seconds to get away.

Again he cursed the jackass who had shot Malik, the idiot who had dumped them here, and whoever was on the other end of that phone call and seemed to be washing his hands of them. Had someone else been given the assignment for which they'd trained for months? *That better not happen.* Jamal knew how to exact revenge.

The nurse was in the back seat where Kasim had dumped her, gagged as he'd ordered with her hands bound behind her back. He placed Malik as gently as possible, resting his head on the unconscious woman's lap.

"I'll drive," Jamal snapped. "Squeeze in the front seat and have your gun ready."

As he cranked the engine, he saw the man who had been with the nurse emerge from the tall grasses that filled the area. The very man he had sent Farid to dispose of. *Fuck!* Where the hell was Farid? He should have known better. Farid was the worst shot of all of them. He was only part of the team because of his other skills.

Fine. They had one chance to get out of here. Jamal floored the accelerator, heading straight for the man, who stood directly in front of them firing straight at them He and Kasim ducked to avoid the bullets that hit the windshield, spraying glass everywhere.

"Shoot him, you idiot!" he swore at Kasim.

But Kasim's aim was affected by his movements to avoid being shot himself. All his shots missed the man, who jumped to the side at the last moment, still firing at them. And there was no sign of Farid.

"He almost hit me!" Kasim screamed. "Get us the fuck out of here."

Shit!

It was a miracle they got past the man without any more hits, but they were in deep trouble. Malik was moaning in the back seat and the car had taken several hits from the bullets. They couldn't drive it anywhere in the condition it was in, which included two flat tires. As the man had jumped out of the way, he had continued to fire and shot them out.

They'd be lucky if they weren't all eliminated for botching this as badly as they had.

"Now what?" Kasim asked as they reached the road that led in from the highway. "We are fucked, Jamal. If that guy is alive, Farid is surely dead, and the shooter will be after us. You have made a mess of this."

"I have made a mess of this? Don't even go there. Anyway, he has no way to follow us right now because we have their car. I will get us another vehicle, so just shut the fuck up."

Lucky for them, there was no traffic at the moment on the side road. There were, however, two houses, set way back from the road, each with vehicles in their driveway. Jamal hotwired one in the first driveway, thanking Allah that he could do it swiftly. When the homeowner came out to see what was going on, Jamal shot him. They got Malik into the new vehicle, but as he reached in for the nurse, he realized she had come to and was kicking out at him.

"What's going on out here?" Someone was screaming at him.

Jamal looked sideways to see a woman rushing out of the house pointing a shotgun at him.

Fuck! Can my luck get any worse?

Leaving the woman in the car, he jumped in the hotwired vehicle, backed up in a spray of gravel and took off like a bat out of hell.

"You left the nurse in the car," Kasim pointed out. "Now we have no hostage."

"Did you want us to get shot while we dragged her out of the car? Just shut up and keep an eye on Malik. We have to find a place to hide for the moment and I have to use one of those phones to call our contact. It's time for him to help us so we can do the job we were brought here to do."

And pray to Allah that we don't get killed along the way.

Chapter Seven

Motherfucker!

Marc ejected the empty magazine from his .9 mm Glock 17 pistol, grabbed a full one from his pocket and jammed it into place as he ran after the car. He'd aimed for the front seat and the two men sitting there, but he'd been a second or two late, giving them a chance to duck down. It pissed him off that he, a reasoned Delta Force solider, hadn't been able to take out his target. Plus, his gut told him Nikki was in that car, even though he hadn't seen her, and he didn't want one of his bullets to hit her. *Damn!* He needed to stop these assholes.

The morning had begun so nicely. After a night of incredible, erotic, fulfilling sex, he'd kissed her good morning and hugged her before she headed to the little restaurant store at the crossroads for the highly recommended cinnamon rolls. As soon as she was out of the door he'd jumped in the shower. Fifteen minutes later, showered and shaved, he was out on the porch drinking a cup of coffee and watching for her. And waiting. And waiting.

Wondering what was taking her so long, he dialed her cell phone, frowning when he got no answer. He found the number for the restaurant on the internet, stunned when whoever answered told him no one like that had been in that morning.

What the fuck?

Okay, maybe she'd had car trouble on the way, but that didn't explain her cell not working. The service out here was good, as witness the strong signal on his own. All his well-trained senses told him something was wrong, that something bad had happened. If anyone had hurt her, they'd better hope they were dead before Marc found them.

Grabbing his Glock and an extra magazine—an automatic reaction—he took off running, out to the little feeder road then up to the store. In his condition it was a ten-minute run, but that didn't matter. She wasn't there and no one had seen her.

Discipline allowed him to push back the swelling fear of what might have happened to her and focus on the situation. He was dead certain she wouldn't just have driven off without a word, without a call or even a text. Not with the way things were going between them. That meant something had happened that had involved both her and her car.

His mind went at once to the next cottage over and the two men they'd seen yesterday. Men who had at once raised his internal sensors.

Relatives of a friend, my ass.

There hadn't been a car parked near their cottage. At the time he hadn't thought much about it, but now he wondered if they'd decided to grab Nikki's car. Had they watched this cottage and waited for someone to come out? What if he'd come out instead of her? Or if the two of them had been together? He'd only seen two men yesterday, but could there have been more? Of course. He should have asked more general questions. Neighborly ones. Except those guys hadn't looked very hospitable.

Okay, regroup and reassess. Do it like a mission. What's the most logical answer here?

Then he remembered that one of the men had shown interest in the fact that Nikki was a nurse. *So.* They needed a nurse and obviously a car. He had no idea how they'd gotten here to begin with but apparently they'd been dumped without transportation. So what the fuck were they doing here without a car and why did they need a nurse? They had to have taken Nikki and her car. That was the only answer for this.

As he came to the slight curve in the road where the path to his cottage intersected, he stepped off the crappy pavement and eased his way through the shoulder-high grass. The cottage where they'd run into the men yesterday was too far away for him to see it from the road, but he immediately went into stealth mode.

As he moved soundlessly through the marsh grass and bushes, he spotted a man creeping towards the cottage, holding a gun in his right hand. It was one of the two men they had seen the day before. *Shock.* He could sneak up behind him as he'd done on other targets, place the barrel of his gun against the guy's skull and ask him where the fuck Nikki was. And her car.

But just then the man turned, as if sensing something, and any advantage was lost. Marc fired twice, both bullets hitting the man dead center of his forehead. He collapsed at the foot of the little stairway. Looking in all directions as he moved, Marc crouched next to the body, searching in his pockets for any kind of identification. There was nothing. Not even a handkerchief.

Okay. His next step was to make his way to the cottage where these guys were holed up.

But just as he started forward, he heard the roar of a car motor and in seconds Nikki's car came barreling toward him at full speed. Feet apart, he braced his gun hand with his other and shot straight at the windshield. *Bam! Bam! Bam!* He fired the shots in quick succession, but only managed to splinter the windshield.

Fuck. That didn't usually happen. Maybe he'd better get in some target practice once they got out of this mess.

He jumped to the side as the car nearly ran him down, braced his feet again and peppered the tires with bullets. Two of them flattened even as the driver gunned the motor harder, the rear end of the car swerving left and right, and turned onto the little feeder road. Marc raced after it, running full out, but even with two flat tires, it pulled away from him. As soon as he reached the road and headed for the highway, he saw Nikki's car ahead parked on the shoulder. He raced toward it, heart thundering, dreading what he would find. Or not find, and he didn't know which would be worse.

When he got closer, he saw the body of a man lying in the driveway of the first house and a woman kneeling beside him, a shotgun lying next to her. She looked up as she heard him pounding on the road and reached for the gun beside her.

"Don't shoot," he shouted. "I won't hurt you. Just give me a minute here." He said a little prayer that she'd listen to him.

But his first priority was Nikki. Was she still in the car? Had they taken her with them? When he got to the car and saw no one sitting up front, he yanked open the rear door. Every prayer he'd ever known raced through his mind when he saw her alive, conscious and struggling to sit up. Two bruises were blooming on her rapidly swelling chin, but she seemed otherwise okay. He made quick work of the gag in her mouth and the rope tying her hands behind her.

"I'm going to lift you out of the car now, okay? Let's be careful because you've got some glass on your clothes. Not much, but I don't want you to cut yourself."

She nodded and clung to him as he extracted her from the mess of the car with extra care. Once he had her on her feet, he shook the glass off her T-shirt and shorts, thanking every god in the world that not much had fallen on her. Being as careful as possible, he began checking her over further for any injuries he couldn't see. Then he pulled her into his arms.

Thank you, God.

"Call 911," he hollered at the woman by the driveway. "Call them now. I'll be right there."

"He's bleeding," she cried.

"Call 911," Marc shouted again. "I'll be right there."

Nikki pressed kisses into his neck.

"I knew you'd find me and save me." She hugged him tighter. "They smashed my phone. I knew when you couldn't get hold of me you'd come looking for me."

He chuffed a laugh. "Yeah, well, I wasn't supposed to lose you in the first place. What the hell happened?"

"They were waiting when I came out of the cottage. I didn't even have a chance to call out to you." She looked around. "Where are they?"

"Gone." He studied her face. "What did they do to you? I don't like the look of those bruises."

"They knocked me out before they put me in the car. And not too well, either. It's okay, Marc. Believe me, I'll survive. They could have done a lot worse."

"I have to check on that guy they hit. Come over here and sit on the grass, okay?"

"I can stand, Marc. Really. I'm okay."

"Humor me, will you? Just this once?"

"Okay, fine. But you remember I'm a nurse, right? I can help you with that man."

He was torn between keeping her out of the way and needing her help.

"Fine. Okay." He gave her a quick kiss then yanked out his cell phone and pressed the speed dial for Slade.

"I thought you two would be hiding from the world." Slade's voice was warm and teasing.

"Forget that shit and get your ass out here right away. And I mean right away. Use the helo. We've got a shitload of trouble and the mother of all clusterfucks. Whatever your so-called friends told you about those guys in the other cottage is a load of bullcrap. Those supposedly friendly dudes kidnapped Nikki and—"

"Kidnapped her?" Slade barked. "Where? How? Is she—"

"I've got her back. Don't worry. They stole her car, which by the way I had to shoot up all to hell. They stole a neighbor's vehicle and shot him in the process. We're gonna check on him right now. I've also got a dead guy outside the cottage we're staying in. I told the neighbor to call 911. If she did, I'm sure a sheriff's deputy is on his way so you need to be here ASAP."

As usual, Slade wasted no time with questions. "On it."

The woman was still kneeling beside the injured man on the ground. She had yanked off her cardigan sweater and was holding it against the wound. The man's chest was covered in blood, but lucky for him it seemed to be coming from his right shoulder.

Nikki slipped past Marc, knelt beside the man and pressed a finger to the hollow of his throat, then breathed a sigh of relief.

"He's got a pulse," she told Marc. "It's erratic but still beating." She looked at the woman, who Marc assumed was his wife. "I'm a nurse. Your husband has a decent pulse but he needs help right away. Using your sweater this way was a smart thing to do."

She rearranged the garment, now blood-soaked but still better than nothing, and kept pressure on the wound.

"I called 911," she told them.

"How far away is the nearest responder?"

"The firehouse is just the other side of the crossroads, so they should be here real quick. They're pretty good at a fast response."

Despite the fact that the woman was distraught and tears streaked her face, she had kept it together. The guy was damn lucky. Apparently when they'd shot at him, they'd done it on the fly, which was probably the only reason he wasn't dead. *Thank god for that.*

"Ma'am?" He knelt beside the woman. "My name is Marc Blanchard. This is Nikki Alvarez. Can you tell us yours?"

"Kitty." She got the name out between gulping sobs. "Kitty Lester." Her face was streaked with tears and her hands were shaking, but Marc gave thanks that she was focused on trying to stanch the bleeding and do whatever had to be done. "They just shot him," the woman wept. "I would have given them the damn car."

He wanted to tell her they didn't give a shit, but that wasn't what she wanted to hear.

"Luckily your husband's still alive," he assured the woman, "but he needs medical attention right away. Let's move back and give Nikki some room to work."

"Emergency will send a sheriff's deputy, too," she told him.

Even as she spoke Marc heard the wail of the siren. Looking in that direction, he saw an ambulance bearing down on them, lights flashing and siren screeching. It pulled up close to where they were both kneeling over her husband.

"Here is the ambulance now. These people will take good care of your husband. Uh, did you get a good look at the men who did this?"

She shook her head. "Not so much. They were already getting into John's car when I ran out the door. I just know they all had dark hair and looked Middle Eastern. Why did they have to shoot him? Why?"

"These are not nice people." And boy, wasn't that just the damn truth. He patted her shoulder. Giving comfort wasn't his strong suit. "But don't worry. We'll get them."

Damn right I will.

A man and a woman in familiar blue coveralls with a paramedic badge on the left side hurried over. Marc rose to make room for them, and as he stepped away Nikki also rose, wiping her bloody hands on her shorts.

He was so damn proud of the way she was handling herself.

"Marc, listen. I don't know if this means anything but they talked about Mexico and a target and San Antonio. And they've been waiting for someone to come back to get them. I think the man getting shot was an unpleasant surprise."

Marc's blood chilled.

"Mexico? San Antonio? Are you sure?"

She nodded. "They're supposed to do something big when they get there, and they're pissed off that someone else might get to do it."

Marc thumbed Slade's number again on his phone. When the connection went through he could hear heavy background noise.

"We're ready for liftoff right now," Slade answered.

"Good. The law will be here any minute. Whoever told you those people were seeking sanctuary here? Not even close. Somebody's lying here."

"God damn it to fucking hell! Okay, you near the crossroads there?"

"Right down the street. And Slade? We have to get the word out on these bad guys."

It was hard to talk over the noise of the helo so Marc hung up.

"My girl over there's been hurt, too," he told the closest paramedic. "Can you just take a look at her jaw? I think all she needs is an ice pack."

"Can she be moved?" the woman asked. "We need to take care of this man first."

"Yes. Let me bring her over here."

He ran back to Nikki, who was sitting there, still looking shell-shocked, her face now swollen and discolored. Anger surged through Marc unlike anything he'd ever felt. If the men who'd done this were anywhere near him at the moment, he'd tear them apart limb from limb. *Literally.* He took a deep breath to calm himself. Going crazy wouldn't help right now.

"Come on, babe. I'm getting you over to the ambulance so they can treat you. Let me carry you, okay?"

"I-I can walk, Marc. Really." She held on to him as she rose, but she had only taken a couple of steps before she stumbled. "Sorry. I guess —"

"Let me do this."

He lifted her up in his arms and carried her over to the ambulance, setting her down on the tailgate. However, he kept his arm around her, holding her while she was examined.

"She needs ice on that face," the woman examining her told Marc. "You were right. And she should be checked over for concussion, but she doesn't seem to have any other injuries." She reached into the ambulance and brought out a canvas tote, pulled out a frozen gelpak and handed it to Nikki. "Be sure to keep this on there. Twenty minutes on, twenty minutes off. If over-the-counter pain relief doesn't work, make this handsome hunk here take you to the doctor."

"I'll keep an eye on her," Marc said in a firm voice.

"I'm okay," Nikki whispered.

He grinned. "And I'm taking care of you. Period."

"Hang on to the rest of these gelpaks." The woman gave them the tote. "Just drop the tote off when you're done."

"Thanks." Marc took it from her and looked at Nikki. "You sure you aren't hurt anywhere else?"

"Of course," she assured him. "My face will be sore for a while and be sixteen gorgeous colors, but I can deal with it."

"Can you tell me what their deal is? Why they grabbed you? Did they say?"

She blew out a shaky breath. "They were mad because they had no car. They got me just as I was unlocking the car to get in."

"But why take you if they only wanted the car?"

"One of them was shot in the leg. They remembered my T-shirt from the day before, the one that had *Nurse* on it. They made me take the bullet out and treat him with what they had. Which wasn't much."

He stroked her hair, trying to soothe her. "What else did they say? Anything?"

"Um, they're supposed to be in San Antonio. Being here wasn't planned. Whoever picked them up was supposed to take them into the city, but I think the guy getting shot screwed up everything. It sounded like whoever was supposed to take them just dumped them out here. They kept talking about their big assignment here in Texas. That it was happening in a few days and they didn't have much time. And I think they mentioned the rodeo."

The sensation of an icy fist gripped Marc's stomach, colder than the stuff Nikki was using on her face. He knew all about the San Antonio Stock Show and Rodeo. Knew it was one of the largest in the country, with a combined daily grounds and show attendance of more than one hundred and fifty thousand. And that didn't count the surrounding area filled with homes and businesses. A great place for terrorists to do a lot of damage and make a statement.

"We need to get the right people involved in this. I'm sure the sheriff will be here any minute and want to talk to us, but Slade's on his way. He needs to know this ASAP and contact the right people. I want to talk to the woman whose husband was shot. Ask her a couple of questions."

"Let me come with you." She drew in a shaky breath and let it out slowly. "I'm good, and maybe I can help."

He knew that, as a nurse, that would be her first reaction. *Damn it.* This was supposed to be a romantic getaway while they explored their growing relationship, not what it had turned into.

"Fine. Come on, then."

He knew she was far from good, but he had to find out what happened. Kitty Lester kneeled by the stretcher, holding her husband's hand, squeezing it, tears running down her face. She looked to be in her forties, best as Marc could tell. She let go long enough for John Lester to be loaded onto a stretcher as he approached. Then she rose from where she'd been kneeling, her face tear-streaked and pale.

"Is-Is that your wife?" She looked at Nikki.

He managed a smile. "Almost." He ignored the stunned look on Nikki's face. "Can you tell me a little more about what happened?"

"We heard some people in the driveway, the car, something. John went out to see what was going on and they shot him." She pressed a shaking hand to her mouth.

Nikki moved closer and put an arm around the woman. Bruised and battered and probably scared shitless, she was still doing her job as the compassionate nurse. Compassionate *person*. At that moment his heart swelled with admiration for her.

"I'm so sorry for that," Nikki murmured.

"It's not your fault." She hiccupped a sob. "We would have given them the damn car."

"Ma'am?" One of the paramedics came back to her. "We're ready to transport him. We'd let you ride with us but someone from Sheriff Gorham's office is on the way and will want to talk to you. He'll bring you to the hospital afterwards, okay?"

She nodded. "Yes. Okay." Fresh tears ran down her face. "Oh, sweet Jesus. Is he going to be okay?"

"We hope so." The man's voice had a professional tone of reassurance. "It doesn't look like any vital organs were hit, but the doctor can give you a better evaluation. We need to get going ASAP."

At that moment, a siren cut through the air. Marc looked down the road to see a sheriff's car racing toward them, lights and sirens on. It pulled to a stop almost side by side with the ambulance. The man who climbed out was a hair under six feet, large, and wearing the light tan uniform of the county sheriff's department. The regulation star was pinned to his left breast.

Just in case there was any doubt, Marc thought.

"Here." He took a fresh gelpak out of the tote he was holding. "Change this for the one you're using. And there's more in the bag." He handed her the bag and looked around. "I wish we had some place for you to sit."

"I'm good. Really."

"The sheriff's deputy is here. He'll want to talk to me and I don't want you to be in the middle of it."

"I'll have to talk to him sooner or later, won't I? You can be sure he'll have questions for me." She gave a slightly hysterical little laugh. "I'm fine, Marc. Truly."

He studied her for a long moment. "You are one of the bravest people I've ever met. And most courageous. Okay, but let's wait until Slade gets here. Hold the ice on your face. I'll be back in a few."

The deputy was speaking to the medical personnel as Marc walked up to him.

"Deputy Al Gorham," he said by way of introduction. "You want to hand me that gun I see in your pocket?"

Before Marc could say anything, Kitty Lester, who kept glancing into the ambulance, shook her head.

"Al, it's not him. He's not one of them." She pointed to Nikki's car. "His girlfriend was hurt by them, too."

"You doing okay, Kitty?" Concern was evident in Al's voice. "The paramedics need to get John to the hospital right away, even though they said they don't think his wound is life-threatening, thank the lord. You gonna ride with them?"

"Yes, if I can." She clasped her hands. "Thank you so much, Al."

"Of course. Anything you need, just let me know. Can you tell me in just a few words what happened? I'll get someone to the hospital after to get more details."

She wiped away her tears. "John heard something in the driveway and went out to check. The next thing I knew, I heard a shot, ran out to see what was happening and John was lying on the ground, bleeding. Whoever those men are, they were driving off in John's car. That's when this gentleman here came racing up."

The deputy gave Marc a thorough head-to-toe look. "That so? Okay, Kitty, you go on and get in the ambulance."

He exchanged a few more words with the paramedics. Then the ambulance took off with sirens screaming and he turned back to Marc.

"I don't recognize you, so how about telling me who you are and what you're doing in the middle of this mess in my county."

"Marc Blanchard." He shook hands with the deputy, then drew Nikki close to him. "This is my girlfriend, Nikki Alvarez. We're staying in the first cottage at the lake." He pointed. "A friend made the arrangements for us."

Gorham gave her an assessing look. "Someone did a number on your face. Can you tell me about that?" He glanced at Marc. "Was it your boyfriend here?"

"Oh, no." She shook her head while Marc did his best not to punch the deputy's lights out. "He would never hurt me."

Marc swallowed his irritation. "She was just checked out by the ambulance crew. She's got a swollen jaw and some swelling and bruises but otherwise they didn't hurt her."

"So why'd they take you?"

"To remove a bullet from the leg of one of their guys." She explained about them seeing her the day before with her nurse's T-shirt. "Plus, they didn't have any transportation. They grabbed me this morning as I was heading out to that little restaurant up there at the crossroads. They never said what had happened."

Marc filled in the rest, including how the men had escaped.

The sheriff looked at the car and frowned. "Damn thing's shot all to hell. You do that?"

Marc nodded. "They came from the cottage just down the lake from us. The guys in the vehicle ducked just low enough that I missed them, though. And by the time I got to the house here they'd just taken off in the Lesters' car."

"I'll need to ask you more about this, but let me make sure one of my deputies is on the way to see Kitty at the hospital. I know she's pretty shook up, but I want to get what she remembers while it's still fresh in her mind. Hold on because I have more questions for you."

He keyed the radio on his shoulder and spoke briefly to someone.

Marc organized his next words in his mind. He had to tell the deputy about the dead guy in his front yard, but he knew that would bring up a whole other complicated set of circumstances.

"Now." Gorham turned back to him. "What else can you add to this?"

"Not all of them got away. There's a dead body lying in front of our cottage. The idiots who got away apparently sent him to take me out."

Gorham's eyebrows arched almost to his hairline. "A dead body? Shit. You kind of buried the lede there, didn't you?"

"I thought we should take care of the Lesters first. Anyway, it was the guy's bad luck that I'm Delta Force, so his chances weren't very good."

A look of respect swept over his face. "Delta Force, huh? I remember you guys from when I was in Afghanistan. But a dead body? This is turning into some kind of asshole clusterfuck, I'll tell you."

"No kidding." Especially if these men might be connected to what they'd been asking about in Niger. "Listen, I have a friend coming any minute to help. In fact"—he looked up—"I think he's here now."

He spotted the familiar dot of a helicopter approaching from the southeast. Gorham looked up also.

"Who the hell did you call that's arriving in a helo? Is there something I should know here?"

"My team leader. As soon as they land, I'm sure he'll answer any questions you have that he can."

Gorham stared at him. "What the hell is going on here?"

Marc said nothing, just watched as the helicopter set down in the big space on the other side of the Lesters' house. The blades were still spinning when the cabin door opened and Slade jumped out. Marc swallowed a smile. His lieutenant was dressed in his Army fatigues and combat boots. Aviator shades covered his eyes and he wore his Glock on his hip. Marc's eyes widened a little more when a second figure hopped out and stood next to Slade. He'd thought Beau Williams was tucked up for the week with his girlfriend, but apparently Slade had pulled him into this.

Then every muscle in Marc's body tightened. *What did Slade learn about our unexpected companions on the lake?*

Chapter Eight

Slade walked up to them, Beau not far behind. *He brought our sniper? What the fuck?* A bad feeling, that he'd been right in his assessment of the situation settled in Marc's stomach.

"And you are?" Gorham asked in a tone edged with hostility.

Slade reached into his breast pocket and pulled out a thin holder that held his Army identification.

"Lt. Slade Donovan. Delta Force. I am Sgt. Blanchard's team leader."

Gorham turned to Marc. "Blanchard, you mind telling me what the fuck is going on around here? You called this guy. You know what this is about?"

Marc started to answer, but Slade cut him off and looked at Marc. "Did you tell him the rest of it?"

"About the dead body? Yeah." Marc shrugged. "I was waiting for you to get here to take him over there."

Gorham frowned. "Why wait?"

"I thought it was more important to get the Lesters taken care of first. This guy isn't going anywhere, and he's part of the group that shot John Lester."

"I need to get someone else out here with me." Gorham spoke into the radio on his shoulder. They could hear the staticky exchange. Then Gorham nodded. "I put out an All Points Bulletin on the Lesters' car, but I did it with a special code we use in case they have something to monitor our system. If anyone spots it, they'll call our office direct. Also, I just radioed for another deputy. He should be here soon."

Marc looked at Slade. "Can we put Nikki in the chopper? She needs to sit and to keep that ice on her cheek."

"I'm good, Marc," Nikki protested. "Please."

"Listen to him, Nikki." Slade's voice was kind but firm. "You've been through a harrowing experience. You don't need to tramp around with us and you certainly don't need to look at a dead body."

"Please," Marc added. "I'm only thinking of you. We still have work to do today and you don't need to be in the middle of it."

"Okay." She blew out a breath. "I think I'd like to sit, anyway."

Slade stayed with Gorham while Marc walked Nikki over to the helo and introduced her to Slade's ranch foreman.

"Nikki, meet Teo, if you haven't already."

The man grinned at her and reached down to help her up into the cabin.

"You're much prettier than Slade and Beau. I'll even share my coffee with you."

As soon as Marc was satisfied she was okay, he rejoined Slade and Gorham.

"Blanchard, can you give us a description of these guys?"

"I only saw two of them, but yeah. Nikki saw all of them, so she can probably tell you more. Then we need to make some decisions on how to handle this."

"This has to do with who those guys really are, doesn't it?" he guessed.

Slade nodded. "I am so pissed at a friend of mine I could spit nails. Let's get this taken care of first."

Gorham studied both Marc and Slade for a long moment. "Okay. You want to tell me what the fuck is going on around here? Why you arrived in a damn helicopter, wearing battle fatigues? And who this guy is?" He pointed at Beau.

Slade had his battle-ready face on. *What the hell?*

"He's another member of our team. I wasn't sure what we'd run into here, and there are things I am not at liberty to tell you." He glanced at Marc. "What began as a little vacation for my sergeant here and his lady has turned into an incident of national security. There are some calls I had to make and I've been told to put a lid on everything. You said you put out an APB on the car, but that's it. If and when you locate it, let me know right away."

He gave his cell number to the deputy, who just stared at him.

"I'm responsible for the safety of the people in my county," he protested. "Whatever this is, I'll give you all the help you need, but I need to be dialed in."

"Understood."

Gorham looked as if he still had something more to say, but he just nodded. "I'll take care of it." He started to walk toward his car, then turned back. "And by the way, did I mention I was in the Army? Two tours in

Afghanistan before I came home to a quieter life, so I can help and I can keep my mouth shut."

The tension in Slade's body eased a little.

"Good. I promise I'll tell you what I can and do my best to keep your people safe. Are you going over this place?"

Gorham nodded. "I'll start as soon as my deputy gets here. We'll do a full check, both at the Lesters' and the cottage they were using, although I don't think we'll find much."

"But if it's all the same to you," Slade told him, "my men and I want to get a good look at the place where they stayed. We might see things you don't." His tone of voice left no room for arguing.

The deputy looked as if he wanted to say something, then just shook his head.

"Okay, then." Slade turned to Beau, who had been standing quietly by all this time, and to Marc. "Let's take a look at Nikki's car first. See if they left anything in it in the short time they used it."

"Maybe we should have Teo take Nikki to the ranch? Get her out of here?"

Slade shook his head. "First of all, I doubt if she'll agree to that. Second, the sheriff is going to want to talk to her. See what she can tell them about these men. Besides all that, I need to talk to her myself. Find out what she remembers from being with these guys. Anything she can tell us will help."

"Fine. But the minute I think there's danger, she's outta here. Now. You want to tell me what the fuck is going on?"

"Okay, enough," Gorham broke in. "What's this is really all about?" He looked at Beau. "Do you know?"

Beau slid a glance at Slade. "It's his show."

A muscle twitched in Slade's jaw and it was obvious he was weighing his options. How much to tell the deputy, how much to keep back. But as they were both aware, a good relationship with law enforcement partners at every level — state, local, tribal, territorial and campus — was essential to the country's domestic defense against terrorism. But Marc knew Slade had an uncanny ability to evaluate each person as the situation arose.

Finally, he gave a sharp nod.

"I got hold of Andy Goodrich," he told them. "He's actually the one who owns that cottage. He sounded weird the second time I called him. I asked him if he was sure the people in that cottage were seeking asylum and just waiting for a safe house to be available."

"What did he say?"

"After I threatened him with everything including emasculation, he said it's actually his business partner's doing. He doesn't know much about it, but he was suspicious of the story the guy told him. In fact, it turns out these people came up through Mexico, which puts a whole new light on it."

Marc felt a chill creep up his spine. "The terrorist training camp."

Slade nodded. "My thoughts exactly."

Gorham's brows nearly hit his hairline. "What the fuck?"

"Keep this under your Stetson," Slade told him, "but I get the feeling Andy is trying to know as little about this as possible. Anyway, I called a contact at Homeland Security and fuck all anyway. He finally told me they got a tip that something big was planned for the rodeo. That a team was being sent up from that camp in Mexico. Bomb specialists."

"So, the rumors we got are all true?" Marc's facial muscles settled into a hard mask. "Fuck."

"Exactly." Slade waved at Teo, who nodded back.

"So what happens now?"

"Yeah," Gorham agreed. "I'd like to know that, too."

"DHS is sending someone to liaise with the sheriff," Slade said. "I need to give him a heads up on that and read him in on this."

"No shit."

"Let's do that now. I told my guy I wanted to wait until I got here and got more details about the situation. He gave me an hour to handle it." He looked at his watch. "And our time's just about up. Let's get him on the horn."

He pulled out his cell and got the number from Gorham, who made the introduction. He was glad the sheriff was also former military and knew what to ask and what to do.

"Okay." He disconnected the call. "Al, he said to do what we have to here, then haul ass out to his office. As soon as my friend from DHS calls me, I'll tell him it's all set and we'll coordinate." He turned to Marc. "While we're here let's pack up everything you guys left in the cabin. I don't imagine you'll want to be coming back here."

Marc snorted. "You got that right."

"Sorry to cut your vacation short, but—"

Marc shook his head. "Don't even say it. Business first. What's Beau doing here?"

"I'm the backup plan." Those were the first words Beau had spoken since he'd gotten off the helo. "Just in case."

"The only one I'd ever want," Marc told him. "All right. Let's get to it."

The three of them rode with Gorham over to the cottage Marc and Nikki had been using. They climbed out of the car and stared down at the body, still on the steps right where it had fallen. They climbed out of the cruiser and both Slade and the deputy snapped several pictures with their cameras.

"Hey!" Gorham picked up a purse and held it with one finger by its strap. "Blanchard, this must belong to your girl."

"It does. I'm sure she dropped it when she was taken, and no one has looked for it since what happened this morning."

This morning? Is it still so early? He'd lost all track of time.

They were methodical as they went about their business, and Marc was glad to see how efficient Gorham was. Shortly a van arrived, bagged the body then went on to the other cottage, the others following. Marc and Slade watched while they dusted and photographed every surface, took pictures and looked in every drawer and closet.

"Looks like someone was hurt." One of the techs held up a pile of bloody bandages.

"Yeah," Marc told him. "One of their guys was shot. That's why they kidnapped my girl. She's a nurse and they wanted her to get the bullet out."

The tech whistled. "Jesus. What a mess."

"No shit."

When the techs were finished and had left with everything, including the body in a black body bag, Slade and Beau went back to the other cottage to get all the personal stuff.

"I'm guessing you'll be headed to the sheriff's office," Gorham said. "You need a ride or you taking that giant bug out there?"

"Got a place where we can land it?" When the deputy nodded, he said, "Then we're good."

Marc packed up all their shit in seconds and dumped it in the cruiser. When they pulled up to the helo again, Gorham turned to Marc.

"I'll arrange to have your girl's car towed to the sheriff's office. He'll want to have our techs go over it with a fine-tooth comb for fingerprints and anything else we might find in there. Don't know exactly how she'll file a claim on it."

"We'll take care of it. As soon as we're done with the sheriff, I'll take care of a rental and we'll go from there."

He could see the deputy struggling with the desire to ask more questions, but he just nodded once.

"Fine. I'll make the call now to get it towed."

Marc and Slade hauled the suitcase and duffel to the helo, where Nikki sat huddled in the back seat. She had a blanket wrapped around her and she cradled a thermos cap of hot coffee.

Delayed reaction, Marc thought. *She might be big and brave and I admire that, but she's still human. Today's stuff isn't on her everyday menu.*

"I take better care of your lady than you do," Teo teased Marc. "Maybe I should take her home with *me*."

"'Yeah. Not happening." Marc leaned in toward Nikki. "How you doing, babe?"

"Okay." She managed a smile. "The coffee helps. Staves off shock."

He studied her face. "I'm going to believe that if you were hurt any worse than this, as a nurse, you'd be smart enough to tell me."

She gave a small nod. "I wouldn't fool around with a head injury, Marc. I'm good. Really. And I'll put the ice back on in a minute."

"Okay. Slade needs to ask you about what happened when they kidnapped you, and whatever you saw and heard while you were there."

She repeated what she had told Marc, adding a few details she'd recalled since then.

"They were very upset," she told them, "because whoever picked them up had just dumped them. I got the sense that their friend being shot was what caused the change in plans. They weren't the least bit happy about it."

"They didn't happen to mention what their big plan was, did they?" Slade asked.

"No. And I didn't think I should ask. But like I said, they mentioned the rodeo, which I guess is a prime target."

"Hundreds of thousands of people," Beau agreed, his face grim.

"All right." Slade took a step back. "Nikki, we have to go to the sheriff's office and I don't know how long we'll be there. I'd have Teo take you to the ranch, but if they have a sketch artist there, I know they'll ask you to sit with him or her and see if you can reconstruct the faces of the men who are on the run. Can you hang with us for a while longer? If it stretches it too much at the sheriff's office, I'll get Teo to ferry you to the ranch."

"I promise to let you know if that happens. Slade, I want to get these guys, too. I don't know how much good I can be with sketches, but I'm willing to do my best."

"Great. I'll hold you to it. Gorham's getting your car towed to the sheriff's office and I'm making arrangements for a rental. When you're ready, we'll take you new car shopping."

Her eyes widened. "Just like that? What am I supposed to tell my insurance company? They'll never believe my story."

"We won't be using them."

Marc had been watching her carefully, making sure she was as okay as she said she was. She was pale from her ordeal, and no doubt still dealing with the shock of it all, but he was so proud of the way she was holding it all together.

"I packed up all our stuff at the cottage," he told her, "and Teo's putting it in the cargo hold of the helicopter as we speak."

"Can I ask one more thing?" She wet her lip, something he'd come to recognize as a nervous gesture.

"Yeah, babe?"

"At some point can someone get me a cell phone to use? They stomped on mine at the cottage." She actually giggled. "When you called me, it really pissed them off."

She could giggle all she wanted, but it made Marc's nerves twang. Something like that could have set off nerves already raw with tension, and he'd have found her body lying there, too. The thought made him sick to his stomach.

"Assholes," he growled. "Sure. Once we get everything taken care of and we have wheels, we can go to a store and pick out what you want."

"I've got one you can have," Slade told her. "I always carry a couple of extra. We'll fix you up with one when we get to the sheriff's office."

Nikki blinked. "You guys carry extra phones?"

Marc shrugged. "Don't ask. But yeah. Not a problem."

"Thank you so much." She smiled and reached out to touch her fingers to his cheek. "You take very good care of me."

Something deep inside him, something that had nothing to do with sex and that hadn't been there in a long time, broke free and floated to the surface. It warmed his heart and, even in the middle of this situation, it settled his nerves.

He shifted Nikki over and climbed in beside her while Slade buckled himself into the copilot's seat.

"See you in a few," Slade yelled at the deputy, who stood watching as the rotors on the helo began to whine.

In seconds they were lifting off and banking to the side as Teo set a course for the location Slade had handed him. Despite the seatbelts, Marc was able to reach his arm around and pull Nikki a little closer to him. The thought of what could have happened to her today made his blood freeze and his heart nearly stop. That he could have lost her made him realize that she had become far more important to him in a short period of time than he had expected. She was the first person who could pull him out of the darkness he'd been in for so long. He vowed to himself to do whatever it took to keep her safe.

Chapter Nine

Once they were away from the crossroads and onto the interstate, Jamal forced himself to dial back the speed he was driving to a reasonable pace. Malik was moaning softly in the back seat and had been for some time. Moving him first to one car then the other had jostled his wounded leg and it had started to bleed again. Taking a chance that this car was not yet out there on a watch list, Jamal stopped at a convenience store and had Kasim get more supplies plus some small bottles of water.

"We have to change cars again," he told Kasim. "They will be looking for this one. We need to steal one that won't be missed for a while."

"And exactly how do you propose to do that?" he snarked. "Maybe now is the time to finally call that number again. Or do you plan to just steal one car after another and run from place to place?"

"Shut your fucking face."

Jamal was in no mood for attitude right now. Everything was going to hell and he had to figure out a way to stop it. He had gotten back onto the interstate, but now he exited and pulled into a small shopping center with a crowded parking lot. He found a space in a row farthest away from the stores and pulled into it.

"Go do your thing," he said over his shoulder.

"Oh, now you want my help?"

No, I'd like to shoot your head off but I can't. And I need to keep my shit together to get this done. And to get help for my friend.

He ground his teeth. "Yes, now I want your help. And please hurry. We need to do this before the owner of the car returns for it. Try the one on the right first. It's black and fairly anonymous."

Grumbling, Kasim climbed out of the car, taking with him the tool they used to jimmy the locks on car doors. On assignments, they often had to switch vehicles — and not with the owner's permission. This had turned out to be one of Kasim's natural talents. In seconds he had the other car unlocked and the motor started. They transferred Malik along with everything else and, that fast, they were pulling out of the parking lot and heading down the access road. When they came to another convenience store, he pulled in, opened the briefcase on the seat next to him and extracted one of the phones. He took a moment to gather himself before pressing the designated number, listening while it rang on the other end.

"Yes?" The same uninflected voice answered he'd gotten every time.

"This is Jamal. We have a crisis."

There was a moment of silence so long Jamal wondered if the man was still there. He forced himself to wait but it wasn't easy.

"What is your problem? You were told to wait at the little house and someone would come for you."

Jamal gripped the phone so hard he was surprised the plastic casing didn't crack.

"My friend was shot. Your man knew that. He needs medical attention. The temporary materials we were given are just that. Temporary. You have just left us waiting there, and that was not the plan."

"The plan changed when your friend was shot. We weren't sure you would be able to handle your assignment, under the circumstances."

Jamal did his best to control his anger. He would not let these people leave them twisting in the wind. He had been assured that every eventuality had been planned for, but it seemed that was not the case.

"We can still do the job. We still *intend* to do the job. If you cannot come for us, we will find some other way. I do not intend for us to be robbed of this glory or to be labeled a failure. Why have we not been taken to the apartment waiting for us in the city so we can begin putting the packages together? Time is short."

Again there was a long silence.

Jamal ground his teeth. This was not going well at all.

"Perhaps this will move you along. You told us no one else would be staying at the lake where we were. You were wrong. There was a couple staying at the cottage closest to us, and he is some kind of thug. He has killed Farid."

"Ya Ibn el Sharmouta." Son of a bitch.

Jamal's thoughts exactly.

"So because the arrangements were less than desirable, my friend is wounded and perhaps dying. Farid is dead. We have people who are now aware of our existence, and—"

"Where are you at this moment?" the man interrupted.

"In the parking lot of a convenience store, in a stolen car." He'd worry about telling them the details, including the nurse and her car, later on. First they had to get to someplace safe.

"Wait."

Wait? What else can I possibly do?

"What is happening?" Kasim asked. "What is he saying?"

"Nothing at the moment, but—"

The voice broke into his sentence. "Tell me exactly where you are."

Jamal looked around for street signs and read them off as well as the address of the store.

"Fine. I will give you directions to a location. Someone will be there waiting for you. He will take you to a new location."

"The apartment we were supposed to be taken to in the first place."

"I suppose we have no choice. My only other option is to kill the three of you and bury the bodies."

Jamal felt a sudden chill. He hoped the man was kidding.

"If you get us to that place, we can do what we came here for. We can do it better than anyone else, and it will be worth all this trouble."

"It had better be. Get moving."

"What?" Kasim asked, as they pulled out onto the street again.

"We are going to meet someone. Hopefully he will take us to our original destination at last."

I only hope he was joking about killing us.

* * * *

Sheriff Chad Schumacher looked like the movie version of a Texas sheriff, Marc thought. He was tall, broad-shouldered and muscular, with a tan square-jawed face and tiny lines at the corners of his eyes that were probably from squinting into the sun. A tan Stetson sat on top of a file cabinet in his office. Al Gorham made the introductions.

"Well," he said, shaking hands with everyone. "It's not every day I get people arriving here by helicopter. You'll give our little neighborhood here something to talk about for a good while." He studied Nikki's face. "I think maybe we should get a doctor in here to look at that."

"No, I'm good. And I have more ice." She indicated the tote Marc was holding.

"I don't know. It looks pretty bad."

Her smile was more of a grimace. "Trust me. I'm a nurse. If I thought I needed medical attention, I'd get it."

Schumacher looked for a moment as if he was going to argue with her, then just shrugged.

"Fine, but holler if you change your mind. I suggest we all go into the so-called conference room. There's a lot more room in there."

"So-called looks to be the right word for it," Slade murmured as they entered.

It was barely big enough for a long table, eight chairs and a counter that held an array of items that Marc didn't bother to catalog. They arranged themselves around the table, Nikki next to him, while Slade introduced their group.

"You sure you wouldn't rather wait in his office, or maybe with his secretary?"

She shook her head. "I want to know what's going on. These animals grabbed me like I was a piece of meat and probably would have killed me if not for you. I want to know exactly what's happening."

"Coffee, anyone?" the sheriff asked. Then he grinned. "Stupid question. Al tells me you've all been up since the sun, so let me get someone to bring it in."

He waited until everyone had been served and had their coffee fixed the way they liked it. Then he sat back in his chair at the head of the table and looked at Slade.

"I got dribs and drabs from Al here, but I'd appreciate it if you would tell me what the hell this is all about. And why I got a call from the DHS Office for State and Local Law Enforcement telling me someone was on the way to see me and they looked forward to working with me." He gave Slade a hard stare. "Would that someone be you?"

"I'm just the advance guard. When I got the call from Marc about what was going on here, I contacted my commanding officer and he put the wheels in motion. DHS is also sending someone from that office to huddle with the county sheriff."

Again, Schumacher looked around the table, returning his gaze to Slade. Then he nodded at Beau.

"My deputy tells me he got off the helo holding a rifle. What's up with that? Why bring a sharpshooter?"

"I wasn't sure what we'd run into at that little lake, and I always like to be prepared."

Schumacher studied him, then looked around the table.

"Okay. Let's get started here. Lt. Donovan, since you seem to be in charge of your little group, why don't — "

"Slade is fine," he interrupted. "We need to be tight with each other."

"Fine. Slade it is."

"Let's start with our last mission to Niger." He gave the sheriff a very concise description of the rumors they'd heard, the tip DHS had received and what they were supposed to search out during their mission. There were plenty of rumors but a distinct lack of information.

"So you couldn't track it down?" Schumacher asked.

Slade shook his head. "That's not unusual, though. We've had other sources working to track it down, but nothing happened until Marc and Nikki came out here to spend what was supposed to be a quiet week."

"I assume the car Deputy Gorham called to have towed in, the one he says is shot up all to hell, has something to do with this so-called quiet vacation?"

"It does. But you'd better hear the rest of it firsthand from Marc and his lady, Nikki Alvarez. Who, I have to say, is holding up remarkably well considering the hell she's been through today. Marc? You want to fill in the details of what's been going on here since early this morning?"

Schumacher listened, not interrupting, while first Marc then Nikki told their stories. When they were finished, he sat for a moment, digesting it all.

"That's quite some ordeal you've had." He looked from Nikki to Marc and back to Nikki. "Sgt. Blanchard, that's quite a woman you've got there."

"First names," Marc told him. "Like Slade said. And yes, she sure is." He grinned at Nikki, whose face turned a delicate shade of pink.

Schumacher looked at his watch. "The guy from OSLLE should be here any time now. At least I've got an idea what we're looking at. The APB on the car turned it up in a shopping center parking lot. We're having it towed back here so my techs can go over it, too. But that means either they were picked up by someone or they hotwired another car. And until someone calls in the theft, we have no fucking idea what it is."

"They were trying to get to San Antonio," Nikki reminded him. "They were going to call their contact and insist he have someone pick them up."

The muscles in Schumacher's face tightened. "If they did that, we've got fuck-all chance of finding them, but we'll keep looking. Miss Alvarez, you gave us a pretty good description of them. We'll take a shot of the dead man, but it would help to have some visuals of the others. Could I get you to sit with our sketch artist and see if we can get some kind of usable drawings?"

She nodded. "Of course."

He got up and left the room, returning shortly with a woman about the same size as Nikki, dressed in jeans and a T-shirt with the logo of the sheriff's office.

"This is Gina," he said by way of introduction. "Nikki, if you'd go with her, please? If you need coffee or anything, she can fix you up."

"I'd appreciate it. Thanks."

He looked around the table. "I'm guessing no one's had breakfast this morning. I'll send someone over to Main Street to the bakery to get some stuff." He chuckled. "Not as good as those rolls at the diner near where you folks were staying, but they're still damn good."

Slade opened his mouth as if to protest, but the sheriff held up his hand.

"No problem." His mouth curved in a lopsided grin. "I hate it when our guests pass out from hunger."

Marc wasn't sure he could swallow a bite or even wanted to, but since he didn't know when they'd get the next chance to eat, he forced himself. He tried to concentrate on the conversation around the table, but his mind was with Nikki, in another room recreating the images of the terrorists with the artist.

She'll do fine. She's got more guts than I give her credit for.

And wasn't that just the damn truth. He kept thinking of her as the frail person he'd first met at the party, but she had a hidden strength that had allowed her to keep her head this morning when everything had turned to shit.

Marc noticed that Beau had contributed very little to the conversation, probably by design. None of them knew what was waiting out there for them or if the terrorists would try to send someone back to finish off Nikki and Marc. Slade's sniper theory was it was better to have them and not need them than the other way around.

He was just about to ask if he could check on Nikki when Schumacher, who had left to take a phone call, came back into the room with a tall man in jeans and a button-down shirt rolled up at the sleeves. He was big and muscular, broad-shouldered, with close-cropped hair and a full but well-trimmed beard. But most of all, Marc recognized a man who meant business and took it seriously.

"Meet Steven Hofler from the Office for State and Local Law Enforcement. He's our DHS liaison for this little party we're having."

Schumacher introduced him to everyone and he took the seat Nikki had been sitting in.

"Good to meet you all," he told them. "Too bad it's not under better circumstances, but if it was, I probably wouldn't be here."

"Steven and I have worked together once or twice before," Schumacher said. "Our county is pretty low-key. Mostly ranches and quiet neighborhoods, even the more low-income ones. But once in a while some idiots think because of that they can sneak through here without notice." He chuckled. "I'd go into details, but then I'd have to kill you."

Slade nodded once. "No problem. We need to concentrate on this one right now, anyway."

"Looks like some dangerous assholes have decided to shake things up around here." Steven looked at Slade. "The brass has determined based on your information that these men are the same ones you and your team were charged with seeking information on in Niger. Convenient of them to show up so we didn't have to go looking for them." He looked around the table. "But they're on a mission that puts several hundred thousand lives at stake."

"You've discovered their goal?" Schumacher asked.

Hofler nodded. "Information was gathered in Washington and confidential informers are still being questioned. Our sources have uncovered information that they plan to set off bombs at the San Antonio Rodeo and Stock Show. Lucky for you, their target seems to be in Bexar County. Unlucky for them. We need to get on top of this."

"You know we'll give you whatever help you need," Schumacher told him.

"I do, and thank you. We don't know which day yet, but plans have to be made. I've set up a meeting for tomorrow morning with Sheriff Vasquez and several of his men. Slade, that meeting includes you and your people, as well as this young lady here."

"Wait a minute." Marc leaned forward. "Let's leave her out of this."

"I'd like to," Hofler told him, "and I understand your feelings. But she spent significant time with the men and can give us invaluable information. Maybe by that time we'll have more feedback, too. Maybe even gotten a hit from the facial recognition software."

Schumacher quirked an eyebrow. "That fast?"

"Remote," Hofler said, "but we're crossing our fingers. In any event, we're keeping everything in-house, not using any of our confidential sources. We don't want one hint to leak out that we're aware of what they have planned. Or, in fact, that the event today had anything to do with it." He tapped the tablet in front of him. "DHS has given me a rough plan as to how we should handle this based on what we've learned so far. Here's what we know and what we'll need from all of you."

* * * *

As Jamal drove into San Antonio, he paid careful attention to traffic and the speed limit, not wanting to attract any attention. He had no idea if the car had been reported stolen yet, but he wasn't taking any chances on getting pulled over. He followed Interstate 10 all the way to downtown San Antonio, as he'd been directed.

He did his best to ignore Malik's moans in the back seat. Kasim had moved to sit with him, holding the man's head in his lap and bathing his face.

I am sorry, my friend, that this happened to you. I never should have gotten you into this.

As if he could have stopped him. If anything, Malik was even more fervent than he was, ready to lay down his life for the cause. It made Jamal sick to realize that might be exactly what he was doing, but not in a way that would bring glory to him.

He followed the exact directions to a parking garage, drove in and all the way to the top level as he'd been instructed. A long gray panel van was taking up two parking spaces, but when Jamal approached, it backed up so he could move into one of them.

He had no sooner opened his door than a man in a tan shirt and brown pants was right there next to him, his face set in a rigid expression.

"I am Salman. You are positive you were not followed by anyone? No one came after the car?"

Jamal shook his head. "I was very careful. Besides, whoever the car belongs to was still in the mall."

"Good. Where is the woman who worked on your friend's leg? You disposed of her, right?"

Jamal swallowed. "We were not able to do that and still get away. We knew getting to where we could prepare for the mission was most important."

The man studied him for a long moment, enough so Jamal began to squirm. The man, with him gave them a hard stare.

"You let the woman get away." His tone was hard and accusatory.

"I tell you, I had no choice." Jamal's temper continued to fray. "If we had tried to move her to the car we borrowed, we risked all of us being shot or captured."

"I am not at all happy with that," Salman told them. The other man nodded agreement. "Fortunately, she has no idea of who you are." He sighed. "But I do not like the sound of the man who was with her."

Jamal shrugged. "What is there to know? Two lovebirds taking a vacation. Lucky for us one of them was a nurse. If you had allowed the driver who picked us up at the border to bring us directly to the apartment waiting for us, none of this would have happened."

"We had to assure ourselves that you were not being tracked. We could not afford for you to lead anyone to our location. The man who shot your friend. What of him?"

Jamal was getting angry. "Listen. We were lucky to get away at all, after you abandoned us the way you did. I did not expect to have a man so cold and focused with a gun staying next door to me. What do *you* think he is?"

Salman thought for a moment but then shook his head. "Never mind. This is Texas. Everyone owns a gun and knows how to use it. We have had someone check and there is no police bulletin out for you, so it seems you have managed to get away clean." He scowled. "But mind you, as soon as they get their shit together, the police will be looking for the two of you. A low profile is mandatory until it is time for the event."

Jamal refrained from saying again that none of this would have happened if the idiot who'd picked them up hadn't just dumped them in the middle of nowhere. And if whoever had been on the other end of those phone calls had made plans to get them into the city right away.

The other man, the one who had not bothered to introduce himself, was still giving them a hard, unfriendly look.

"And you are positive no one at all knows of your assignment? There were no slipups?"

"I said no and I meant it," Jamal snapped.

"That is critical. We cannot do anything to give them advance notice and allow them time to prepare for this. You should have killed both that man and that woman."

"And you should have brought us into the city at once, despite Malik getting shot. We could have gotten him into whatever place we are staying without alarming anyone, but you refused to adjust for it. We did the best we could under very bad circumstances."

"Very well." Salman sighed. "But I don't like loose threads. We will just have to be extra vigilant. This will be a major statement on our part and nothing must stop it. Come now. We need to move all of you into the van. We'll leave the car here. It will be days before anyone wonders about it or reports it. Let's go. We must hurry."

The other man, whose name they still had not been told, was already helping Kasim move Malik into the van, where a mattress had been placed on the floor. Salman dropped each of the cell phones on the ground and smashed them with his foot, scooping the remnants into a plastic bag he pulled from the van.

"Let's go," he said.

"Wait." Jamal held up his hand. "The bag in the car. There is medicine in there for my brother. And more bandages."

"He won't need those. We have a doctor we are taking him to. Get in. We have to move at once."

Jamal wanted to ask him, if they had a doctor, why he hadn't been able to bring Malik into the city to be tended to, but the man's attitude didn't invite questioning. Instead, once they had Malik settled, Jamal found himself and Kasim scrunched into the back of the van with his brother. At least he could crouch on the floor beside the wounded man and do his best to keep him comfortable in these insane circumstances. Salman and the other man sat in the front.

No one spoke as they left the parking garage and circled through the downtown area. Staring straight ahead through the windshield, Jamal saw signs everywhere promoting the San Antonio Stock Show and Rodeo. Jamal tried to take in as many of the landmarks as possible to orient himself. He had the sickening feeling that his 'hosts' would prefer that he knew little or nothing about his surroundings.

As they left downtown, he managed to see the area they were in through the windshield. They drove through a part of the city that was all small houses and converted buildings, and included a mix of small stores, what the Hispanics called bodegas, as well as neighborhood cantinas, where people were gathered on the sidewalk. He finally got up the nerve to ask a question.

"Are we going to stop at the doctor first? I'd like to be there when he treats my friend." With Farid dead, he felt an additional responsibility for Malik.

"First we drop you off. People are waiting for you and you need to make sure we have all the materials for you."

He needed to make sure? He had been told these people knew what they were doing and would have everything required. At the training camp, they had experimented with different types of explosive devices and come to the conclusions that pipe bombs would best serve their purpose. They had a longer target range and more explosive effect. He had received a map of the San Antonio Rodeo and Stock Show grounds, with target areas marked. It was up to him and his group — which now seemed reduced to two — to decide which ones would go where and to place them.

These people had supposedly acquired all the materials and would provide them with housing and transport them to the grounds on the day of the attack. Then they would arrange safe passage out of the city. He was, however, beginning to have a very bad feeling about this whole thing.

When they reached a two-story blue house, Salman pulled up to a chain gate leading to the rear and tapped the horn. At once one of the men sitting on the steps jumped up to unlock the gate and swung it open. Salman drove to the end of the cracked driveway and stopped at a flight of stairs by the rear door. The man who'd opened the gate hurried up to them. Salman leaned over the back of his seat.

"Ashar will show you where everything is and make sure you have food. We will be back shortly."

"But my friend," Jamal protested. "I told you I want to go with him to the doctor."

"And I told you we would take proper care of him. We will deliver him to the doctor, where he has medicine and instruments to take care of him. You do not need to hold his hand. You need to get busy on your assignment."

"If I needed to get so busy," Jamal snapped, "then why did you leave us out at that godforsaken place so long? Why did you not come for us sooner?"

"You are here now," Salman said, ignoring the question. "And you left a mess behind you. You'd better hope it does not interfere with your mission."

"My mission will be flawless as long as my friend is cared for."

"Then you'd better get your ass upstairs and get to work and let us get to the doctor."

Kasim followed Jamal as he reluctantly exited the van but the look he gave his friend echoed Jamal's thoughts.

Big goatfuck.

Chapter Ten

Nikki leaned against Marc as he unlocked her door and guided her inside. Today felt as if it had been a week long. Her jaw throbbed, her muscles ached and she felt as if she'd just fought her way out of a nightmare. She was proud that she'd kept it together back at the cottage then all that time in the sheriff's office. And finally getting the rental car, which Marc and Slade handled without her having to do a thing. Now she was more than glad to feel his strong arm around her and the comforting warmth of his presence. She had finally reached the frayed end of her rope.

After Marc dropped the keys on the little table in the foyer, she let him guide her into the bedroom. With a gentle press of his hands, he urged her down onto the edge of the bed.

"Stay right there a minute," he told her. "Don't move."

She managed a weak smile. "I'm not sure I could if I wanted to. By the way, thanks for handling the car rental for me."

He shrugged. "That was all Slade. He's the one with all the connections."

"But you made sure it happened, so big thanks to you."

He cupped her chin in his warm hand and tilted her head up. "I'll be sure and find an appropriate way for you to give me those thanks."

He brushed a soft kiss on her lips, the gentle touch just what she needed to ease the awful tension that had gripped her all day.

"Mmmm. That sounds good to me." She swallowed. "Do you think those sketches will be of any help? It was so hard to remember what each of them looked like, but I did remember most about the guy who was in charge."

"And he's the most important one. Hofler sent it to Washington for them to run through their facial recognition software. I'm sure they have the most extensive program. If his picture was taken anywhere, we might be lucky and get a hit. Plus, we've got the headshot they took of the dead man. We hope that will get a hit."

"God, I hope so. The thought of them running around loose, getting ready to create a disaster, chills my blood."

"Mine, too, darlin'." He placed a gentle kiss on the bruise on her cheek. "You're gonna need a lot of makeup to cover that for a while."

She shrugged. "I'll think of it as a badge of honor. Meanwhile I desperately want a shower."

"I've got a better idea. I have a mission to get rid of all that tension and stress that's got you tighter than a rubber band."

She gave a ladylike snort. "You know that's gonna take some doing on your part. I think the whole day, from the time I walked out of the cabin until we got back here just a few minutes ago, is like one nightmare that won't go away." She studied his face. "And we have that meeting first thing in the morning, right?"

"I wish I could figure out a way to keep you out of that."

"I understand and agree, but Steven was right. I spent time with them. I can help. And believe me, after what went down, I truly want to." She sighed. "A month ago, if someone had told me I'd be involved in stopping a terrorist attack, I'd have asked them what they were drinking. God, Marc. I feel as if we've stepped into a nightmare and I can't wake up."

He crouched in front of her. "Trust me, darlin'. I have just the cure for you. And, by the way, you have to be one of the bravest women I've ever known. Most people would fall apart if they went through what you did, but you kept your head. Didn't fall apart. Didn't give them a reason to kill you."

"Oh, well." She swallowed back a hysterical giggle. "Believe me, I wasn't about to give them any reason to turn one of their guns on me. But all joking aside, nursing trains you to be alert in any situation and never show emotion except for sympathy. Can't fall apart in front of the patient or the family."

"Then I'm grateful you had good training all those years." He kissed the tip of her nose. "Just sit for a second. I'm working on a plan so you can finally let down. Let it go."

"What are you doing?" she called, when she heard him moving around in the bathroom.

"Working on my plan," he shouted back. "Just hold on."

Nikki lay back on the bed, her arm over her closed eyes, trying to let the images of the day fade from her brain. She'd gone through all the gelpaks of ice and while her jaw wasn't nearly as swollen, it still throbbed like a bitch. She couldn't decide if she wanted ibuprofen or wine, but she knew she needed something.

As she lay there, the day began to fade away and sounds disappeared into the background. She was startled when she felt Marc's hands at her waist, tugging at her shorts. Her eyes flew open.

"Wait. What—"

"Ssh," he soothed. "Just relax. It's all good."

He unbuttoned her shorts and slid them down her legs then followed them with her panties. She sucked in a breath when he placed a soft kiss at the top of her mound, but then the next instant he was pulling her up to a sitting position. She lifted her arms while he tugged her T-shirt over her head and divested her of her bra. One more little caress, a lick of his tongue on each nipple, before he lifted her in his arms and carried her to her bathroom.

One of the things that had sold her on the apartment, in addition to the large rooms, was the oversized tub in the master bath. Bubbles were frothing in the water and the scent of lavender drifted in the room, soothing her jangled nerves at once.

"I think I did a number on your lavender bubble bath," Marc told her. "The directions said it's soothing and I wanted you really relaxed."

"Mmmm," she hummed, and leaned back. "I do believe this will do it."

He propped the little bath pillow behind her neck. "Just keep your eyes closed. Don't move. I'll do all the work."

Nikki was more than happy to accommodate him. She closed her eyes, inhaled the exquisite lavender scent and felt the edge of peace steal over her for the first time all day.

"Keep your eyes shut," Marc ordered. "No matter what, do not open them."

In a moment she felt the caress of one of her primo soft washcloths stroking her arm. Her shoulders. Her chin. Then across the upper slope of her breasts. Even in her tense, exhausted state, her nipples hardened into tight little points and the pulse in her sex throbbed with a low, insistent beat. What was it about this man that he only had to touch her now and erotic need coursed through her body?

He stroked the cloth over her shoulders again and her breasts, taking his time, dipping it in the water and squeezing the drops in a sensual dance over her skin. The warm water was like a cocoon, the lavender-scented air both hypnotic and an aphrodisiac. She was content to lie there, the events of the past hours forgotten, while Marc seduced her senses.

Her eyes popped open when he dipped his hand between her thighs, the tactile feel of the washcloth kissing the soft skin of her mound and the crease where thigh and hip met. An uncontrolled moan burst from her when the cloth was replaced by his fingers stroking her slit, caressing the skin. She bent her legs, planted her feet on the bottom of the tub and tried to raise her hips to give him better access.

His low, rough laugh was an aphrodisiac in itself, stroking her senses and ramping up her need.

"Relax," he murmured again. "Stay still. Don't do a thing. This is all on me."

But staying still was close to impossible, especially when he moved his fingers back between the lips of her pussy, a leisurely movement that was driving her insane one increment at a time. She reached down to wrap her fingers around his wrist when he began to caress her clit, rubbing the tip of a finger over it, giving it a light pinch then stroking again.

When he nudged her thighs with his hand, she let them fall apart, silently offering every bit of her body to him. He teased her opening, glided his fingertip over her clit, slipped his hand up to give each nipple a gentle pinch. Then he left every erogenous zone hungry for his touch as he kneaded her muscles in gentle strokes. Between his incredible massage and the scent of lavender that invaded her nostrils and soothed her body, the tension flowed like a slow river from her body.

She leaned her head back, eyes still closed, and just gave herself over to the relaxed feeling. The last twelve hours had seemed more like twelve days, and this was exactly what she needed to get it out of her system. The fear that had wound itself around her when the two men had grabbed her that morning had not let go until she and Marc were back here at her place. Even in the safety and security of the sheriff's office, with Slade and Beau in full battledress, she'd kept expecting something to happen.

But now here she was, relaxing in this great tub, with Marc soothing her and pushing everything to the back of her mind. Who would ever have thought this man who had been in a dark place for so long could be so intuitive, unselfish and caring?

She was drifting on a cloud of sensuous lassitude when the pinch of his fingers on her clit brought her back to the present. Another pinch. Then he slid his fingers deep inside her and curled them before slowly easing them out.

Her breath caught in her throat. She tried to close her thighs together, trapping his hand, but he just gave her another of those low, erotic, guttural laughs.

"Didn't I tell you to just relax and let me do all the work? And remember to keep those eyes closed."

He threaded the fingers of one hand through her hair and tugged her head toward his own. Leaning a little closer, he ran his tongue over her lips, licking the seam. She opened her mouth and welcomed him inside, dancing her tongue with his, drinking in his taste.

She was so lost in the excitement of the kiss that at first it didn't register that he'd slid two fingers into her again, using his thumb to tease her clit. Delicious shivers raced over her body, intensified by her inability to close her thighs and squeeze. The day's bad stuff feathered away like disappearing smoke. She moaned into his mouth at the fluttering in her internal muscles, the signal that an orgasm was building.

Marc plundered her mouth, licking every bit of it, sliding his tongue over hers, coaxing her to do the same. And all the while his hand was busy at her sex, fucking her with his fingers while he tormented her clit.

The orgasm exploded without warning. One minute she was rising on a tide of need, the next her sex was clamping down on his hand, muscles spasming, her entire body shaking with the force of it. Marc was right there with her, driving her through it then coaxing her down from the high, his mouth still fused to hers.

At last the tremors subsided and her pulse slowed its erratic beat. Marc lifted his mouth from hers.

"Open your eyes, darlin'." His voice was low and hot.

Nikki fluttered her eyelids open and stared into Marc's aged-whiskey eyes where heat and humor danced together. She smiled at him and lifted a hand, laying it against his cheek, loving the rough feel of his late-day scruff.

"Thank you." She whispered the words, afraid if she spoke too loudly, she'd break the spell he'd woven.

He grinned. "My pleasure."

"Actually, I think it was all mine."

"Let's get you out of here. I'm not nearly finished with your relaxation treatment."

Her pulse sped up a notch.

"Oh? Exactly what else did you have in mind?"

"You'll just have to wait and see. Here you go."

He lifted her out of the tub and stood her on the mat. While the water drained, he wrapped her in one of the big bath towels taken from a hook and dried her with a tenderness that almost brought her to her knees. Finished, he carried her into the bedroom where he ripped back the covers on the bed and placed her on the sheets.

"Hang on a minute."

She heard him rattling things in the kitchen. Then he was back holding a glass of the white wine she'd had chilling. He propped her up with the pillows fluffed behind her then handed her the goblet.

"Take it slow," he joked. "Don't want you getting drunk before I get back."

She sat up so sharply a little of the wine sloshed over on her hand, and she licked it off.

"Back from where?"

"The shower. Can't make love to my best girl smelling like a garbage pit."

Her heat clenched. "Best girl? Is that what I am?"

"Moving too fast for you?" He sat on the edge of the bed and cupped her chin in his palm. "I think today was worth at least a month of taking it slow. Danger does that to you. When you were missing and I couldn't find you, I almost had a heart attack."

"Me, too. When I realized what was going on."

"I know it hasn't been that long for us, Nikki, but when I'm not on a mission with the team you're all I think about. I can't say I never thought I'd feel this way about anyone again, because this is more than I ever felt before."

"Oh, Marc." She stroked his face. "I'm —"

"Ssh." He touched his fingers to her lips. "Don't say anything now. I know it's happening for us, even if you aren't sure yet. And I thought I'd be the very last person ever to feel this. To risk my heart again. So let it be 'best girl' for now and we'll see where it goes from there."

The words bubbled up in her throat but stuck there before she could get them out. Instead, she leaned forward and pressed her mouth to his, trying to put her feelings into the contact. She was stunned that with his history, he was already wanting to take this step. She wanted it, too, but she'd lost one love who'd died. Marc didn't have a disease, but he had a career that put him in constant danger. They'd never discussed it and now wasn't the time. She wasn't sure she had as much courage as he did, but didn't want to ruin what they had going on either. Especially not after today.

She let out a slow breath. "I'm good with that. Now go take your shower. I can't wait to see your naked body."

He chuckled and saluted. "Yes, ma'am. On my way, ma'am."

Nikki leaned back against the pillows, sipping the wine, thinking how much better the day had ended than it had begun.

Marc let the hot water sluice down on him, washing away the dirt and tension of the past hours. Had he pushed it too far with Nikki too soon? He hoped not, but after the almost paralyzing fear of losing her today, he was filled with more emotion that he knew what to do with. Than he'd ever felt in his life. And that wasn't like him.

This was so different than it had been with Ria. That had been all fire and flame, so intense it had consumed him. As he thought about it now, standing under the water, he realized that almost all the memories he had of their time together had to do with sex. Even when they went out, to dinner or whatever, she was all over him, teasing him, seducing him with an almost frantic need. In hindsight he realized it was the drugs, ramping her up and blocking everything else out. She was addicted to sex as much as she was to the drugs themselves.

They'd never made love. They'd *fucked*.

And now, with Nikki, he knew the difference. It was the emotion, something he'd always been good about hiding. The sex was different, too. Less frantic, although much more intense. It was more about giving than taking. Touching. Feeling. Sensing. When he slipped his cock inside her, the feeling outweighed any other emotion he'd ever had. They joined together. Became one.

This week, in his mind, was all about exploring what they had to see if it was real. But when she'd gone missing then had been in critical danger, any questions had been answered. If anything had happened to her, the fallout for him would have far surpassed Ria's betrayal. The reality of his feelings for her had smacked him hard.

As he scrubbed himself with her body wash, he felt as if her hands were the ones cleansing him. He closed his eyes, remembering her fingers on his chest, brushing his tight nipples. The lick of her tongue across his abdomen. The warmth of her palm cupping his balls. The heat of her mouth as she took his shaft into it. And the incredible sensation of sliding into her pussy and feeling those tight muscles clamp around him.

He had it bad.

He wasn't at all sure how to take things to the next level. He knew Nikki still harbored dark emotions from the death of her fiancé. Was she ready for a deeper relationship with him? Could they make it work with him in Delta? He knew that not everyone was cut out for that life.

Jesus, Blanchard, shut the fuck up. You've got a few steps to go before sending out wedding announcements.

Maybe so, but it wasn't too early to put all he had into showing her how he felt. He finished rinsing off, dried himself and strode into the bedroom where Nikki was stretched out on the bed waiting. For him. His cock, which he had forcefully diminished to half-mast in the shower, swelled with need at the sight of her naked body and the simple classic beauty of her face. The stormy gray eyes looking out from behind a thick curtain of lashes flared with desire, despite the god-awful day. Her rosy nipples just begged to be sucked and the sight of her glistening sex almost made him come standing there.

Almost. But not quite.

Not until he'd had his fill of every inch of her, inside and out.

He took another long look at her, assessing the bruise on her jaw. The gelpaks had kept the swelling way down and the wine, he was sure, had dulled the edge of the pain. Was he being a selfish animal because all he could think of was making love to her? Maybe he should let her sleep.

"Shut off your brain," she told him. "I can smell the smoke, it's working so hard."

"I just want to be sure you're okay. I want you so bad, but you've had a very rough day. I need to put what you're feeling first. We can make love any time."

Her smile was like an arrow straight to his heart.

"I won't be okay if you don't get up here with me, Marc." She pushed herself up on her elbows. "Yes, I've had a frightening day. Yes, it could have been a lot worse. But don't you understand? This" — she waved her hand between the two of them — "is what makes me feel better. Feel whole again. Come here, Marc. Let's love each other and shut out the world."

He blew out his breath in a soft *whoosh*.

"Okay, then."

He climbed onto the bed, kneeled between her thighs and took another moment to drink in the sight of her. When she ran her tongue over her lips in a slow sweep, he couldn't wait any longer. He lowered his head and touched his mouth to hers, licking the place where her tongue had touched the soft skin.

Delicious.

Hungry for more, he eased his tongue inside her mouth and lapped every surface. She slipped her own tongue over his and drew him into an erotic dance that fired every one of his nerves. He scraped his teeth over the surface of her skin, eliciting an sensual little moan from her, so he did it again. She slipped her hands up along his arms and shoulders until she was able to thread her fingers through his hair, holding his head in place. He took the kiss even deeper, urged on by the sexy little sounds she was making. He only lifted his mouth when he needed to breathe again.

Her mouth was kiss-swollen and shiny, her eyes flaring with hunger and need. He took a tiny bite from her lower lip before dipping his head to capture one rosy nipple between his own lips. When he had worked it to a rich, dark rose, he turned his attention to the other one, giving it the same treatment. The sexy little moans that Nikki kept making only ramped up the need raging through him.

He coasted his lips down the soft skin, loving the faint lavender flavor of the bathwater that clung to her. He paused to swirl his tongue in her delightful belly button, then slid lower on the bed so he could trace a line from one ankle up the inside of the leg, over to the other leg and down the soft flesh to its ankle.

Her moans grew louder and were punctuated with little sounds that made his balls ache. At last, he lifted her legs to rest on his shoulders, stared for a hard moment at the glistening pink of the lips of her cunt, then with a light touch traced the tip of a finger the length of her wet slit.

"Oh, god!" The words burst from her and she lifted her hips toward his touch.

He inhaled the sweetness of her musk then flicked the tip of his tongue over her clit. Then he did it again. And again, before pressing the pink lips apart and thrusting deep inside her hot, slick channel. *And holy shit.* Every nerve in his body fired as her taste coated his flesh. Taking her clit between thumb and forefinger, he pinched it as he worked his tongue in and out in a quickening rhythm.

Nikki hooked her ankles behind his neck and thrust herself at him, her little whimpers growing louder as he worked his tongue faster and faster. He drew his mouth back and thrust two fingers inside her, scissoring them, curling them so the tips scraped the sensitive sweet spot. He added a third finger, still working her clit, increasing the speed of his movements.

When her inner muscles clenched harder, he slipped his little finger down between the cheeks of her ass, just barely touching her opening back there. He bit down on her clit and it was enough to send her over the edge. She flooded his hand with her liquid, arching up to him, as spasms rocked her. He rode her through it until the last flutter subsided and she went limp. Then he kissed his way up her body until he reached her mouth, pressing his lips to hers and sharing her taste with her.

He slid his mouth across her undamaged cheek to take a soft nibble of her earlobe. Then, bending her knees back, he drove into her very wet pussy, immersing himself completely with one thrust.

Holy fucking shit!

He had to close his eyes and grit his teeth to keep from coming then and there. This was more than hot sex. There was so much emotion around and between them that everything was intensified. Nikki locked her heels at the small of his back, pressing him more tightly into her hot, wet sheath, her inner muscles clamping down on him until he had to work hard to maintain control. He didn't want this to be over before it had hardly begun.

Drawing in a deep breath, he began a slow in-and-out movement, his cock so thick and swollen it filled every inch of her. As he picked up the tempo, her body again responded to him and tensed as another orgasm began building.

"Don't hold back," she whispered. "I'm ready again."

Okay, then.

He increased his pace, her slick flesh heating his shaft. In and out. Back and forth. With her legs wrapped around him, she held him to her and matched his rhythm. The muscles at the small of his back tightened and his balls drew up, and he exploded, erupted into her welcoming body with the force of a rocket. Tremors shook him, shook them both, as they climaxed together.

It seemed to go on forever before they both began to slide down from the high. Marc held her to him, not knowing whose heartbeat was shaking them harder or whose breath was raspier.

Then they were quiet. Nikki slid her legs from around his body and he fell forward, catching his weight on his forearms. When he opened his eyes, she was looking directly at him with her eyelids lowered, cheeks rosy, face flushed with satisfaction, and…something else. A deep emotion he hadn't seen there before. Or was it just wishful thinking on his part?

As he was trying to figure out what to say, she wet her lips.

"Am I imagining things or is this…different?"

"It's different." He answered her without thinking. "And not because of what happened today. Although, when I thought I might have lost you, I was afraid my heart would stop altogether."

He brushed his mouth over hers. When the tip of her tongue came out so she could lick him, a shiver skated down his spine.

"What's happening here, Marc? Are we going too fast?"

He shook his head. "I think we're going at just the right pace. Our week in paradise kind of got shot to shit, and I don't know what the rest of this week will bring, but damn, Nikki. I want this, whatever it is."

"Me, too." She ran her fingers through his damp hair. "I don't know what it is, either, but can we take it one day at a time?"

He wanted to tell her he wanted all the days, but he knew she was dealing with a lot more issues than he was.

"We can take it any way you want. As long as we do it together."

Chapter Eleven

How did this all turn upside down? And why am I being kept from Malik? Do they think I won't finish what I need to do? I'm sure they are going to kill Malik. I am only sad that he will not die with glory and honor.

Jamal sat at the big dining room table, these and similar thoughts running through his brain as he did his best to focus on his work. What he was doing was complicated enough by itself and distractions weren't helping. But twenty-four hours had passed and he still hadn't seen Malik. Salman kept assuring him his friend was receiving medical attention, but Jamal wasn't so sure. He wanted to lay eyes on him to reassure himself. And he did not like the attitude of Rafiq at all.

The surface of the table was covered with the materials he would need to assemble the improvised explosive devices. On the wall directly opposite where he sat was a huge diagram labeled *San Antonio Rodeo Grounds*. It looked exactly like the one he'd memorized during the weeks at the training camp. He was sure by this time he could find his way around the grounds blindfolded. He was equally sure Salman, or someone, would drill him down on it many more times before they actually went to the location. There could be no room for error here.

He looked down at the table again, gathering what he needed for the next device. Pipe bombs had been deemed the most effective for the size of the crowd they were targeting. Salman had obtained several eight-inch lengths of pipe, plus the caps. Two large open boxes of nails sat side by side, and next to them containers of powder and fuses. Beside those was another container with red bandanas. They had been told this would be the most effective way to camouflage the pipe bombs, wrapping them in something half the people at the rodeo would be wearing.

And, finally, a large box of burner phones. It had been decided to set a base phone and clone all the others to it. The phones would be connected to the fuse and the charge from the phones would detonate the bombs. One phone call and the rodeo grounds and buildings would be a mass of explosions. It was hoped that those not killed by the explosions would trample each other in their haste to get out of the way. But in any event, the number of deaths would be massive.

Assembling the bombs and setting the phones was simple enough. They'd been able to do it blindfolded by the time they left the camp in Mexico. Six or eight pipe bombs made a significant explosion, but whoever was running this operation wanted to make a real statement, cause significant damage and death. Salman had introduced him to a couple of strangers who he was told would be replacements, so his team was now back up to four people. They needed that many and each would be carrying several pipe bombs of significant strength into the rodeo grounds. Tonight they would be meeting to learn more about the layout of the rodeo grounds and begin preparation. It was crucial that they were familiar with it so that no mistakes would be made.

The plan was to place them in various spots in the AT&T Center where the actual rodeo took place, the Freeman Coliseum where the dozens of vendors would be attracting thousands of people and in the carnival area, which would be filled with people at the rides and games. There would be children in the latter area and for a moment that gave Jamal pause. But then he reminded himself those children would grow up to be the enemy, so better to get rid of them now.

He and Kasim would be ferried into the rodeo grounds in food trucks, carrying the bombs in knapsacks and placing them one at a time at the sites marked on the huge wall map. He looked across the table at Kasim and for an infinitesimal moment, they exchanged a meaningful look.

Something stinks here.

On the surface it all looked fine, but everything had changed so much since they'd left the camp in Mexico. Malik getting shot had been no fault of theirs, yet from the moment it had happened, it had been treated as a huge error on their part. Being hidden in that stupid cottage had been a disaster. He wondered if anyone would have come for them if he hadn't forced the issue.

Once again, he reviewed the situation in his head, dealing now with a combination of unease and desperation. Their original orders had them headed to San Antonio, just the four of them. Someone would take them to the designated apartment where the necessary materials would be waiting there for them and they could get to work. The person in charge would familiarize them with the layout of the rodeo grounds and on the date of the event, people would drive them to the rodeo and they'd complete their task.

Instead, here they were in a very unpretentious two-story house in a neighborhood not so different from the one where he'd lived in his home country. Only the building materials were different. He and Kasim were sharing a small bedroom on the second floor, and every room seemed to be filled with some men who didn't appear to be at all friendly. In fact, they seemed downright suspicious.

Who were these men? No one had bothered to explain their roles in this, or which of them was a permanent part of the group here in San Antonio. Did they think Jamal had shot his own friend? Then killed Farid, another friend? Deliberately tried to sabotage this job?

Also, no one had yet explained how they were expected to get the bombs through security. He was sure guards would be at every entrance to the rodeo grounds, so how were they supposed to avoid the metal detectors? Did they have other ways to accomplish this? Why didn't they tell him? He was, after all, one of the team making the ultimate sacrifice. The more he got into this, the less he liked it. These were supposed to be experienced people, but they didn't impress him that way.

At first, with Salman and Rafiq angry at the turn of events and accusing them of stupidity and nearly ruining a crucial mission, he'd worried they'd just be shot and the mission given to someone else. He had insisted he and Kasim could prepare with no problem.

Rafiq had agreed with obvious reluctance. This was set up to be a major statement, just like others across the country. Enemies called them terrorists or extremists, but in fact they were soldiers of Allah, ridding the world of infidels. It was an honor to be chosen for this and he didn't want any idiots to fuck it up.

"How are you coming?"

Jamal jumped at the sound of the voice, scattering the nails he'd been sliding into a pipe with a loud clatter. Rafiq, who owned the house, had come into the dining room and snapped the question at him.

Jamal focused on his task to keep from snapping at the man.

"All is proceeding well. One more day and I should have enough for all the knapsacks."

"Good, good." Rafiq studied the surface of the table. "Do you have everything you need?"

"I do."

"This is the most important thing you will have ever done in your life." Fire burned in Rafiq's eyes. "More than five thousand Muslims live in San Antonio alone. Everywhere in Texas people protest our being here, even our just being alive. We must show them that we have the power and the strength. That it is our mission to rid the world of infidels and they must join us. We must make the world ours."

The world!

Jamal's heartbeat sped up at the words. Yes. Soon it would be theirs and he would have destroyed a significant number of infidels in the process. He could not mourn Malik and Farid. He would take their memories with him as he and Kasim made a statement the entire world would acknowledge.

He put down the pipe he was holding and looked at Rafiq. "I might do a lot better if I could see my friend. I do not understand why he was not brought here after the doctor saw him. Is there some kind of problem?"

"It is very crowded here." Rafiq spoke in a flat, almost toneless voice. "The doctor says he needs quiet and rest."

"Where is Salman, the man who brought us here? I want to speak to him."

"Salman has other responsibilities. I am in charge here. Make the bombs. When they are ready, we will take you to see your friend."

"That is not acceptable." Jamal pushed the half-filled piece of pipe away from him. "If I cannot see Malik, then I demand to speak to him on the telephone. I am doing Allah's work here and for that I should get to reassure myself that my friend is on the mend. His brother was killed by infidels, so I have extra concern for him."

Again, Rafiq studied him in silence. "Fine. I will call and make sure he is awake and you can speak to him. Keep working. I will be back in a few minutes." He pulled his phone from his pocket as he walked out of the room.

Jamal wanted to ask why the man couldn't just make the call then and there. However, he had a sense that these men would kill Malik, if indeed he wasn't already dead, so he just nodded. When he and Kasim had been brought to the house, the suitcase with their weapons had been locked into a closet. These men had no idea he and Kasim, anticipating something like this after all the other fuckups, each had a weapon squirreled away. From now on, he would wear it underneath his loose shirt so it was ready at all times. It didn't hurt to be prepared, especially when the circumstances had changed so much.

He would give the man another half hour. Then he would find him wherever he was in the house and demand to talk to Malik. If they killed him, they'd have to find a replacement for the job at hand. And it just meant he'd rise to heaven a little sooner than expected.

He handed the filled length of pipe across the table to Kasim to finish, picked up another one and scooped some nails into it. Maybe he'd make one to stick in his pocket, one he could set off if things got too out of hand. Although it might not be sacrificing himself for the greater good, it would satisfy him in heaven to have exacted revenge.

* * * *

Sheriff Enrique 'Ric' Vasquez was big, as tall as Slade but broader and wider. His thick black hair framed an oval face that was defined by dark brown eyes and thick brows. And those eyes looked as if they'd seen enough of the dark side to last a lifetime. Marc knew the man had been sheriff for four years now, a deputy before that and prior to that a Force Recon Marine. Yeah, he'd been to hell and back in a number of different places and ways and knew what he was doing.

Although his greeting was cordial, there was no joy in his expression. His county was being invaded and Marc could tell he was fucking pissed.

The man ushered them all into his conference room, where someone had made coffee and set out a tray of pastries. Every seat at the table was taken. In addition to Sheriff Vasquez and Steven Hofler, there were four other men who had yet to be introduced, two in plain clothes, and two obvious sheriff's deputies in uniform, Marc, Slade, Beau and Nikki.

"Good thing he has a big conference room," Nikki whispered to Marc.

"No kidding."

Vasquez cleared his throat. "Okay, everyone. Let's get settled with coffee and whatever and get down to business. We've got a hot potato on our hands that I want to contain so we'd best get started." He looked at the men to his right. "You all know each other, but let's introduce you to the Deltas. Gentlemen, say hello to Detectives Adam Gorsh, Rob McRae, Greg Handler and Joseph Trainor, and senior deputies Frank Novak and Ward Benton. Joe will be the team leader of this group, Slade, and he'll be working in tandem with you. You will both lead the planning and execution of this action. Slade, the floor is yours."

Marc noticed two things. Joe Trainor didn't appear to be happy that he wasn't the single top dog and that Slade caught it right away. But Lieutenant Donovan wore the mantle of leadership well, and did whatever it took to get the job done. He didn't care who had what title as long as it didn't interfere with the mission. Planning missions—and this definitely fell in that category—was one of his many strengths.

And both of them had been trained to follow leadership, execute action plans and to put aside personal feelings. There was no room for them in times of conflict and this was a conflict.

"You've all met Steven Hofler from the Department of Homeland Security. Actually, he's with the division that coordinates with area law enforcement. He's going to tell you why we're all gathered here."

"We have a major crisis brewing," Hofler began. "Sad to say this is not a new story. Homeland Security monitors absolutely everything everywhere and analyzes all the bits and pieces of conversation. It's critical that we smell out any hint of trouble so we can decide how to deal with it. Sometimes we get the word in time, others like now we're running to play catch-up."

"As I understand it," Trainor said, "the latter is why we're here. There's a bad situation brewing right in our back yard here."

Hofler nodded. "We picked up chatter about a team from Agadez, Niger, being smuggled into this country via a terrorist training camp that's working in Mexico."

"Any particular place in San Antonio?" one of the deputies asked.

"Yes, damn it. Word is the sole purpose of the team is to create an incident at the San Antonio Stock Show and Rodeo. As you all know, last year the event topped the two million mark for visitors. In other words, this would be a massive bombing, so we needed to find ways to verify it. Chief Vasquez reminded me that on any given day that place is packed to the gills, so an attack would take a lot of lives and do a great deal of damage."

Hofler pointed to Slade. "We checked with JSOC — Joint Special Operations Command — and learned a Delta Force team was about to leave on a mission for Agadez. The team is led by Lieutenant Slade Donovan." He nodded at Slade. "I'll let him present his people and fill you in."

Everyone nodded when Slade introduced Marc, Beau and Nikki.

"Like the man said, the people at DHS who monitor this stuff reported there was way too much chatter about it. But they needed a way to chase down the rumors, try to verify them. I was told to make that another part of our mission to Agadez, but we drew a blank there. In Agadez, all we had were the same rumors and no one was talking. We returned from the mission without getting any valuable information."

"So how did we get to where we are now?" Trainor asked.

"We got lucky, although I'm not sure Marc Blanchard and Nikki Alvarez would think so." He indicated both of them. "They were supposed to be vacationing at Lookout Lake, in a cottage owned by a friend of mine, when they ran into some unexpected visitors. There are only four cottages on that lake, and the others were supposed to be unoccupied. Imagine their surprise when they discovered the cottage closest to the one they were using was occupied by some people who looked very out of place. And definitely weren't your average vacationers. So I called my friend."

He repeated to them the details of that conversation.

"I'm embarrassed to say I took it at face value, until the situation went sideways." He rubbed his jaw. "I guess I need to be more careful of who my friends are from now on."

"So how did you connect those people with whatever is going on?" one of the men asked.

"Just by accident, although it was a pretty harrowing accident for Nikki and Marc. It seems one of the team members was shot crossing the border, just as they were being picked up. They were stranded at the cottage and needed help for him."

He went on to fill in the details of Nikki's kidnapping, the fact she was almost killed, Marc's killing of the man waiting to ambush him and the shooting of the neighbor as the remaining men made their escape.

Marc held Nikki's hand when she gave them more details about her very frightening episode. He saw the skepticism on all the faces being replaced by grudging admiration for the way she'd handled herself and kept her head.

"You're a smart young woman," Vasquez said, as the others nodded. "And very courageous. We'd like to keep you out of this as much as possible, but you've spent the most time up close and personal with these guys. We'll give you full protection but you're going to be very critical in identifying them."

She squeezed Marc's hand. "I want to do whatever I can."

"And I'll be handling her protection," Marc announced in a voice that brooked no argument. *Damn straight I am.*

"Do we have any idea just who is on this team?" Frank Novak asked.

"Working on it," Hofler said. "Miss Alvarez's car has been gone over inch by inch. We've pulled fingerprints and anything else that could give us some identification. Not that we expected it to. None of these foot soldiers have prints anywhere. However, we do have a headshot of the dead man, plus Miss Alvarez worked with a sketch artist to give us likenesses of the other three as close as she could come. Homeland Security is running them through every possible facial recognition software we have. If we're lucky, he—or any of them—got their picture taken somewhere, sometime, and we have a starting point. Meanwhile, we also have copies of these for you."

He handed out packets to everyone containing copies of the photo and sketches.

"Scan these into your phones so you have them with you at all times. Maybe we'll get lucky and spot them at the rodeo grounds before they get a chance to do any damage."

"That's like hunting the proverbial needle in a haystack," Trainor reminded him.

"I agree, but we need every resource, no matter how farfetched." Vasquez looked at Nikki. "If not, our best resource is Miss Alvarez, who has unfortunately for her been up close and personal with this group."

"DHS is also looking for a money trail to see if they can find out who's pulling the strings on this one," Hofler added. "We don't hold out much hope, though. Most likely the funds come from overseas and don't go through any bank transfer. We're pretty sure they chose this particular target because of the size and the statement it would make. For all we know, they have a series of attacks planned on or around the same time, but we have to be concerned with this one."

Vasquez cleared his throat. "Sheriff Schumacher called here to tell us John Lester is still in critical condition, but it looks like he'll make it after all. He's going to hold off on filing any charges until we clean up this mess here. If we're lucky, there won't be anyone left to file charges against. So, let's go over what we know. There is an attack planned for sometime during the rodeo. The event is eighteen days long and every day brings its own special crowd. No one day stands out as more likely than any of the others, so we'll have to be prepared every single day."

"I've been a couple of times," Slade offered. "When I was in town. I know the security force is huge."

Vasquez nodded. "Two of our neighboring counties have deputies that join the force for that period of time, plus police from this city and from the Texas Rangers. More than one hundred and fifty in all, with a commander for each shift." He rattled off the names of each shift commander. "But their duties are pretty much what you'd expect. On a typical shift, officers might direct traffic, staff security booths, check vehicles for parking permits, ensure horse trailers leave with the animals they brought in or reunite lost children with parents or school groups. Sometimes they might break up a fight, or even catch a purse snatcher. But nothing out of the ordinary. Steven, you want to take it from here?"

Hofler cleared his throat. "What the sheriff is leading up to is that these people on the rodeo police shifts will continue as always. They will not be part of our special team, although they will provide support if and when needed. For one thing, the terrorists will avoid anyone in uniform. Their most likely weapon will be pipe bombs and they won't want to be placing them where uniforms can see them. So we have to be invisible. Blend in. And follow DHS protocol as we take these bastards down."

"I think it's a given we're all prepared to do that," Vasquez told him.

The others murmured agreement.

"All right, then. I want to thank all of you for your cooperation and for working with my team on this." Slade looked around at each person. "I understand this is your territory. I'm not looking to step on anyone's toes. Just know this. We hunt these guys on a regular basis, have extensive knowledge of them and just want to bring all of that to the table."

Marc noticed Joe Trainor relax a little, and the same with the others. Slade was good at avoiding pissing contests.

"We have a couple of things in our favor," Slade went on, "which we're going to need. First is the fact that Miss Alvarez spent enough time with these men to be able to identify them for us. We'll have her in disguise riding in one of the golf carts patrolling the grounds. We're hoping that camouflage will be good enough that the terrorists, preoccupied with their mission, will pay little or no attention to her."

"And if they do?" Novak asked.

"Marc Blanchard will be riding with her. He'll be fully armed and in mission mode. If I were in her shoes, he's the man I'd want protecting me. For the rest of it? We need to plan this all with extreme attention to detail, something I know you're all used to."

Marc was aware that Nikki paid careful attention to everything they discussed, absorbing everything that was said. It amazed him that she was as focused on this as she was, something so far out of her normal purview. But he had been learning a lot of things about Nikki Alvarez since what was supposed to be a romantic getaway had begun. The emotionally damaged woman had a core of inner strength that amazed him — although, as he thought about it, that was probably what had gotten her through the death of her fiancé without retreating from the world altogether.

Lucky for me, he thought, since it shocked the hell out of him that he was falling in love with her, something he'd been sure would never happen. Certainly not after Ria and her scorched-earth policy where his heart was concerned. No, not his heart. His cock and his pride. This thing with Nikki? He'd better not fuck it up. He just hoped this crisis didn't derail everything.

Reaching beneath the table, he took her hand in his and clasped it. She gave him an answering squeeze and his tension eased a little, at least as much as it could given the situation.

Vasquez fetched a large rolled-up sheet of thick paper and gave it to the two deputies, who taped it to the wall. It displayed a very detailed map of the entire landscape of the Rodeo—every building, outbuilding, exhibition, whatever.

"Here's the map of the layout you asked for, Slade. Let's get down to it."

"Thanks. I need to know where the entrances are, if someone can mark them off, and who uses them."

One of the deputies uncapped a black magic marker.

"These gates are where the public enters the premises." He made black Xes at the spots. "There are scanners at every one of these stations." He slid his hand to one side of the diagram. "These are potential trouble spots. It's where everyone with a truck enters— contestants hauling horses, ranches bringing steers, other ranches bringing animals for the judging, concessionaires, food vendors, you have it." He added several more marks to the sheet.

"So explosives could be hidden in any of those vehicles." Slade frowned. "Do you have enough people to visually check every vehicle that comes through those gates?"

"We'll get whatever personnel we need," Joe Trainor told him. "Believe me, we know this is no time to scrimp on personnel. Pardon the pun, but this isn't my first rodeo."

"Joe's worked with us before," Hofler told him. "He'll be your point person for that."

Marc looked over at the detective. Trainor was doing his best to look cordial but it was obvious he didn't like his knowledge or experience being questioned.

"We'll also have helicopters doing flyovers," Vasquez told them. "They'll be using long-range binoculars. And Mr. Hofler informed me that DHS has undercover people scouring the community for any clues. This team had to have some place to get to when they arrived, besides the cottage. Especially since Miss Alvarez tells us she heard them bitching about the fact they got dumped at that cottage instead of being taken to San Antonio as originally arranged. It seems one of the team getting shot had everyone's balls in an uproar." He looked at Nikki. "Apologies, Miss Alvarez."

She gave him a tiny smile. "No worries. I'm a nurse. I know what balls are."

A little chuckle danced around the table.

"Lieutenant Donavan and I have set up a meeting with the rodeo grounds operation manager." Vasquez looked around the table. "Joe, you need to be there, too."

"And we need to include Deputy Novak in that," Trainor told him. "You know he's more familiar with every kind of vehicle that comes through one gate or other than anyone else in this room." He paused and glanced at Slade. "If that's okay with you."

Marc saw a muscle twitch in Slade's cheek. Slade didn't like people yanking his chain or questioning his ability to do his job. As he told members of his team time and time again, there was no room for egos in Delta Force. To Slade, that translated to every other type of mission, but he was also smart enough to know that pissing off people whose help he needed wasn't a good idea, either.

"I'll take the help of anyone who can contribute. We're going to run this like a mission and everyone will have a role. No egos here. Certainly not mine."

He went around the table, checking what each person's assigned responsibility was. Marc knew the man wasn't foolish enough to shift someone from a job he was familiar with.

At the end of an hour, Slade pretty much had things in place, along with lists of how many people he'd need and where, and where they would come from.

"We need to get eyes on each vehicle entrance," Slade told Joe. "And narrow it down, if possible, to the most likely means of sneaking the bombs into the grounds."

"Is it possible the bombs might be made of plastic?" Novak asked. "That makes them less detectible."

"They specifically mentioned pipes," Nikki interjected in her soft voice. "The one in charge thought I couldn't hear them."

"That's their standard, anyway," Slade confirmed. "The other possibilities are suicide vests and we can't rule them out."

"I've seen the massive damage they can do," Joe told him. "You're right. We have to be prepared for anything."

"Okay." Slade sat again. "I think maybe all of you need to be in the planning meeting. You each bring something to the table or you wouldn't be here, so let's get busy. Then, Joe, I think you and Deputy Novak and I, along with Marc and Beau, need to take a trip to the rodeo grounds and look at each of these spots ourselves. The event starts tomorrow. I want eyes on everything before the public swarms in."

Trainor nodded. "Let's do it."

Chapter Twelve

Jamal had not slept well the previous night, worries about his friend making him restless. He kept imagining Farid's body in the tall grass by the lakeside cottage, and Malik, pale and shaking as he lay in the back seat of the stolen vehicle. He had a devastating feeling he had failed his friends, two brothers whom he had been close with since childhood. He was still plenty upset that Malik had been taken off somewhere and not kept in this house with everyone else. Anything could be happening to him.

Kasim, too, had been agitated and they had both risen early, determined to see their friend today. Jamal wanted answers. Now. He needed to be focused to do this most important of assignments and he couldn't be when thoughts of his friends kept taking over his brain.

Today, after morning prayers, he marched into the kitchen to find both Salman and Rafiq preparing their breakfast.

"I want to see my friend. I want to lay eyes on Malik."

Ashar, who seemed to float in and out of rooms, was quietly making coffee, but it was obvious he was listening. What were they all concealing? Jamal had a very bad feeling.

"I understand." Rafiq's voice was flat.

"No, you don't. You think we are stupid and easily led but we are not." He clenched his fists to keep himself under control. "You were supposed to call and check on him and it does not seem as if you have even done that."

"Forgive me." Rafiq came to stand beside him. "I have just been so immersed in making sure all the details of our project were in place that I somehow forgot to tell you. He is healing well, but it is taking some time."

"I want to see him," Jamal demanded. "We have been here two days and I have not even spoken to him. How do I know you did not kill him?"

The other two men exchanged glances.

"The bombs are all assembled and ready to be packed," Jamal continued. "We are waiting for the materials from you for the vests. Tomorrow we are supposed to go to the rodeo and walk the ground to identify the best places to leave each one. I am not going there until I see Malik."

"Then perhaps you will not be going anywhere at all," Rafiq sneered. The placating tone had disappeared from his voice.

Jamal had already figured out that this man was running the show, although he had expected someone a little smarter.

"Fine. Then you two or your friends can carry the bombs in and blow yourselves up." He turned to walk back into the dining room.

"Wait."

Salman's voice stopped him. "What?"

"You are right." This man's voice was softer, more placating. "We thought it best that you direct all your focus to your work and that your brother be undisturbed to rest and heal. But perhaps it would be better for both of you to have a brief visit. Right, Rafiq?"

Rafiq's lips curved in a smile that was lacking in real sincerity. "Of course. You are right, Salman. I have been inconsiderate. I will arrange it now."

Jamal's heart settled back into a steadier beat. He still did not trust any of these men. They did not exude the feeling of brotherhood as had the men at the camp in Mexico, or those who had recruited him and his friends. He had come here filled with pride that he would be sacrificing himself for the good of his fellow men. Now he worried someone else would get the glory and he and Kasim would be just a couple of dead bodies for infidels to find.

But he made himself nod, forcing a calmness he did not feel.

"Thank you. I will wait for you in the living room."

He poured coffee into a mug and carried it into the other room, telling himself it would all work out. He had to believe that. Malik would heal, find a way to return home and tell everyone how Jamal and Kasim had sacrificed themselves for the glory of Allah. Martyrdom was the most exalted thing in Islam and his family would be honored that he had been chosen for this. Despite his earlier threat, he did not want to be cheated of the honor. He would also be doing it for Farid, who did not have the chance to go to heaven, and for Malik, who might not survive this.

"Well?" Kasim was waiting for him. "What did they say?"

"Rafiq is calling now to make sure Malik is awake. Then they will take us."

He was standing at the window with Kasim, sipping his hot coffee, when Rafiq came into the room.

"Come. The doctor says your friend is awake. It is a good time to visit him."

"We will both come," Jamal insisted.

Rafiq looked as if he wanted to say something but then changed his mind.

"Fine. Let us go."

They climbed into the van that was still parked in the back. Salman sat behind the wheel, Rafiq in the shotgun seat, and they backed down the driveway. They drove along narrow streets filled with houses much like the one they were staying in, punctuated with neighborhood stores of various kinds, many with people hanging out in front. When he saw convenience stores, he knew that a lot of them were owned by people from his country who had come here, legally or not. He thought in a wistful moment how nice it might have been to own one himself and take care of his family.

But the thirst for revenge against the infidels burned hot and bright, fed by the flames of the speeches he'd heard. If he had not been told he was chosen by Allah who knew where he would be?

While he was ruminating, the van pulled into a driveway next to a small tan house.

"We are here," Rafiq said. "Let's go."

They climbed a short flight of stairs to the front door and walked into a small hallway. To the left was a room obviously being used as an office, containing a desk, a computer, a filing cabinet and some chairs. Across the hall was what looked like an examining room, with the usual equipment. *Not much*, Jamal noted, but then he was used to sparsely outfitted clinics.

The man who had opened the door for them led them to a room at the end of the hall, opened that door and stepped aside so they could enter. Salman stayed in the hallway but hovered near. Jamal elbowed everyone aside and pushed his way to the side of the bed. He was appalled at Malik's condition. He looked as if he'd lost weight just in the short time since they'd crossed the border from Mexico. His skin had an unhealthy pallor and his breathing was very shallow. His injured leg was heavily bandaged and was propped on two pillows.

When Jamal took his hand, he opened his eyes and his lips curved in a weak smile.

"Hello, *sadiqaa*. It is good to see you."

"As it is to lay eyes on you."

A sick feeling settled in the pit of Jamal's stomach. What were they doing to his friend? The bullet had been removed. With a doctor's care, he should be getting better.

"I need to get better," Malik told him.

Jamal could not have agreed more. His friend was sending him some kind of silent message, so he bent down low, putting his ear at Malik's mouth.

"But I believe they are going to kill me." His mouth barely moved, the words a bare whisper. Jamal's stomach knotted.

The man who had ushered them into the room nudged him upright.

"Do not get too close to the patient. We do not want to risk making his infection worse."

"Worse?" Jamal parroted. "The bullet is out. He should be getting better. I was told that is why he is here, under a doctor's care, instead of with us."

"The infection had already set in. Whoever removed the bullet caused great problems."

Jamal ground his teeth. The nurse had known what she was doing, had been well aware of the rudimentary nature of the supplies they had, but had done the best she could. He was sure of it. If Malik was dying, it was because of something done to him here.

"Where is the doctor?" he asked. "This man is worse than when we brought him in."

"Not true. And the doctor is away on a call."

"You have seen your friend." Rafiq closed his fingers over Jamal's elbow. "We must go."

"But he is not doing well," Jamal protested.

"He is doing fine."

Kasim had not said a word, just stood there and stared at their friend. Now he looked at Jamal and gave a faint shake of his head.

"I want another doctor to look at him."

Rafiq turned Jamal so the two men were practically nose to nose. "You are on a mission for Allah. You were chosen with great care and months were spent on your training. Do you think he would want you to throw it all away?"

"But—"

Rafiq put his hand on Jamal's shoulder and for the first time the cold look in his eyes was replaced by one filled with hot fervor.

"You must focus on the assignment. Think of the pride your family will take in the completion of your mission. Think of the infidels who raided your village and killed your friend for no reason. That is the reason you accepted this assignment. Whatever happens to your friend is Allah's will. If it is so ordained, you will join him in heaven. Please. Come. We must prepare."

Jamal was so conflicted. He couldn't decide if he liked these people or not, or if in fact they had given any kind of care to Malik. Maybe they were just keeping him alive so Jamal and Kasim wouldn't bail on them at the last minute, or to use as some kind of leverage. *Then why have we not been allowed to see him before this?* Nevertheless, he had to put all that out of his mind now. Malik had sent him a silent message. He would honor it.

Besides, Rafiq's words had inspired a new fire inside him. This was the feeling he'd had back in Niger. When the United States had built a base in Agadez to house and operate armed drones, he and his friends had been so furious they could hardly think straight. How dare these people set up shop in the very country where they would be launching instruments of war to kill people like Jamal's family and friends?

Did they think everyone in the country welcomed them with open arms? Just because the government fell into bed with them for millions of dollars didn't mean the populace approved of it. He and his friends had made a plan, reaching out to others who shared their beliefs, who resented the intrusion of strangers into their country. Little by little they had begun to stockpile explosives for a great raid on the base.

But somehow the word had leaked. Jamal had never found out how or who had such loose lips. But the infidels had arrived, had searched every bit of the village to find the explosives. It had been unfortunate that those compiling the materials hadn't stored them in stable situations. As the soldiers had begun removing them to waiting trucks, a spark had set off the first detonation and it had grown into a full-fledged conflagration.

When at last it had been contained, parts of the village had been left in ruins. The 'less fortunate' areas, as some idiot had said. 'Poor' was how Jamal and his friends described it. They had all grown up with hope in the midst of poverty. Now their hopes lay smoldering in piles of rubble that had once been container houses built with sweat and hard labor. Some were houses crafted of all-wood and others were built with painstaking effort from palm fronds, raffia matting and wood.

Gone, leaving families homeless.

No one had ever blamed the men who had collected the explosives for not storing them in a proper manner. No, all the blame had lain with the foreign soldiers who had stormed in and dragged them out in a careless manner. He'd vowed vengeance then, and in a big way. His burning rhetoric was what had led the recruiters to him and his friends. The blaze of hate inside him had rekindled with a big swoosh. His anger had been a white-hot flame. When he had been approached for this mission, he'd accepted without any hesitation. And because the other three were his good friends, they'd been recruited as well.

Almost before they could turn around they'd been shipped off to the training camp in Mexico where their ability with firearms had been refined and they'd been educated in the building and use of explosives.

At the end of each day, after evening prayers, one of the leaders in the training camp would gather everyone together for a fiery speech and vitriolic denunciation of nonbelievers. Infidels. Traitors to the cause. At the end of each of these he'd been inspired, his blood thirsty for retribution. The four of them, their tight little group, would sit in their tent afterward, wondering what their assignment would be and how many of the infidels they would in fact be able to kill.

All of that had rattled through his brain as he'd tossed and turned in his bed. Vengeance was primary. *So be it.* His personal feelings must be put aside for the successful completion of his mission. He would trust Malik's future to Allah. Perhaps his situation was simply another contribution to the winning of this never-ending fight.

He let out a slow breath.

"Yes. Of course. Let me just pray a moment."

He glanced at Malik and the two of them knelt and prostrated themselves on the floor beside the bed, reciting the Islamic prayer to heal the sick. Then they rose and looked directly into Malik's eyes which burned with religious fervor.

Go with Allah. Kill the infidels.

They each gave a brief nod before turning and leaving the room. Jamal didn't know what this whole charade was about.

He turned and marched out of the house, Kasim behind him, Rafiq and Salman bringing up the rear. Rafiq spoke in an undertone to the man who had shown them into the bedroom and who had not spoken one word up until now. Then they were in the van and headed back to the house where they were staying.

* * * *

Joe Trainor had called and set a meeting at the rodeo grounds with the event operations manager and some of his staff. Joe and Slade each drove their vehicles from the meeting. Novak rode with Joe and Slade had Beau, Marc and Nikki with him. When they arrived, they discovered the chairman of the board that governed he rodeo was there as well.

"I'm hoping you can fill me in on this," he told Joe. "The rodeo has been going on for generations and is an icon of the area. As chairman it's ultimately my responsibility for whatever happens here."

"And we want to make sure you're fully informed," Joe told him. "And here's the gentleman who can answer all your questions."

He introduced Hofler and the chairman got all his questions out.

"I'm going to trust you all to do your jobs," he said at last.

"We'll do our best," Hofler assured him. "We're hoping the visible presence of nearly two hundred law enforcement officers on the security staff might be some kind of deterrent, although with terrorists it doesn't seem anything gives them pause. However, we have our own little group here, which includes the county's finest top officers plus members of a Delta Force team."

"I can't ask for more. Okay, then. I'll let you get to it. Just please keep me in the loop."

Now they all stood with the operations manager and some key staff members at Gate G of the AT&T Parkway. They had decided to start there, since it was the gate that all the vendors used to come and go and Slade wanted a visual of the process.

Marc looked at the group standing on the pavement at the rodeo grounds and tried to assess the situation. Anyone observing might think it was mass pandemonium, but he knew from all his years in the military it was in fact chaos organized with precision. The food operators were setting up both inside one of the large buildings and in the large open area outside that facility. Loaded hand trucks were whisked around everywhere and people yelled orders to workers.

People shouted back and forth. In the carnival area set up in one corner of the grounds, the games and rides were being given a final run-through. And over it all was the continuous sounds of animals—cattle lowing, goats bleating, horses whinnying.

Marc took it all in, memorizing every detail, looking at it through experienced eyes. What he saw wasn't an entertainment venue but a massive target for terrorists, with hundreds of thousands of lives on the line. Whoever had picked this as a target had chosen well. They would have one fucking hell of a job containing this. He was glad the large security force would be tasked with the general safety of the people so Slade and the team could concentrate on finding the terrorists and taking care of them before they did any damage.

"We announced over the general address system before you got here that we were starting our usual security checks today," the operations manager told them. "I needed a reason for all of you to be here scoping things out. I assume you didn't want to raise anyone's suspicions?"

"Good thought," Joe Trainor said. "I figured you'd cover our asses some way."

"And that was the easiest. Now. There'll be guards on the gate here checking the credentials of every vendor who comes through here. Joe, you know what a tight ship we run here."

Trainor nodded. "I do, but this knocks everything up a lot more notches. We're going to have people here with wands checking under, over and around every vehicle. Maybe even inside, if we think something is suspicious."

"Shit, Joe." The manager shook his head. "That will take forever to get them in here. We work hard to avoid a jam as it is."

"Would you rather have a bunch of pipe bombs in here blowing everyone and everything to kingdom come?" Slade asked.

The manager rubbed a hand over his face. "'Course not. You know that. I was just thinking out loud. I'll figure out a way to keep things moving and also not piss off the vendors, since we sure as shit can't tell them what the fuck's going on."

"Let's follow the path the vendors take to their parking lots and also how they move their merchandise into their booths."

They spent the next hour in golf carts crisscrossing the entire area, checking everything from the food sites to the livestock barns. Then they walked both the Freeman Coliseum and the AT&T Center. The entire time everyone had their cell phones out, checking the photos in case by some stroke of luck they spotted one of the terrorists. All Marc could think was what a nightmare this was going to be. And they still had to check the exhibits and other ancillary facilities.

Marc sat in the back seat of one of the carts with Nikki, holding tight to her hand, watching Beau in the front seat scan the rooflines of every building. He obviously had to pick his place. He was only one man, after all. Trainor and Hofler had both said they would provide additional snipers but Marc knew his friend trusted no one but himself. Still, he could only be in one place at a time, so it was critical they plan on the ground where the terrorists would most likely be moving and go from there.

"We can't eliminate the possibility of suicide vests, either," Slade said when all the carts had come to a stop to compare notes. "That's become a signature of these attacks. The final big blowup. Whatever plan they have for bringing in the pipe bombs, they'll be using the same means to get the vests in."

"Hofler's bringing us more people with security wands," Joe reminded him. "Frank Novak here will be leading a team of deputies who have trained for just such a thing. They won't be in uniform and they'll be circulating everywhere checking everyone out. And they'll also have the pictures on their cells."

"And you trust their abilities," Slade persisted.

Trainor huffed his impatience. "I know where you're coming from, Donovan, and I can't argue with that. If I were in your shoes I'd feel the same way. But let me assure you, our men don't want a disaster any more than you do. Like I said, these men have been specially trained for this kind of situation, plus I have my own two guys here."

As they stood there the cell phone in Slade's pocket vibrated and he yanked it out. He looked at the readout before he answered it.

"Hey. I know you were tied up with family stuff, and your leave's not over yet. I just thought I'd give you a shout-out in case you were getting bored."

He smiled at whatever the answer was.

Marc leaned over to whisper in Nikki's ear. "I'll bet that's Trey and he's done with his family obligations. Maybe we got lucky after all."

"How soon can you get here?" Slade asked the caller, then paused to listen. "The rodeo grounds. Okay. Hang on. I'll tell you what gate to use and where to meet us. Yeah. Right." He double checked the information with the operations manager, then repeated it. "Okay. Good copy."

"He's coming," Marc said as soon as Slade disconnected the call.

Slade nodded.

"Who's coming?" Joe asked.

"Trey McIntyre, the fourth member of our core team. He's Beau's spotter and a crack shot himself. He's been visiting with his family. "

"I hope I don't have to worry about a bunch of you running around shooting off your guns," the operations manager said, a scowl creasing his forehead.

Joe snorted. "Have you ever known us to do that? Anywhere?"

"No, but this is different."

"Exactly," Joe agreed. "This is different."

"What about the rest of the security?" the manager asked.

Marc noticed Slade doing what he always did in situations like this — watch and wait. He said he always got more information that way and also figured out how not to step on anyone's toes while still taking charge.

Joe pointed his thumb at Frank Novak. "Frank is going to be in charge of the law officers for this part of the operation. Sheriff Vasquez called you, right?"

The operations manager nodded. "My chief of security will coordinate his crew with you, Frank. But as you know, they're all peace officers in uniform, so your guys are not likely to go anywhere near them."

"My people will all be in civilian clothes, blending as much as possible."

"Do you happen to have cameras installed around the grounds?" Slade asked.

"We do," the manager told him. "We installed them last year. Let's go take a look at the monitoring station."

Marc was pleasantly surprised at the high-tech setup. He always thought how much better it was to work with people who had their shit together.

Slade turned to Hofler. "This should be our command center, don't you think?" He glanced at Joe. "Your opinion?"

"I agree. We'll have comms set up with everyone on our team. This will give us eyes on everything from here and a way to keep in touch."

"The bomb squad will be set up and ready so if we spot something—and I hope to fucking hell we do—they can deal with it at once."

By the end of another hour Trey McIntyre had joined the, and been given a tour. They had marked another map of the grounds with places to put security checks and station members of their group. They also set up a routine to coordinate the patrols. They all had their assignments.

"We open day after tomorrow," the operations manager reminded them. "Tomorrow will be our busiest pre-opening traffic day. If anyone is going to sneak anything in, that's when they would do it."

"I don't think the terrorists themselves would sneak in with the vehicles," Slade told him. "They'd just need a friendly truck driver willing to hide their stuff so it passes security into the rodeo grounds. Then they could walk in with the rest of the public and retrieve the explosives."

Again they went over security at the public entrances and how many people would be checking where the vehicles were parked for anything that looked even the least suspicious.

"Remember," Marc added. "They've been training for this for quite a while. And surviving is not an option for them. Suicide is considered an honor."

The operations manager scratched his head. "That whole philosophy baffles me."

Trey snorted. "Join the crowd. Listen. Has anyone thought about bringing dogs onto the grounds? They could save us a lot of time, right?"

"Yes, and yes," Joe answered. "But here's the deal. We don't want a bunch of guys walking around with bomb-sniffing dogs every day and scaring the shit out of everyone. So yes, we will have dogs here, but they will be comfortably housed in special trailers until we need them. If Nikki spots any of these guys, we'll put the dogs to work right away."

"And you'll have enough to cover the entire grounds?" Trey persisted.

"We will. This is a joint operation with several agencies. We'll make it work."

"Okay, good. Thanks."

"All right," Joe said, "everyone's got their assignments. Slade, you comfortable with the setup?"

"I am. We still need to check for the optimum location for Beau and Trey. The idea is to try and spot these men before they get the bombs placed. Certainly before they set any of them off. But if push comes to shove, we need to take them out before they pull the triggers. Joe, you and I will be in the electronics room monitoring the cameras and watching for anyone that sets off alarms. We'll be depending on Frank and his crew to physically eyeball people, which will be damn tough in the crowd."

"It's difficult not knowing which day they'll decide to hit."

Slade nodded. "No shit. These guys don't necessarily use logic. So, tell everyone to be prepared for long days ahead."

"No problem."

"Okay, then." Slade looked at his watch. "Let's rendezvous at the vendor gate at five tomorrow morning. Everyone dress down to fit in. And look sharp."

When they reached their vehicles and everyone but the Delta Team and Nikki had left, Slade turned to each of them.

"I think we need to meet somewhere private. Everything we went over today is well and good, but we all know how easily an op can go sideways. We need to make our own preparations. I'd say let's head for the ranch, but we're all here in the city."

"We can go to my place."

Marc was startled when Nikki spoke up. She'd been noticeably silent through the entire process.

"You good with that? Having us there for a head session?"

"Of course. We need to do whatever it takes to stop this, and my place is the most convenient."

"Thank you."

Marc took Nikki's hand and gave it a gentle squeeze, the kind that always eased any worries or panic.

Like now.

"Yes," Slade agreed. "Thank you."

"Okay, then." Marc looked at his team leader. "Slade, if you'll get us back to our wheels, we'll head on over."

"You all have the address?" Nikki looked at the other team members. When they nodded, she added, "We'll stop at that great bakery near my complex and get some goodies."

"I'll take care of it," Slade told her. "It's the least I can do."

Marc was very aware of how silent Nikki had been for most of the meeting. Even though she'd spoken up to offer her place for them to gather, he still had no idea what was going on in her brain. As soon as they were alone in their rental car he intended to find out.

Chapter Thirteen

Suicide vests had been on the final list Jamal had seen of the supplies they'd be provided with. The possibility had been discussed back in Niger and certainly at the training camp in Mexico. Up until now, however, he hadn't seen them. He began to wonder if perhaps whoever was really running this had had a change of heart. But, after they all said their morning prayers, Rafiq sent the other two men to the garage. When they returned, they had several boxes, which they placed on the dining room table. Rafiq indicated that Jamal and Kasim should help empty them.

The box on top held two padded canvas vests, each with multiple inside pockets. The other boxes they opened and removed the contents with extreme caution—sticks of dynamite, fuses, bags of shrapnel and nails and plastic bags to stuff them into so each little vest pocket was filled to capacity. Once the detonator was activated and the dynamite exploded, the dispersal of the shrapnel and nails would do incredible damage to anyone it hit.

"For your trip to heaven and the virgins waiting there for you," he halfway joked. "This is a very important assignment for you and Kasim."

"And an honor," Salman added.

Jamal looked across the table at Kasim, who gave him a slight nod.

Yes. Also for Malik and Farid.

"These vests, as I am sure you know, will provide additional impact. We are going for maximum effect here. You will each have a detonator to control, but I will hook them up to cell phones also." He looked from one man to the other. "Just as a failsafe, you understand."

"I understand." *In case we change our minds at the last minute, but that isn't going to happen. We are committed.*

He was fine with this. Now looking forward to it, in fact. After all the trouble they'd had getting to this point, he welcomed the opportunity at last to martyr himself for Allah and bring honor to his family. He would be in heaven where he would receive his glorious reward.

Rafiq walked over to the map of the rodeo grounds taped to the wall. Despite the fact that Jamal told him how much time they'd trained for it at the camp, he insisted on spending a portion of each day going over it again, drilling them on the locations of everything.

"You cannot be too well prepared," he said over and over. "You will have one chance to get this right. If you forget where you are, or go to the wrong place to retrieve the equipment, all will be lost. We have set this up to make a bold statement, Jamal. We cannot fail at this."

He meant I cannot fail. Or Kasim.

"There will be no failure," he assured Rafiq. "We are well-trained and one hundred percent committed."

"Fine. Then you will appreciate the continued attention to detail. Now."

Rafiq circled two places in red.

"These are the most optimum spots to set them off. The Freeman Coliseum will be filled by that time with people trying to escape the other explosions. Same thing for this little cluster of buildings here. Tomorrow Salman will accompany you to the rodeo. You will all enter separately but then meet together past the gates. Salman will personally show you where you'll be retrieving the supplies and vest and where you will be planting them. The map is a guide, but seeing it in person is better."

"Yes," Jamal said. "I agree."

"I will also be at the rodeo that day, waiting for everything to be in readiness. I will give you a cell phone, Jamal, with one number programmed into it. Once all the pipe bombs have been placed, call that number. It will alert me. Salman and I will then call each of the numbers on the phones affixed to the bombs to generate a series of explosions. Then, while everything is mass confusion, go quickly to these two locations. Open your vests, offer your prayer to Allah and hit the detonator switch."

"Will they have security precautions against bombs?" Kasim asked. "I mean, even after they are planted?"

Good question, Jamal said to himself. He should have thought of that himself. And why hadn't they been alerted to the possibility?

"No more than the usual security methods are being employed," Rafiq assured them. "We have checked with the people bringing your equipment onto the rodeo grounds and they have paid careful attention to every briefing. If they hear something, they will let me know. But since we won't be bringing anything through the regular gates and the materials will all be hidden and disguised, there will be no way for them to detect anything." He gave Jamal a hard look. "Especially since you assure me that no one knows of these plans."

"Just to repeat." Salman walked in from the kitchen. "You said you never mentioned your assignment in front of the woman at the cottage?"

"That's correct." Jamal hoped to hell he was right. He was pretty damn sure they had avoided the subject, although his stomach knotted at the possibility something had slipped.

"Then they have no reason to be on alert any more than normal. We will keep in touch with our contacts, but so far there has been no word of anything. Also, there is nothing on the news about the man you shot. Perhaps that is in an area of no news importance."

"The man who killed your friend must also be of no significance to us or there would be chatter everywhere. We are hooked into all the pipelines and things are silent. You seem to be off the radar. Just keep putting those vests together."

I am going to die, Jamal thought. *Am I prepared to do this?* The tiny thread of fear disappeared as once again rage at the infidels coursed through him. Yes, he was more than ready. It would be the ultimate revenge and assure him his place in heaven.

"We understand," he told Rafiq.

"Good. Good. Then the two of you had better get to work preparing them." He sighed. "It is unfortunate that your two friends are not able to be there with you. The impact would have been doubled."

Yes. Too bad that Farid had been killed by an infidel's bullet and that Malik was now dying from a similar cause. There was no glory in that. But he and Kasim would avenge them and send a strong message not to fuck with his people.

"Breakfast first," Salman told them, coming in from the kitchen. "While we eat, we will go over the final arrangements for delivering you to the rodeo and the security process at the gate. You will have to memorize where the knapsacks with the bombs are being held." His smile was more arrogance than friendliness. "It is obvious we cannot write it down for you."

"We can remember," Jamal snapped. He was really tired of the man's attitude.

"Fine. Let us get to breakfast then."

Jamal ate quickly, food being the last thing he was interested in. Excitement curled inside him as the hour of their mission approached. He would finally be able to honor his family and the friends he had lost. He ate sparingly then hurried to the dining room to begin preparing the vests. Flexing his fingers, he went to work.

* * * *

Nikki was silent as they headed toward her apartment complex. She had so much going on in her mind. She had deliberately said nothing while they toured the rodeo grounds and discussed the details of their plan. Instead she'd absorbed everything and let it run around in her head.

She was well aware of what Delta Force did and the dangers the men faced. But somehow, when it was remote, the dangers didn't seem quite so real. The one thing she hadn't considered when she'd moved forward in this relationship with Marc was how life-threatening his career was. But listening today as they all discussed optimum locations for shooting, making sure no one walked around with a bull's-eye on his back, all the little things that went into this, it really hit her hard that she could lose him at any time.

And, of course, there was the necessity of protecting her. She had agreed, against Marc's objections, to serve as their spotter, riding around in a golf cart pretending to take event pictures. And since he wouldn't allow anyone else to serve as her protection, he was putting himself in harm's way for her. Her rational mind knew he did things like this on a regular basis, but her emotional one didn't want anything to happen to him.

It had taken her so long to get past losing Jon. Of course, part of that was her despair at not having been able to nurse him back to health. Never mind that he'd had a debilitating disease that hadn't been discovered until it was too late. She had carried the burden on her shoulders for a long time. Not until Marc had come along and the two of them, wounded souls, had begun to heal each other had she thought she was ready to embrace life again.

He was fast becoming everything to her—lover, friend, companion, confidant—and the sex was beyond anything she could ever have imagined. But it wasn't until that morning that she'd realized the constancy of the danger he lived in. Marc shooting up the car, Slade and Beau arriving in the helo, Beau with his sniper rifle, had brought home to her with clarity that on a mission their lives were on the line every single minute.

Faster than she could have imagined, she was falling in love with this man. What if something happened to him while he was off protecting the world? Could she live through it again? Was she becoming a coward now? But what was the alternative? Was she willing to give up what they had now because it might end too soon, and never have it at all?

"All right, darlin'." His warm voice broke into her thoughts. "Out with it."

She shifted in the seat next to him. "Out with what?"

"Whatever's been on your mind since we started touring the rodeo grounds."

"It's…I'm fine." She had to get her act together. The last thing she wanted to do was serve as a distraction to him because of her wimpy attitude.

"No. You're not." He reached over and took her hand. "Answer me this. Do we trust each other? Can we tell each other things?"

"Yes," she answered after a long moment. It stunned her to realize how open they could be with each other, but even so, she couldn't tell him this. He had to focus on what he was doing, not on her.

"Then tell me what's on your mind, or I'm stopping the car on the side of the road and telling Slade we'll be late."

She plastered what she hoped was a real smile on her face and looked over at him. *Think fast*, she told herself.

"I guess it's just this is the first time something like this has really hit home with me. I mean, the fact that there are people like this who deliberately come to this country to kill as many people as possible." She swallowed a sigh. "I know 9/11 was the ultimate and we'll never forget it or recover from it. But this is up close and personal for me. I have to be honest. Those men yesterday scared me to death. They aren't rational."

"No kidding. God. I hate the fact that you had to go through that. If I hadn't been in the shower, or been more suspicious of them, or — "

She leaned over and put her hand over his mouth.

"Hush. That was not your fault. I should have been more aware." She managed a smile. "And in the end, you saved me, right?"

Just as she'd known he would. It was all that had kept her going during her time in that cottage and when she'd been tied up in the car.

"Nikki, we're going to get these guys." He lifted her hand to his mouth and placed a light kiss on her fingers. "This is what we do in Delta. Get bad guys like these. Then everyone will be safe."

Yes, but will you?

She found a smile from someplace. "I know you will. I believe in you. And don't worry about me. I'm still processing it all."

Suck it up, girl.

The very last thing she wanted right now was to give him a hint of her misgivings. She hated that she was such a coward, but her feelings for Marc had intensified so fast and were so deep that if she lost him she wasn't sure how she'd recover.

When she'd lost Jon, she'd been sure she'd never dare to risk her heart again. Then she'd met Marc, a lost soul like her, and, unbelievable as it was, the darkness had faded. They were so perfect together in every way that she kept waiting for something to go wrong. On the one hand, she wanted this more than anything. On another, she wondered if she had the courage to really take the next step. She hadn't really thought much about the constant danger Marc was in until today. But riding in the cart with Marc and Slade, listening to them all discuss containment of explosives, minimizing targets, examining the necessity of kill shots, had brought the reality of it home to her. And Marc would be in twice as much danger because he would be out in the open with her, protecting her while she tried to lay eyes on the terrorists.

"You're quiet again." He deep voice pierced her thought cloud. "Should I be worried?"

Not when you need all your concentration for the job ahead. This is my problem. I'll deal with it. But not until after we get past this crisis.

"Not at all." She squeezed his hand again. "I read once that men going into battle abstained from sex because it drained their energy and concentration."

Marc chuckled. "That's an old wives' tale, and we don't have any old wives around here. In fact, I think I read somewhere that good, hot sex stimulates your nerve endings and makes you more battle-ready."

"I think you just made that up," she teased.

His chuckle was low and sexy, and just the sound she needed right now.

"But it sounds like a good idea." He glanced over at her. "Right?"

Yes. If nothing else, they could lose themselves in each other's bodies.

"Yes," she agreed. "It does. But are you sure?"

"Sure as I am of my own name." His voice had deepened to that timbre it always did when they made love. "I say we lock down all the details in this meeting right now then spend the rest of the day forgetting about anything in the world except for the two of us."

"Sounds good to me." And it did. She wanted every minute of intimacy with him they could squeeze in, just in case...

No. She wouldn't think about that. Not yet.

Slade, Beau and Trey were leaning against Slade's pickup in the parking lot of her apartment complex. Slade was balancing a large box that she knew had to be from Dough Ray Me. That had been her favorite place from the day someone had recommended it to her. She was always grateful that she didn't have to watch her weight so carefully, because her willpower where their goodies were concerned was nonexistent.

"Consider this our rent for using your apartment." Slade grinned as he showed her the label on the box.

"Sold. And thank you."

Nikki made coffee as soon as they walked into the apartment, and plated the pastries, which she carried to the dining room table where they'd all gathered. She started to walk toward her bedroom, but Slade called to her.

"You should sit in on this, too, Nikki. You'll be an integral part of this, and it's vital that each person on the core team knows exactly what's going on."

"Thank you." She slid into the empty chair next to Marc. "I think."

"Yeah, you may not be so ready with the thanks when this is all said and done. But let me say first, we are all pissed off at what happened to you yesterday, and more grateful than we can say that you are willing to be a part of this. Marc has seen these guys, but not as up close and personal as you have. You may be the only person who can pick them out for us."

"If it will get them off the streets and save people's lives," she told him, "then it's worth it."

He nodded. "Okay, then. Let's get down to business."

Despite herself, Nikki was fascinated listening to them as for the next hour they plotted the most intricate details of how and what and when. She understood why they wanted to do this without the rest of the people around. There were parts of a Delta Force op that no one else was trained for, no matter how good they were, and Slade and his men wanted to prepare for even the tiniest details.

By the time they'd gone through two pots of coffee and all the pastries had been eaten, Nikki's head was spinning, but it was clear to her that every eventuality had been discussed. The problem would be preventing the dispersal of bombs before any one of them could be detonated.

"Again," Slade said, "top of the list is anyone wearing a backpack. That's the accepted method of transport for improvised explosive devices. IEDs. Also, the weather is predicted in the high eighties, so look for anybody who is wearing a bulky jacket or heavy shirt that can conceal a suicide vest."

"Trey and I are going to scope out everything ourselves tomorrow morning," Beau interjected. "We'd really like to have a helicopter do a flyover for us so we can get a bird's-eye view of everything and also take photos. It will help us decide where to plant ourselves."

"Good idea," Slade agreed. "I'll have Teo get you in the ranch helo at whatever time you say. Where do you want the pickup?"

"Someplace where we won't have a lot of people watching and asking questions."

"Okay. Let me ask Teo. He usually knows where to find those places. I'll call or text you as soon as I get back to the ranch." He sat back in his chair. "I'll be bringing plenty of ammo in the truck, and hoping to fucking hell we won't have to use it. Anything else?"

He looked around the table and everyone shook their head.

"Then I guess we're all set. Nikki, thank you for the use of your apartment. And most of all, thank you for putting yourself out there to help us catch these guys."

"It's okay. I have a vested interest here."

Once the others were gone, Marc turned to her and cupped her face with his big, warm hands.

"You are the bravest woman I know." He brushed his mouth over hers.

"Oh, I'm scared." She gave a little laugh. "But mad, too, at what they did. And what they're planning. But I can only get through it because you'll be right there with me."

"That's a given, darlin'." Another butterfly kiss. "But didn't you forget something?"

She frowned. "Like what?"

"Like you only have four days of vacation time left before you have to go back to work."

"Oh, that."

"Yes," he chuckled. "That."

"I'm calling my supervisor in a minute to tell her I had an emergency come up and I need the next three weeks off. I've hardly ever taken vacation time since…" She stopped. "Well, since forever. And they won't fire me. Trust me. No one else is crazy enough to work all the shifts for everyone else the way I do."

"And that's something else we need to talk about, but not now."

"Oh?" She quirked an eyebrow. "What are we talking about now?"

"Some physical therapy I think we both need." He licked her mouth. "Then I want to go over every detail of what's going to happen just relating to the two of us for the next however many days it takes to get these assholes."

She smiled. "I can for sure get on board with that."

Chapter Fourteen

"No tub?" Nikki asked as Marc led her to the shower and turned on the spray.

"Uh-uh. This time I don't want anything between us but water."

He was out of his clothes before she could blink, and in seconds had added hers to the pile. He wanted them both naked. Now.

"In a hurry, are we?" she teased.

"To shut out the big, bad world and think about two things—us and pleasure?" he growled. "You better believe it."

He adjusted the spray so it was soft and fine, like a rain shower.

"Close your eyes," he told her, "and just enjoy. Forget about everything except this, right now. Us."

She closed her eyes and leaned her head back, the water kissing her skin. He hoped it was washing away the tension and disaster of the past two days. He poured some of her scented body wash into his palms and rubbed his hands together to create thick lather. Then, starting at her neck, he worked his way down her body, massaging each of her muscles as he did so. Shoulders. Arms. Back. Stomach. Legs.

God! Just touching her was an incredible gift. He had no idea what stroke of luck had connected them, but she brought the first light in a long time into his life, and he wasn't about to let it go. He wasn't stupid enough to believe no problems would crop up. Everything else aside, they were both still unpacking a lot of emotional baggage. But whatever it was, he'd make sure they worked through it. Because they were worth it. *She* was worth it.

When he slid his hands between her thighs, she gasped and opened her eyes. He looked up to see her watching him and his mouth curved in a hungry smile.

"Eyes closed, darlin'. Tight shut."

She drifted them shut again and let out a sigh that he felt in every part of his body. Especially his cock, which was standing at attention with such rigidity that he worried if he bumped the shower wall, it would break off.

Now he slid his hands up to her breasts, the hot, slippery feel of them so erotic he felt it all the way to his balls. He plumped her in his palms and squeezed with a gentle motion of his fingers. Just that simple contact pushed back the memories of the past two days and the thoughts of what was yet to come. He tucked them into a box and slammed the lid down. Nothing existed but him and this incredible woman.

He brushed the pads of his soapy fingers across her nipples, feeling them harden at once beneath the contact. He squeezed them, gave a light pinch and was rewarded to see the increase in the beat of her pulse at the hollow of her throat. She cried out in protest when he moved his hands away.

"Ssh," he soothed. "There's more to come."

But not yet, he wanted to say. Not until he had her so relaxed, so undone, that the pleasure would go on and on and on. He slid his mouth over hers before taking a gentle bite of her lower lip. She sighed, a sound that vibrated throughout his body, so he did it again. Then he turned her so she faced the wall and placed her palms against the tile so she could brace herself.

Adding another dollop of the shower gel, he massaged the body wash into her shoulders, down her back, and along her spine. He ghosted his fingers over the curve of her gorgeous ass down to her legs, then knelt and nudged her thighs apart. With the same slow, leisurely movement, he stroked each leg up from ankle to thigh and down again. When he brushed the lips of her cunt with his knuckles, she moaned and pressed herself against his hand.

Not yet, he told himself again. *Not quite yet.*

Coating his fingers with more shower gel, he then slid them between the cheeks of her ass, stroking up and down, feeling the hot, puckered opening. What he wouldn't give to plunge his cock inside her there, feel that scorching heat and those tight muscles around his shaft as he fucked them both into oblivion.

Soon, he reminded himself. *One thing at a time.*

By the time he'd attended to every inch of her, his entire body was one big hard-on, but Nikki was relaxed and limp as she leaned against the shower wall.

He turned her to face him again, then dropped down to his knees and lifted one of her legs over his shoulder to give him complete access to her. Using this thumbs and forefingers, he opened the lips of her cunt as though he was exposing the core of a flower, took her clit between his teeth and bit down with a gentle pressure.

Nikki moaned her pleasure and dug her heel into his back to balance herself. When her swollen bud was fully teased, he ran the tip of his tongue around her opening before thrusting it inside. She was so wet, and he knew it wasn't just the shower. He curled his tongue to taste every bit of her inner walls, lapped at her clit again then returned to fucking her with his tongue.

Her sexy little moans were as much of a turn-on as teasing and feeling her, so he did it again. And more. He adjusted her position so he could continue to fuck her with his mouth while he clasped the cheeks of her ass and separated them just enough that he could slide his fingers into that tempting place between them.

She continued to make those delicious sounds that only made him hotter as she rocked forward against his mouth and back against his fingers. He could tell she was close, so he increased the pressure and speed. Then he bit down on her clit again and she exploded, pouring her juices onto his tongue, her buttocks clenching hard against his fingers. He banded one arm around her to hold her to him as spasm after spasm rocked her.

Then, at last, the tremors subsided and her body was lax against the tiles. He rose and placed a soft kiss on her lips. Then, sliding his tongue into her mouth, he soothed her and stroked her until she was calm again.

"Well." Her eyes opened but they were still heavy-lidded with passion. "That was some shower."

He chuckled. "There's more where that came from. Can I coax you into bed so I can slide into you and feel all that delicious wet flesh around me?"

"Let's dry off. Then I have a better idea. "

He couldn't imagine what on earth that could be, but they dried each other carefully, swipes with the towels punctuated by kisses that were hot and hungry. He was astounded that despite her orgasm just seconds ago, Nikki was aroused again. They could barely keep their hands off each other as they fell into bed, covers kicked to the foot of the mattress. But when Marc started to reach for the condoms in the nightstand drawer, she stopped him.

"I have a better idea. You've been doing all the work. Now it's my turn."

She caught him so off guard that when she nudged him onto his back, he just tumbled into place. Although still shaking a bit in the aftermath of her release, she prodded his legs apart, knelt between his thighs and circled his cock with her slim fingers.

When she lowered her head, he tried to stop her.

"Wait. Nikki. No, wait. Please. You don't have to —"

But she knocked his hand away and closed her mouth over him, sliding her lips from tip to root and back again.

Oh, sweet Jesus.

Although in their short relationship he'd done this to her several times, he'd never hinted that she should reciprocate. For one thing, he knew a lot of women didn't like it. For another, Ria had always done that whenever they got in a fight and she wanted to get past it. Change the environment. She'd discovered early on that she could drive everything out of his mind when she closed her lips around him.

Would those bitter memories ruin what could be special with Nikki? Could he relax and enjoy it?

"Quit thinking." Her words were muffled as her mouth was still closed around his shaft. "Please let me do this for you, okay?"

His head fell back on the pillow and his arms dropped to his sides. Nikki hummed as she slid her mouth up and down his cock, pausing now and then to lick the soft skin of the head, punctuating it with brief dips of her tongue into the little slit. Heat surged through him, lighting him up like a Fourth of July firecracker and his hips automatically rose and fell with the rhythm of her mouth.

He had already been teetering on the edge before this, but now his body was screaming for release. As if sensing it, Nikki slowed her movements, eased back and licked the warm flesh with a lazy movement of her tongue. When she went back to it in earnest, he wove his fingers through her long, thick hair, pulling it to one side so his view of her mouth was not obscured.

The sight of those plump pink lips closed around his hot shaft, the feel of her tongue, the delicate way she sucked him yet still drew on him with force. *Jesus.* Whatever he'd done with Ria wasn't even in the same ballpark as this. This—*this!*—was the stuff erotic dreams were made of. He closed his eyes and gave himself over to sensation.

Need rose within him, hot and fluid, surging through his body. He held it together until she slid her hands between his thighs, cupped his balls and gave them a gentle squeeze. At the same time she drew her teeth the length of his shaft then sucked hard.

And he exploded.

Fuck!

He didn't know if he shouted it or just heard it in his head, but his entire body convulsed and shook as spasm after spasm gripped him and his cum spurted into her mouth. She stayed with him until the end, sucking until there wasn't a drop left in him, squeezing his balls in a rhythmic motion. And swallowing. All he could think was nothing that had come before had ever been like this. *Nothing.*

It seemed forever before his body finally gave up the ghost. Every bit of energy had been sapped from him. Nikki looked at him, a knowing smile curving her lips. Despite the harrowing experiences of the past two days, there was a little spark in her eyes.

"Good?" She licked her lips, a slow, easy swipe of her tongue.

He could not believe that his very limp shaft began to harden again.

"Are you kidding? Good isn't even close to describing it." He reached up and pulled her down to him, cradling her against his chest. "When this is all over, darlin', we are definitely discussing our future. I know we both have unpleasant histories but I think we can build something good together."

"Okay."

But what did it mean that she took so long to get that word out? A feeling of unease threaded through him, pricking at the happiness he was finding despite the situation they were all involved in.

He wasn't going to worry about it now. They had a crisis to get through first. But he for sure wasn't walking away from this. And he wouldn't let her, either.

Tugging her forward until she lay across his chest, he put his arms around her and kissed her forehead. When she snuggled against him, the tight feeling in his chest eased a little. Whatever this was, he'd find the answer so they could move ahead together. For the first time in forever he was actually looking forward to the future.

* * * *

Jamal put the final touches on the suicide vest, closed the flaps and set it inside a box. Across from him, Kasim did the same. In an hour a friend of Rafiq's would be here to pick up all the explosives, including the vests, and secure them in a hidden compartment in his food truck.

"This is where the truck that we are looking for will be parked." Rafiq marked a red X on the big map. "Tomorrow the two of you and Salman will attend the rodeo like any other citizens. We have tickets for you. Salman will give you the guided tour, show you how to retrieve the explosives from the truck and plan out their route for the placement of the bombs. You will know exactly where everything is and how to get to it."

Jamal frowned. *Is it just this simple?* "Won't someone question us being around there?"

Rafiq gave him a look of disgust. "Do you not believe we have thought of everything here? It will be mass chaos there. When you return the day after opening, you will arrive as workers for this vendor. No one will be wondering about a couple of men getting supplies from a truck. The man helping us has a false back in his truck, concealing a locked cupboard that looks like a solid piece of metal. And the spicy aroma of the food will be enough to disguise any lingering odors of the explosives."

Salman had walked into the dining room as Rafiq finished his explanation. He nodded at the other man's words.

"Tomorrow we will be just average people going to the rodeo. We will check out all the buildings, buy some food and look at trinkets. Check out both the Freeman Coliseum and the AT&T Center. We will even take pictures, like tourists. Pictures that we can look at back here and memorize again."

Rafiq looked at each of the men, fervor hot in his eyes. "It is important that you not fuck this up. Instead of heaven you will be cast into hell, and your families will suffer."

Jamal was too familiar with the suffering inflicted on the families of those who failed their missions. From the time he'd been a child, he had seen ISIS teams march to the homes of people he knew, drag families out into the street and behead them or shoot them down. Often the person accused was forced to watch members of his family whipped and tortured in other ways before everyone was killed.

To some, this might have been a reason to try escaping. To Jamal and his friends, it meant a purification, as they'd been taught from an early age. His heart was committed to ISIS as the one path to being blessed by Allah and achieving the highest state in heaven. Killing infidels would bring him and Kasim a great reward. Rather than fearing his death, he embraced it, as did his friend. He was only sad that Malik and Farid would not be joining them, but he would pray for their souls.

Chapter Fifteen

Marc and Nikki arrived at the rodeo grounds at eleven-thirty the next morning, thirty minutes before the gates opened. Everyone was already there, gathered outside the operations manager's office

Steven Hofler gathered everyone inside the office before they started out for the day. "First thing," he told the group, "is we got an identification on the dead body about an hour ago. His name is Farid Abadi."

"Any history on him?" Slade asked. "Or word about the guys with him?"

"Unfortunately, not yet, but I promise you, they are all over it."

"Is he part of a group?" Joe Trainor asked. "Do we know who his friends are? Who the other three guys in that cottage with him were?" He glanced at Nikki. "The ones who captured Miss Alvarez?"

Marc felt rather than saw Nikki tense at the words.

Hofler shook his head. "Not yet, but we're still working on it. They'd be the ones he would have been sent to Mexico with." He paused. "We should all keep in mind the chaos and death we'll be facing if we can't find these men in time."

"I'm sure you don't need me to tell you," the operations manager commented. "We'd sure appreciate it if you caught these guys before we get into any of the evening hours."

"Believe me when I tell you we want to catch these guys as fast as possible ourselves," Steven Hofler all but snapped at him.

"I'm just sayin'," the manager told him.

Marc realized the man had the entire facility as well as all the employees and volunteers to be concerned about, but he thought the manager should be damn glad they'd caught the news about this before anything could happen. And that they had a full-out plan they were implementing to shortstop disaster.

He was convinced that Day One of what he was calling the Rodeo Bomb Tour would be busy but uneventful. The consensus was that the terrorists would spend that day scoping out the site and making their plans.

"We don't open until noon today," the manager reiterated. "After that it's eight o'clock every day. We're open the first three nights until ten. After that we close at nine."

"They'll be marking spots to conceal the bombs for optimum effect," Hofler reminded them. "They won't want to place them just willy nilly. And they'll be dressed to blend in with everyone else, so even with the sketches, it will be difficult to identify them."

"Everyone has those sketches, right?" Slade asked, looking at the group.

They all nodded.

"Okay. The regular security force will be visible at all times." He pointed to a man standing close to Trainor. "Sheriff Andy Morrell heads that group and shift captains report to him. They will all be visible, wearing uniforms and many also with Stetsons on their heads. Our guys will want to avoid them at all costs, so if you happen to spot anyone in the overwhelming crowd that looks like the deputies make them nervous, keep a sharp eye on them."

"You've all got your assignments." Hofler looked at the group. "Let's get some coffee and get started."

Slade was standing by the cart Marc and Nikki sat in, one arm leaning on the top.

"Hold on until everyone else is gone," he told them in a low voice.

The group dispersed, Hofler going off to the electronics office so he could track everything with the on-site personnel. Then it was just Marc's team and Nikki.

"What's up?" Trey asked.

Slade looked at Trey and Beau.

"Yesterday we couldn't seem to agree on the best vantage point for the two of you. Beau, you're liable to be the point of last resort. We'll have the dogs sniffing all day for bombs, which we hope will make things difficult for these guys. We'll even have them in the Freeman Coliseum and the AT&T Center. But these insane fanatics could decide any statement is better than no statement at all and try to place them outside."

Beau nodded. "Trey and I talked about that after the meeting yesterday. We had the same thought." He pulled out a copy of the map they'd all memorized. "If Plan A fails for them, this looks like the optimum place for them to place their stuff."

With the tip of his finger he drew a line through the area in front of the Freeman Coliseum, indicating the cluster of shows, food places and family activities. Just off to the left but still within the danger zone was the big carnival setup.

"Yesterday we talked about us getting up on the roof of Expo Hall, but the Freeman gives us a wider range," Trey pointed out. "Get us up there with radios so we're in touch at all times and we'll be good to go."

Marc felt Nikki's hand on his arm.

"Yeah, sugar?"

"Marc, it's broiling in the sun up there. I'd hate for them to get dehydrated or burned alive."

"Good thing we have a nurse along," he teased. "I promise you it's way hotter than this over in the sandbox. And Slade will be sure they have plenty of water. No worries."

He could tell she was still bothered, and he loved the fact that she was concerned about his teammates. Again he wondered if he should stash her away in the electronics room until the end of the day. *Who knows what these nut jobs might do, especially if they recognize her?*

As if she knew what was running through his brain, she shook her head.

"You need me out here, Marc. I'm the only one who's spent enough time with them to recognize them. And I don't look anything like myself, right?"

He had to give her that. She wore faded jeans, a rodeo T-shirt and a rodeo ball cap set atop a wig of curly black hair. Even he wouldn't recognize her, except that he'd memorized every inch of her body so well that no disguise would trick him.

Slade had reminded him that the terrorists had also gotten a look at him during the boat discussion, so they'd outfitted Marc with a rodeo T-shirt and a straw cowboy hat.

He swallowed a sigh.

"Fine. But you aren't leaving my side for a second. Got that?"

"I'm sure she does." Slade grinned at her. "She's pretty damn savvy, the way she kept her shit together at the lake."

Nikki gave him a tiny grin. "Thank you. Just as long as I don't have to do it too often."

"Okay." Slade slapped his hand on the roof of Marc's cart. "I'll get Trey and Beau over to the coliseum and check in with the others. Hofler and Trainor and their crew will be checking every possible place these nuts could pick to place a pipe bomb, then checking it again. Hofler says he believes they'll do the deed tomorrow. He's got experience with this stuff, so I won't argue with him. You two take off now. You've got your route and your stuff. And be sure you hydrate yourselves, too."

"You got it."

They'd needed a reason for Marc and Nikki to be riding around everywhere for however many days it took for this thing to go down. Trainor was actually the one who'd come up with the idea of taking pictures for a magazine that would showcase the rodeo. The chairman of the board was only too glad to sign off on it after they filled him in on what was happening. No way did he want his pride and joy, a historic, multi-million-dollar event, disrupted by terrorists.

Marc drove them once around the rodeo grounds to make sure he was familiarized with every inch of it. In Delta, because his life always depended on it, he'd learned to absorb information quickly. Then they started on their 'assignment', stopping at vendors and exhibits so Nikki could snap photos, even as she managed to sneak shots of the crowd. In case she missed the people they were looking for, they could check the pictures.

"What if this whole thing is a mistake?" she asked, when they stopped for a moment. "What if this isn't their target after all and we're wasting time and resources?"

"Anything is possible," Marc agreed. "But JSOC would have checked out the rumor before they passed it on to our team."

He'd worried about the effect of this whole thing on her, but she was one hundred percent focused on her job. She was also damn good with the little digital camera someone had gotten for her, as well as charming and joking with the people whose pictures she took.

Periodically he would find a shady spot to park in that still gave them a wide view of the outdoor area. They could take a few moments to scan the crowd and see if they got lucky and spotted anyone. Whoever these guys were, Marc was convinced — as were the others — that they'd scope out the place today and try to blend in with all the other rodeo-goers. That meant there was a good chance they could spot them at one of the outdoor vendors or activities.

By noon they had covered a good section of the grounds, familiarizing themselves in greater detail than the day before. Getting people used to seeing them so they didn't look out of place. That was the key. To not set off any alarms while they scoped things out.

It was straight up noon when Marc pulled the cart into the shade of an overhang and stopped. He reached into the back seat of the cart and lifted the small cooler he'd packed that morning.

"Food and water," he said. "And a few minutes' rest."

Nikki uncapped her water bottle and took a long drink. "This is like finding the proverbial needle in a haystack."

"That it is. And while the sketches you helped with are great, they aren't the same as real photos, so we're having to pick faces out of the crowd that we hope look like these."

She sighed. "I wish I could have done better."

Marc took her hand in his, lifted it to his mouth and pressed a kiss to her knuckles.

"You did great, Nikki. Better than ninety-nine percent of people. You remembered things that most folks wouldn't even have noticed. So don't sell yourself short."

"Well, I hope they do what we need them to. The more I look at the crowds packing in here, the more frightened I get at the damage these men can do."

"I think we all feel that way," he told her. "Some of the stuff we see overseas in the sandbox could give you nightmares for years."

"I'm so torn," she told hm. "I'm so proud that you're out there doing your best to protect people and get the bad guys. At the same time, though, I hate that you have to be there, putting yourself in danger."

"Someone's gotta do it, darlin'." He cupped her chin and turned her head so she faced him. "I'm proud to be doing this and I promise I'm more careful than I am crossing the streets here. Okay?"

She hesitated for a moment, long enough for him to wonder what was going through her mind. But then she nodded and even smiled.

"Okay. And we'd better get back to work."

Marc packed the trash back into the cooler and pulled out into the crowd again. He was focused on identifying the terrorists, but one tiny part of his mind still wondered what was bothering Nikki. Whatever it was, he'd fix it before he had to leave again. He'd found the woman who made him whole once more and gave his life meaning unlike anything he'd ever known. He'd do whatever was necessary to make it work.

* * * *

Rafiq dropped them off just before the gate officially opened.

"You can ease yourselves into the crowd. Do not all go on together, but make your way to the spot I marked and go from there. There is safety and disguise in numbers."

The three of them—Jamal, Kasim and Salman—blended into the crowd waiting to enter, passed through security with no trouble and met at the designated spot. Even though Jamal had studied the huge maps and diagrams of the event grounds, he still could not help marveling at the size of it as well as the numbers of people in attendance.

"Be sure to note the heavy presence of the rodeo security force," Salman reminded them. "Lucky for us, as Rafiq explained, they wear their uniforms, so they are easy to identify. You have your programs?"

Rafiq had told them each to purchase a program as they entered. That way they could look like regular attendees checking locations as they walked around. Kasim had a ballpoint pen with him to mark off the spots that Salman said were optimum for bomb placement. And Jamal took pictures with the cell phone he'd been given, forcing himself to adopt the posture of any of the thousands of eventgoers doing the same thing.

"It is best to place them in this area where all the food vendors and exhibits are located," he told them. "The vests should be detonated in the Freeman Coliseum and one of the expo halls. We will look at both of them and decide which one would give you the best effect."

They stopped shortly after noon, to buy bottled water and something called noodle buckets with chicken. They sat at a bench behind a tree to eat.

"Who are those people riding around in that cart?" Kasim asked, pointing to a golf cart carrying a man and a woman.

"It looks like they are rodeo employees," Salman said. "When they were taking pictures at one of the vendors, I walked over to listen to what they were saying. It seems they are taking pictures for a magazine the rodeo is putting together. Why?" He gave Kasim a sharp look. "Do you recognize either of them?"

Kasim shook his head. "No. I just want to make sure they aren't taking pictures of the crowd."

"Don't worry. I won't let them anywhere near you. Even though tomorrow is your last day on earth, it would not do to have your picture show up someplace. Any of our pictures. Who knows what could lead back to Rafiq and me and the others?"

Jamal squinted at the cart as it passed them heading toward the carnival. A thread of unease wriggled through him, but he didn't know why. Neither of the two people looked familiar to him. How would anyone know to search them out here, anyway? He did not remember if any of them had mentioned the rodeo when the nurse had been in their cottage.

By mid-afternoon, they had covered the necessary portions of the event grounds and marked where the bombs were to be located. Jamal was ready to get out of this crowd of infidels and back to the place where they were staying. Perhaps he could persuade Rafiq to have someone take them to say goodbye to Malik. If not, he would just keep him in his mind. He had already accepted the fact that Malik would not survive this. Then he would say his evening prayers, memorize the map and prepare for tomorrow.

Allah be with me.

Chapter Sixteen

At seven in the morning, Marc's cell phone rang. He groaned as he rolled over, not wanting to separate himself from the warm, naked body of the woman next to him. He grabbed the phone and punched Accept.

"Yeah?" he growled.

"It's Hofler. Bring your lady and get your asses down to the sheriff's office. Meeting in the conference room in one hour."

He disconnected before Marc could reply.

"What is it?" Nikki murmured from beneath the covers.

"That was Hofler." He repeated the short message. "I hope to hell it means he's got something for us so we aren't flying so blind."

"I hope so, too. I'd like to get these men caught before they can blow anything up."

"You and the rest of us, darlin'." He kissed her cheek. "Come on. We'd better get ready. Hope he's got some good pastries to feed us."

Hofler and Vasquez were already in the conference room when he arrived, along with the rest of his Delta Team. Joe Trainor and Frank Novak were also just walking in.

"The others will be here in a moment," Vasquez said. "Help yourself to coffee and a roll and have a seat down at this end of the table. Agent Hofler has some interesting and helpful news."

Marc noticed then that a screen had been set up at one end of the room and Hofler had a computer open in front of him.

"Good," Trainor said. "We could use some."

"Amen," Marc added.

"Then you'll be happy to know we've had success with the photos you and Miss Alvarez took. Agents from both my office and DC flew in late yesterday and we spent a good part of the night looking through the photos you took. I had also sent them to DC so they could scan them and see if anyone matched up with photos in their database. "

"And?" Slade prompted.

"See for yourself."

Hofler pressed a key on his computer and four pictures hit the screen at the same time. They all stared at them. Then four more pictures took their place and finally two shots. Next to him, Marc felt Nikki tense and she reached for his hand.

"It's him," she said in a low voice. "One of the men at the cottage."

Vasquez turned his sharp eyes on her. "You know one of them, Miss Alvarez?"

She nodded. "From the cottage. Someone called him Jamal. That's him in the brown T-shirt. I don't know why I didn't notice him yesterday."

"You were snapping crowd pictures as fast as you could," Marc reminded her. "He blended in so well. It was difficult to determine ethnicity in the crowd. If he had stood out in any way, you would have noticed him."

"But we've got the pictures now," Hofler reminded her. "And an identification, thanks to an undercover agent we've got in the camp in Niger. His name is Jamal Baqri. He's the designated leader of the four-man team sent to Mexico for training then smuggled into this country. Our sources tell us today is their target date, so it's a good thing we identified him."

"But what about the other men?" Nikki asked. "I know one of them was injured. He may have died of infection if they didn't get him to a doctor. Marc shot another one, but that still leaves the fourth one. I think his name is Kasim."

"We couldn't face match him," Hofler answered. "But we did get lucky with another one." He tapped a key on the computer and brought up two more pictures. "See the man in the black T-shirt with the very curly hair? His name is Salman Abidi. He's part of a crew led by a man named Rafiq Pasha. We've had our eye on him for some time. Then he upped and disappeared. We were pretty sure he was still in San Antonio. When this whole thing came down the pike, we upped our search for him. Figured he'd squirreled himself away waiting for these guys to arrive from Mexico so they could get their plan in motion."

"But...why did they need someone else to do this?" Nikki asked. "Couldn't he just have done whatever this is himself?"

Hofler shook his head. "He's not a doer. He's a planner. He puts everything together and whoever is highest up on the ladder sends him the grunts to carry it out."

"So they're the ones who blow themselves up," Slade guessed.

"Got it in one." Hofler took a swallow of his coffee. "We've already got dogs at the event, stashed away in one of the cattle barns. What we need you to do, Miss Alvarez, is ride around there today with Marc, spot either of the men from the cottage and let us know what they're doing."

"Not an option," Marc growled. "I'm not putting her in any more danger. Why can't you just look for them on the camera feeds?"

"Because by the time we send out the word where they are, they could have moved to another spot."

"But—"

Nikki put her hand on his arm. When he looked at her, he saw the fear in her eyes but also determination.

"I'm the only person who has seen them close up. You'll be right with me. Nothing is going to happen to me. Okay?"

"Once she identifies them and where they are," Hofler said, "the rest of us will take over."

"I hope you're including us in that," Slade told him. "This is what we do for a living, dealing with these lunatics."

"I'm counting on it. So. We have a camera at the main gate to see if we can spot them entering. We'll try to follow them electronically after that but if we miss it, the next thing is to look for anyone wearing a backpack."

"Then what?" Novak asked.

"One of you will track them," Hofler explained. "If they conceal a package someplace, we've got the dogs to sniff for bombs. We may have to track them a little, gathering up what they've left, because when we drop the net on them we want to make sure they haven't sent a signal to detonate the explosives."

He paused to take another swallow of his coffee.

"The pattern is for them to strategically place pipe bombs around the area, then use cell phones to set them all off at the same time. Last time this happened, in Paris, while the bombs were still exploding the men who placed them opened their shirts to expose suicide vests and detonated them. If we stop him too soon he may just get to the main event right then, before we can clear people out of the way."

"Oh, god." Nikki squeezed Marc's hand, hard.

"And you want me to bring my girl into that?" Marc wanted to snap someone's head off.

"We just need her to help us with a positive identification. Like I said earlier, as soon as we see them enter the grounds we'll start following them. We'll have the dogs. As they place each bomb, we'll be able to pick it up and put it in the special container. I promise you. We'll have eyes on the main gate and the electronics will be all over everything."

"If you have the electronics, why do you need Nikki?" He had a bad feeling about this. Getting her away from this was a priority for him, but it didn't look like that was going to happen."

"Marc, I told you. It's fine. The cameras can't cover everything at once. Let's just do it and get it over with."

* * * *

At the house in South San Antonio, everyone was up early for the big day. After morning prayers, they all had a breakfast of sweet rolls and coffee before preparing to leave for the rodeo. Last thing, Jamal and Kasim donned the long-sleeved plaid shirts, rolling up the sleeves so they wouldn't look quite so out of place. They would fit loosely over the suicide vests when they were finally able to slip them on.

Rafiq had insisted on going over the details with them one last time. Jamal was losing patience but realized it was important to lock everything down. They would have only one chance to get this right. Salman would go. Also, but like the day before, he would stand in line separately. They had decided the best place to rendezvous, after which Salman would take them to get the explosives.

Unlike opening day, beginning today the gates and some food vendors would open at eight o'clock, with attractions opening at ten. They had discussed several options and agreed that noon would be their zero hour. After placing the pipe bombs, Jamal and Kasim would make their way to their final targets, one of them to Freeman and the other to the expo hall. As soon as the pipe bombs began exploding, they would each find a spot where they could garner everyone's attention, open their shirts to expose the vests and detonate them in simultaneous explosions.

"I will find the right spot to get their attention," Jamal assured the others.

"As will I," Kasim added.

"Good, good." Rafiq studied both of them with a hard look. "No mistakes today."

Jamal shook his head. "Will you trust us for this mission? We have trained for it for months. We will not fail, not you, not Allah."

"Then we are all set. Let's get into the van. I will be driving so Salman can move freely into the grounds." He paused. "And I will find my way into the area where I will await your phone call."

"Then let's get going. Come on, now."

They left through the back door, down the stairs and into the van. Then they headed for the rodeo grounds.

It was after eleven o'clock when they arrived. As they had the day before, they each entered the grounds separately, presenting their tickets and passing through security. Salman wandered off away from them, pretending interest in all the displays that were set up. Jamal and Kasim made their way slowly and separately to the truck Salman had shown them the day before, pausing to look at different exhibits and activities as they moved along. Dressed in the jeans and T-shirts they'd been given, they entered the big truck, found the false back and stuffed the bombs into knapsacks. Next they donned the vests and covered them with the plaid shirts, sleeves rolled up.

They didn't speak to each other during the process. Then, backpacks hooked over one shoulder, they moved away from the truck one at a time, as if each was heading for a specific errand. Jamal hoped Kasim had his shit together. So many things had gone wrong with this that he would not rest until the final explosion. Then he would rest in heaven.

'You must look like you are here to have a good time,' Rafiq had insisted over and over. 'Do not do one single thing to call attention to yourselves. Carry your knapsacks the way you see others doing it. Even stop here and there to purchase a trinket and stuff it in the backpack. It is important to maintain the illusion.'

As he moved through the grounds, he stopped at the designated locations and placed the bombs. He took his time as he had been instructed, making sure no one knew what he was doing, stopping to check out some of the activities along the way. When he placed the final bomb, he stopped for a moment, wishing he could check with Kasim. However, Rafiq had confiscated all the cell phones they'd been given and the one in his pocket was to be used only to signal for the detonations.

He was close to the entrance to the Freeman Coliseum, moments away from notifying Rafiq then entering the big building and setting up the detonation of his vest. He supposed it didn't matter much if they went off at the same time. Perhaps it might even be better if they didn't. Having devastating explosions in two separate places made for more mass confusion.

As he started toward the entrance to the building, he spotted the cart carrying the two people he'd seen yesterday, the girl with black hair and the guy with the cowboy hat. Now he recalled that he'd seen them earlier when he'd made his way out of the lot where the truck was parked and back into the area of activity. She was still taking pictures and he was still playing chauffeur. He'd been so focused on his assignment, and they'd appeared so ordinary, he hadn't thought anything of it.

But they were taking shots of the crowd and he sure didn't need his damn face in someone's picture. Without appearing too obvious, he'd managed to walk away from them and wander among the various vendors until he could get back on track again. He started to head again toward the Freeman Coliseum and…

The cart turned sharply toward him. He stared at them and his heart almost stopped beating. Why hadn't he looked at them with greater care yesterday? The black hair might be a distraction, but her makeup had worn off in the heat and the bruise on her jaw was unmistakable.

It was the damn fucking nurse.

And they were so close to him. Too fucking close.

He backed away, hoping they didn't recognize him. Hoping to get to the Coliseum. Turning away from them, he yanked out his cell phone and pressed the number to signal Rafiq. He resumed walking, still with his back to them.

I pray to you, Allah, to give me these last moments to complete this assignment, for your grace and glory.

Any minute now the first of the explosions would go off. Any second. Any...

But nothing was happening. All he heard was the noise of the crowd, the music from the carnival and the voices of people selling their wares. What had happened with the bombs? He tried calling the number on his cell again, but nothing happened. Nothing connected. His heart rate speeded up and a sick feeling settled in the bottom of his stomach.

What the fuck is going on?

* * * *

They all entered the rodeo grounds through one of the back gates and gathered at the operations office. The operations manager took Beau and Trey up to the roof of the Coliseum where they would wait, as snipers did, for the moment when a shot might be needed.

Hofler and Slade went over the rest of the assignments one more time before sending everyone on their way.

"I still think you could have done it from the safety of the electronics room," Marc growled.

"It's okay. It will all be over soon. You heard Agent Hofler. They've got highly trained personnel all over the place, and the bomb dogs to sniff out the explosives. What can go wrong?"

Marc snorted. "Don't ever say that, darlin'. It's a sure sign everything is about to go FUBAR."

Nikki glanced at him. "FUBAR?"

"Excuse the language, but it means Fucked Up Beyond All Repair."

"But we're going to prevent that," Hofler said. The others around the table nodded. "Okay. I have pictures of these men for everyone, so let's get to the fairgrounds and everyone take their places."

Marc knew Slade was champing at the bit to be out where the action was. But he was also a good leader, and knew the best place for him was in the electronics house, making sure their crew out there had everything covered.

"My men have their assignments," Joe Trainor told Hofler. "They'll be on top of this."

Hofler nodded. "I appreciate that you've got your best on this. Make sure their radios are all working and on the same channel. The first person to spot either of these guys, call it in. Both Lieutenant Donovan and I will be ready."

Marc and Nikki set off in their golf cart, wearing their disguises from the day before. Marc hoped the fact Nikki continued to be so quiet had more to do with the tension of the situation than anything else. Something was wrong and he was going to find out, but first they had to get past this.

The gates had been open an hour when one of Trainor's men spotted Jamal making his way from a far parking lot with a backpack hanging from one shoulder. Everyone on the crew was wearing an earpiece to enable them to hear everything going on, so they all heard the message.

Static crackled in Marc's earpiece. "Tango One looking to begin unloading backpack. Dogs on the way."

Where? He wondered. *Where the hell was he spotted?*

A few minutes passed. Then…

"Tango Two leaving his packages. Handlers on the way with dogs."

The plan was to make sure the terrorist was out of sight after each drop-off before bringing the dogs to sniff the packages. After almost thirty minutes, they had collected six bombs and the men were still moving.

"Don't spook them." Slade's voice was low in everyone's ear. "We want to get the bombs so the only thing we have to deal with is the suicide vests, at which these guys are experts."

"We've got it," someone said in a reassuring tone.

Marc's earpiece came alive again. "Here is the current location of Tango One."

Marc lifted the tiny radio to his mouth. "Got it."

"Marc." Slade's low voice. "Can you head that way to confirm?"

"On it."

"Someone else is homing in on Kasim so you stick with Jamal."

Then they lost sight of the man for a moment. One minute he was there, then he was gone, swallowed up by the growing crowd. Marc turned the cart around and suddenly, there he was. Right in front of them.

"Got him," he murmured into his radio. "Have you got us on camera?"

"Roger that," came Slade's voice. "Joe, you got it?"

"We're on our way," Trainor said in a soft tone.

Marc eased the car closer to Jamal, but not so close as to trigger something. He saw the exact moment Jamal knew who they were, and wished he could tell Nikki to get out of the cart and run, but they were past that. Recognition flared in the man's eyes and he looked around as if expecting something. Then he pulled a cell phone from his pocket and pressed a button before Marc could react. But when nothing happened a puzzled look spread across his face, replaced by one of panic.

Joe Trainor and two of his men had approached from another direction, quietly getting everyone's attention, which was no easy feat. Then they began moving people out of the immediate area and back as far as they could push them.

Jamal backed up, trying to ease himself into the crowd behind him, but by now several of the security guards had shown up and were pushing everyone out of the way. Jamal hit the button on the phone several times more, real panic slashing across his face now. When nothing happened, he dropped his backpack and opened his shirt to reveal what was underneath.

"Do not move away," he shouted. "Everyone stay where you are."

"Fucking shit," Marc said in a low voice. "Suicide vest."

"What?" Nikki stared at the man five feet away from them. "Oh, my god, Marc."

A canvas vest was zipped from his waist to his pecs, sticks of dynamite peeking out from its many pockets, all hooked to something at his waist. A wire snaked from the zipper to a small cylinder in his hand, something Marc recognized as the detonator. If the man took his finger off the button, he and a good portion of the crowd would end up in pieces right there on the pavement.

Trainor and one of the deputies started to approach the terrorist, but Hofler appeared and waved them back. Marc saw them all quietly continuing to move the crowd and give Jamal as wide a space as possible. It wasn't going to be enough. Jamal's eyes widened as he looked everywhere.

Something had to be done.

"Marc." Nikki's voice was little more than a whisper.

"I see it."

There it was, the slight tensing of Jamal's muscles in the arm holding the switch. There wasn't much time. Marc eased himself out of the cart and moved very slowly toward the man. He hoped Hofler wouldn't get in his way, because he needed Jamal's full attention.

"Come on, Jamal." He spoke in a low, measured tone. "Let's let everyone get out of here and we can help you get that vest off."

"No." The man gave his head a violent shake. "It is my mission. Why did the bombs not explode? They were supposed to explode."

"Dogs." Marc eased closer and closer to him. From the corner of his eye he saw Trainor doing the same thing, but also staying out of Marc's way. "We discovered your plot and managed to get the bombs before they could be ignited. Give it up. Let us get you home to your family."

Something he knew was never going to happen.

"I am disgraced," Jamal cried. "I cannot ever see my family again."

Marc was less than two feet from the man now. Taking a deep breath, he leaped forward and closed his hand over Jamal's, keeping his thumb pressed over the other man's on the ignition switch. The force of his leap drove them both to the ground. As Jamal tried to yank his hand free, Marc heard the *crack!* of a shot and a hole appeared in the man's forehead. He sent up a silent prayer of thanks to Beau and Trey as he yanked the detonator from the dead man's hand.

He collapsed forward onto Jamal, keeping his thumb pressed on the button. *Fucking A.* He'd done it. Prevented the vest from exploding. Lying on the dead body wasn't much fun, but he couldn't release the button or it would all be over.

"We've got it, Marc." A familiar voice spoke to him and he turned to see Slade crouching beside him. "The bomb disposal guys are here."

Even as he spoke the words, a strong hand closed over Marc's and slid something between his thumb and the trigger. A thumb eased his out of the way and he breathed a sigh of relief as he realized one of the bomb squad had locked heavy tape over the pressure point.

With great care he eased himself from his position on top of the body and pushed himself to his feet.

"Good job." Hofler was beside him, shaking his hand. "We've got it all under control now."

Marc looked around and saw several members of the rodeo security staff dealing with the crowd, pushing everyone back even further to allow the bomb squad to do its work.

"We got Kasim and Rafiq, too," Slade told him. "And all the bombs have been neutralized. Crisis past."

"Thank god." Marc blew a sigh of relief. He looked over at the cart where Nikki sat waiting for him. She was still as a statue, her face white with an expression that gave him a distinct feeling of unease. He knew he should have fought harder to keep her out of this.

"Go ahead and get Nikki away from here," Slade murmured in his ear. "I'll square things here. Hofler will want a debriefing, but we can put that off until tomorrow."

"Thanks." He looked from Slade to Nikki and back again. "I think I need to get her home and help her deal with this."

"Just be sure and tell her we're all very grateful for her help."

"Will do." He hopped into the cart, backed it up and drove it away toward the parking area. He hoped to hell that whatever was wrong, he knew how to fix it.

Chapter Seventeen

'I can't do this, Marc. I can't deal with the danger.'

The words played over and over in Marc's head, like a bad tune he couldn't erase.

'You put yourself in such dangerous situations. What if I lose you like I did Jon?'

He had tried his best to make her see the difference between a situation he could control and an illness that no one had control over, but it didn't seem to make much difference. He had to find a way to handle this.

Slade had called, and Marc had told him they were dealing with some issues and could he please hold off the dogs until tomorrow. Hofler had called him, and he'd sung the same song to him, telling him he needed some room to deal with personal stuff. He didn't give two fucks about anything else. Nikki and this thing between them was his priority. His *only* priority.

'You put yourself in situations that can turn deadly at any minute. I don't care how much practice you've had, you can't eliminate all possibilities of harm. Look how long it took me

to get over Jon. If I lost you, I'd never recover. I can't take that chance.'

He'd tried his best to ease her fears, to make her understand that his training would always protect him, even as he had to admit to himself that with any op there was a chance he'd never return. He'd used every option he could think of—a massage, a hot shower, telling her how he felt about her—everything, but nothing had worked.

They had both slept fitfully, albeit in the same bed, even though she'd rolled away from him, sending a silent signal. He'd tried again in the morning, but nothing had seemed to be working.

At last, with all his choices exhausted, he'd packed his stuff, called the ranch and asked Slade if he could camp there for a few days. He hated to intrude on Slade and Kari, who were still in the honeymoon phase, but he knew if anyone could understand, it would be them. The lieutenant had married a real gem there.

"Hofler's having a debrief at Sheriff Vasquez's office," Slade reminded Marc. "I was planning to call you, anyway, to see if you wanted me to pick you up. I know you're not in the mood for this, but you really need to be there. How about if I pick you up in thirty and we'll head over?"

"Got it."

No matter how shitty his life might be, he never ducked out on responsibility or a mission debrief. And wasn't that what this was? A mission?

"I'm not throwing in the towel on this," he told Nikki as he tossed his gear into his duffel. "I'm just giving you some space." He paused. "To think about this. About *us.*"

"All the thinking won't help," she told him, her voice low and flat. "I told you. I just can't put myself in that situation. Not ever again. I thought I'd never get over Jon. I know for sure if anything happened to you, it would finish me off."

"Space," he insisted. "I know when you can back up and think about this, you'll know how special this is between us."

"I already know it's special," she cried. "That's the problem. I have to cut this off before it destroys me altogether."

She was silent as he packed his gear, but the moment he carried his bag into the living room, she retreated to the bedroom and closed the door.

Damn.

He meant what he'd told her. He wasn't done with this. He'd never thought to find what he and Nikki had together, not after the stupidity of Ria. And now he was going to fight for it, doing whatever he had to do to make her take down the walls she'd put up.

When Slade pulled up in front of the apartment building, Marc tossed his duffel into the back seat and climbed in the front.

"Stay as long as you need," he said without asking questions. "We've only got a couple more days until we have to leave." He studied Marc's face. "And Kari and I are here if you want to talk. Or not."

"Thanks," was all Marc could manage.

He kept his shit together during the debrief. He for sure didn't need to air his personal problems with a bunch of hard-assed cops and agents. Steven Hofler gave them a full after-action report.

"As we suspected, Jamal and Kasim were part of a four-man team sent here after six months at a training camp in Mexico. We're all aware that one of their team was shot crossing the border and another was killed by Delta Force team member Marc Blanchard as they escaped the cottage where they stayed.

"They were plagued by problems from the git-go, especially when two men ended up having to carry out an assignment meant for four. Still, if we hadn't learned about this, and if we hadn't had invaluable help identifying them, they could have done incredible damage. Hundreds of people would have been killed or injured and the fallout would have gone on for days, maybe even weeks."

Vasquez cleared his throat. "Marc, we owe you and your lady a huge debt of thanks. She's a smart woman who kept her head even when she was kidnapped, and helped us a lot with this." He smiled. "A definite keeper."

Marc couldn't agree more. Now he just had to find a way to get Nikki on board.

Hofler went on to tell them that the injured terrorist had been found near death from infection and was currently under guard at a hospital. Rafiq and his crew had been rounded up, and Homeland Security was continuing to follow threads to see where else they led.

"By the way, Slade. Tell your sniper that was some shot."

Slade nodded. "I will. He never misses."

"I've seen plenty of snipers, but not all of them could be that precise from that distance. He saved a lot of lives. I'm impressed." He looked around the table. "A good day's work all around. I'm sure each of you knows the disaster this could have been if the terrorists had succeeded. The death toll would have been in the hundreds, the rodeo would have been damaged for a long time, and the terrorists who come to this country or are already living here would celebrate a victory and at once plan the next one. Excellent teamwork. Thank you all very much."

At last the meeting was over, everyone was thanked and they could leave. They were about ten minutes outside of San Antonio when Marc realized he had to tell Slade what was going on and ask his advice. It wasn't something he felt comfortable doing, but the realization that he might lose the one woman he wanted for a lifetime was enough to make him step out of his comfort zone.

"That sucks," Slade agreed. "Believe me, I know what it's like to find the one woman who is it for you then run the risk of losing her."

"I can't change who I am," Marc told him. "If I did, I would lose my own identity and that would kill the relationship for sure. So what do I do?"

"That a tough dilemma, Marc." He was silent for a moment. "Would you mind if I ran this past Kari? She's got a solid head on her shoulders."

Marc had to agree with that. Kari Donovan was a top assistant prosecutor in Bexar County and dealt with thorny situations all the time. She, too, had been faced with the challenges that went with a relationship with a member of Delta Force. And she hadn't had anyone guiding her through it. He hoped to god she had some answers here.

"That's a toughie," she agreed, as the three of them sat over beer while Teo grilled steaks for dinner. "Some women aren't cut out for this, and you have to understand that. Especially when you consider what she's already been through."

Depression grabbed him at the thought. He'd survive this if he couldn't change her mind, but nothing would not be the same. He couldn't believe how much he loved her, or how dark his life would be without her.

"Let me ask you this. And, Slade, don't you say a word. Would you leave Delta Force if it meant you could be with Nikki?"

Marc had to think about that for a long minute. Delta was his life. He'd been in the military since he'd enlisted at eighteen. That was nearly fourteen years ago. Everything that he was he owed to the military, especially to Delta. It had shaped and defined him. What else would he do with his life?

But then he thought about never being with Nikki again, and he realized that if push came to shove, he'd do it.

"Let's just say if all other options are exhausted, it's definitely on the table."

"Marc," Slade began.

But Kari held up her hand. "It was just a question. That's all." She took another sip of beer. "But let me mull it over. Maybe I can figure out the answer."

"We leave in a couple of days for our next mission, Kari. It will be weeks before I even get a chance to see her again. If she'll even give me the time of day by then."

"That might be a good thing. Let her have some peace." She leaned forward and touched his hand. "And it also gives me time to think about this and find a chance to talk to her."

"God." He blew out a breath. "If you can do that, I'll be in your debt forever."

She grinned. "Might be fun to have one of Slade's guys owing me. Just in case he misbehaves, you know."

"I'm not sure that's such a good idea," Slade growled, but then he winked at his wife.

Marc pushed down a surge of jealousy. This was what he wanted with Nikki. What he thought they'd have. How the hell did he get past this?

He was still asking the same question three days later when the team rendezvoused to report for their next mission. He wanted to call Nikki with an intense desperation. Just one contact with her before he left. But he settled for texting her.

Leave time is over. Be back in eight weeks for a long weekend. Will miss you so much. I'll do whatever you want. Love, Marc.

Then he climbed onto the waiting helicopter and with an ingrained discipline forced it all out of his mind.

* * * *

Nikki read the text so many times over the next couple of weeks that every word was burned into her brain. He'd do whatever she wanted. Did that mean he would give up his military career for her? If so, what would he do? She knew that had been everything to him since he was eighteen. Could she live with it if she allowed him to do that for her?

She was glad they were so busy at the hospital, so she had little time to dwell on it. She offered to take extra shifts, immersed herself in her patients and worked hard enough that she could fall into bed at night and sleep. But her dreams were anything but restful. Sometimes she'd dream about Marc getting killed on a mission. Other times she'd dream about life without him, cold and lonely and empty.

And she read and reread that text.

How much do you love him, Nikki?

Wasn't that a key question? If she loved him enough, how could she ask him to give up his life for her? Couldn't she suck up her fears? But then the panic would grab her and she saw herself destroyed by yet another loss.

You are pathetic, Nikki Alvarez. You don't deserve to have anyone in your life.

At the end of three weeks, she was still no closer to finding an answer. She missed Marc with an unholy need — his touch, his warmth, his smile, his laugh, the way he made her feel so special. Even more than Jon, if she was being honest. They were two wounded souls who had come together and found something extraordinary. Could she really give that all up?

She was curled up on the couch indulging in another pity party when her phone rang. The number that popped up was unfamiliar. For a moment her heat stopped beating. Was it about Marc? Had something happened?

Well, answer the phone, dummy, and you'll find out. Whatever it is, deal with it.

"Hello?"

"Nikki? This is Kari Donovan. Slade's wife?"

Slade's wife? Holy shit! Did something really happen to Marc?

"Yes. Of course. Um, is everyone okay?"

Kari chuckled. "He hasn't been physically harmed, if that's what you're asking. I was calling to see if you might be free for lunch this week? I don't know what your schedule at the hospital is."

Lunch? Nikki held the phone away for a moment and stared at it.

"Uh, lunch?" *Right. Sound like an idiot.*

"Yes. I was hoping we could get to know each other a little better."

Nikki rubbed her thigh, a nervous habit she'd picked up. "Um, Kari, that is really nice of you. But if it's because you think Marc and I are a couple, you should know…"

"That you don't plan to see him anymore? Got that. I just thought it would be nice to have lunch."

Maybe she had some kind of message from Marc he'd sent through Slade. What could it hurt? And she liked Kari a lot, the little she knew of her.

"I'm off for the next two days, as it happens. Do either of those work for you?"

"As a matter of fact, tomorrow works just great. How about noon?" She named a restaurant on the Riverwalk.

"Sounds good. See you then."

She tossed and turned all night and fretted all morning about what was behind this lunch. She couldn't get rid of the feeling that there was still something wrong. Maybe Marc had decided she wasn't worth the effort after all and asked her to deliver the message so he didn't have to see her again. *But Kari wouldn't have put it off until tomorrow if that were the case, right?*

God, she was such an idiot and a mess. Why would Marc Blanchard want to be with a ninny like her, anyway?

The next day she spent an hour putting on her makeup and deciding what to wear. If Kari was delivering the news that Marc had decided to wash his hands of her, she at least wanted to look nice.

The other woman was already waiting for her at the restaurant when she arrived.

"I always like to sit by the river here," she told Nikki, grinning. "It's festive and relaxing at the same time. Oh, and here's our waitress. How about a cocktail? I allow myself one at lunch when I'm not on the clock."

"Yes. That would be nice." She ordered a frozen margarita and sat back in her chair, trying to relax.

"Nikki, I'm not here to deliver bad news," Kari assured her. "In case that's what's worrying you."

"I'm not really sure why you're here," Nikki said.

"Let's order and we can talk."

The waitress delivered their drinks, wrote down their orders and hurried off. Nikki took a long sip of the frozen concoction in front of her.

"I'm sure you know Marc spent the last couple of days of his leave with us," Kari began.

"I do. And I guess he told you why."

Kari swallowed some of her drink and set her glass back down.

"I can't say I disagree with how you feel. I feel the same way about Slade. I worry about him every single minute he's gone."

Nikki frowned. "Then how do you deal with it? How do you handle the fear?"

"I guess it's a question of what's important and what counts in your life." She paused, studying Nikki's face. "Not too many people know that Slade and I met five years before we reconnected here in San Antonio."

Nikki stared at her. "You're kidding."

Kari grinned. "Not even a little. But those five years when we weren't together were some of the longest in my life. I missed him every single day."

"And what about when they were out on a mission? Don't you worry yourself sick?"

"Deployment takes its toll on everyone. But these men are operators. This is their life. They don't stay home and go out on a mission once a week. This is a choice they make."

Nikki looked down at her plate. "So what are you saying? That I should just give up on Marc because he's not going to leave Delta?"

"I'm saying you can find a way to have what you want. Is it easy? Hell, no."

She paused while the waitress set their plates in front of them. Nikki had suddenly lost her appetite, but she nibbled on the tortilla chips, mostly to have something to do.

"I know." She whispered the words.

"One thing that long absence from Slade taught me? That having him in my life, even with the dangerous career he has, was way better than not having him at all. That every moment with him is precious. And that I'd rather have limited time with him than unlimited with someone else."

"But don't you worry about him getting killed?"

"Of course I do." Kari took a forkful of food and chewed slowly. "But he could work in an office and get killed crossing the street. He could fall down on wet pavement and break his neck. Any number of things could happen even if he wasn't a member of Delta."

Nikki had been refusing to look at it that way, but Kari was right.

"Here's the thing," Kari went on. "If you love him, if you cannot see any color in your world without him, if your heart is empty when he's not in your life, then you have to find the courage to take that step. And to make every moment between deployments count like ten. Because you know damn well it's worth it. Or do you want to look down the black tunnel of your life without him?"

Nikki stared at the woman across from her. "How'd you get so smart?"

Kari laughed. "Sheer dumb luck. Oh, we had our glitches in the beginning. But what we have now is so worth whatever we had to give to get it." She leaned across the table. "Just think about it, Nikki. What's better, all of him in part of your life or none of him in your life at all?"

She saw what the woman was saying with startling clarity, and in an instant her answer was right there. Not having Marc in her life would destroy her. She'd dealt with tragedy once. She could do it again, if it meant having this amazing man with her at all.

"Do you know when they'll be back?" she asked.

"According to Slade, they have five days off at the end of the next six weeks." She grinned. "We can count the days down together."

For the first time in days, Nikki found herself smiling. She touched her glass to Kari's.

"Here's to a great future with great men."

"Amen to that. And don't forget, we can commiserate together while we wait for them to come home."

"I'll drink to that."

* * * *

When you get your five days off, have someone drop you at my place. Just let me know what day that will be.

Marc stared at the text yet again. When he'd messaged Nikki so many days ago and hadn't heard back, he'd just assumed, reluctantly, she was letting him know it was over for real. But he was far from giving up. He'd figure a way around this, somehow.

Then, two weeks later, she'd sent him a message.

Stay safe. Come home, in pieces or otherwise.

He had no idea what to make of that one, so he showed it to Slade.

Slade shrugged. "Guess she wants you however she can get you."

"But she said unless I left Delta it was all over."

"Maybe she changed her mind. Whatever, we have details to go over for tomorrow so let's get to it."

He wondered if Slade was being cagey for some reason, but then he didn't have much time to think about it.

He began to check his cell with an unfamiliar obsession, irritated when no other messages came through. But then he got another one.

Hope you're staying safe and taking care of my favorite parts.

What? The? Hell?

Then nothing again until the last day of their mission.

By my count you're flying home tomorrow. Be sure someone drops you off at my place.

Again he showed it to Slade.

"I'd say you'd better do what she says."

"But what if she's just going to tell me she can't do this?"

Slade cocked an eyebrow. "Would she go to all the trouble just to dump you? Again?"

"I don't know. I hope not."

"I guess you'll find out tomorrow."

When Teo picked them up in the helo, he handed a key to Marc. "I was told to give this to you."

"Told by who?"

He shrugged. "Someone I didn't want to argue with."

"We'd better drop him off first," Slade chuckled. "Before he drives himself and us nuts."

The drive seemed endless, even though he knew it wasn't. He thanked Teo and Slade when he hopped out of the truck with his duffel and marched into the apartment building. At the apartment he stood for a moment, nerves jangling, before he finally unlocked the door. The living room was empty and he didn't hear any sounds. Was she at work? Had he gotten their signals crossed?

"Hello?" he called out.

"In here."

The voice came from the bedroom, and was accompanied by a sudden drift of music. Marc followed the sounds, curious about what he'd find. What he saw froze him in his tracks, his jaw dropped and his dick, which had been out of circulation, was so hard so fast he was afraid to bump into anything.

Soft music came from the radio on the nightstand and the covers had been folded back on the bed. Nikki lay on the silky sheets he remembered, completely naked, legs bent and spread apart so every glistening inch of her sex was exposed.

"Holy fucking shit!"

What the hell else could he say?

"Come here." She crooked a finger at him.

He dropped his duffel and hurried over to her. "Nikki? What's going on?"

"I want to give you a proper welcome home. Come on. Get naked."

If he was dreaming this, he hoped no one woke him up.

"I need a shower," he told her, stripping off his clothes.

"Later. We'll take one together." He climbed onto the bed and straddled her, wanting to lick and touch her everywhere. "I've spent too much time waiting. I want you inside me. Now. Then I'll answer your questions."

He touched her glistening slit and found her ready and wet. Drawing in a breath, he spread her folds to open her and eased himself inside.

Jesus Fucking Christ!

He'd never expected to feel this again, so the pleasure was doubly intense. God! She was so tight around him he wasn't sure how long he'd last. He'd give up anything for this. For her. But what the hell was going on?

"Okay. This is as far as we go until I get some answers. What's going on?"

She reached up and pulled his head down to her.

"A very wise person made me understand that I couldn't live my life in fear. That having you and losing you was not nearly as bad as not having you at all. And I realized that Delta Force has made you the man you are, so why would I want to change that?"

"A wise person, huh? Anyone I know?"

"My lips are sealed." Then her smile disappeared. "I'm not saying it won't be hard, but if we do this together, we can make it work." A sudden anxious look flashed in her eyes. "Right?"

He grinned. "Right. My thoughts exactly."

"I love you, Marc. I want whatever we can have together."

"I plan for us to grow old together, so count on it."

He leaned down more to brush his lips against hers and ran his tongue gently over her mouth.

"Mmmm," she crooned.

"Mmmm is right. But time for talking's over. We need to get started on the rest of our lives."

Locking his gaze with hers, he began to move, thrusting inside her with long, slow strokes. The more he moved, the more she urged him on. He picked up the rhythm, thrusting faster, in and out, her wet cunt feeling like heaven. When he increased his pace, she wound her legs around him, locking her ankles at the small of his back.

"More," she urged. "Faster."

He gave her faster and it all overtook him as he pounded into her, harder and harder.

"Yes," she cried out. "Yes. Like that."

The moment he felt the tremors begin inside her, he thrust once, twice and let himself go, just as her inner walls pulsed and milked him and her body convulsed and shook with her climax. He held her close to him as they throbbed together and he filled the condom with spurt after spurt. Her legs around him held their bodies tight together in a climax that went on and on and on.

At last the spasms slowed and finally subsided. Their rough breathing seesawed in the air and he wasn't sure whose heartbeat he felt, his or hers. At last, they were finished, but still he had his arms wrapped around her, unwilling to let her go.

"I love you," he whispered.

"I love you, too."

Marc gathered his thoughts. He knew what he wanted to say and hoped she was on the same page as him.

"I can't promise you it will always be easy, but I will always love you and come home to you."

"And I'll always be here waiting for you."

Okay, here goes.

"Marry me, Nikki. Be my wife."

She smiled at hm. "Just say when."

"I don't have a ring for you."

"I don't care."

Happiness surged through him like a tidal wave. "I've got five days. Think we can make it happen?"

"No sweat. I know a prosecutor who can cut red tape for us."

"Well, then. How about that shower? I believe shower sex is in order to celebrate."

"Lead on," she told him. "I'm yours."

And those were the best words he wanted to hear.

Want to see more from this author? Here's a taster for you to enjoy!

Corporate Heat: Where Danger Hides
Desiree Holt

Excerpt

Hell and damnation.

Taylor Scott never swore, but after this week — this day — she'd acquired a number of words not previously found in her vocabulary.

She hitched her five-foot-four-with-heels body onto one of the two vacant barstools. Turning sideways, she looked at herself in the mirror behind the bar. She saw a tumble of auburn hair and emerald-green eyes. The conservative navy suit and silk blouse looked only slightly the worse for wear after the day's confrontation. The heavy gold hoops in her ears shone even in the subdued light the cocktail lounge afforded.

Not bad, she thought, critically assessing herself. *Not a showstopper.* Breasts too small, hips too wide, thighs a little plumper than she'd like. But she made the best use of her assets. Certainly not someone to get tossed out into the street, so to speak.

She wasn't much of a bar sitter — not even a bar visitor, truth to tell — and she'd really wanted one of the small tables, only they were all full. But she needed a drink, something to make her forget the fact that in the short span of seven days she'd learned her entire life had been a lie. The letter from her grandmother was folded in the pocket of her jacket, a slim sheet of stationery filled with words that had destroyed everything she'd believed about her life up until now.

"What can I get for you, miss?"

Taylor snapped her head up. The bartender had placed a cocktail napkin on the bar in front of her. Now he waited patiently for her, this stocky blond with eyes that said he'd seen and heard it all and an expectant look on his face. What did one drink to get drunk? Her experience was limited to a small selection of good wines and Bloody Marys at Sunday brunches. *Wait.* The partners in the investment firm where she worked always drank Jack Daniel's at corporate functions. Black, whatever that meant. She guessed it was as good a choice as any.

"Jack Daniel's Black, please." She tried to sound authoritative.

"Rocks or neat?"

She frowned. *Why does ordering a drink have to be so complicated?* "Oh, um, rocks, please."

She was hyperaware of her surroundings. The walls of the bar were a rich, polished oak as was the paneling of the bar itself. The tables were oak planking, with chairs covered in soft-looking leather. The lighting, discreetly recessed, gave patrons the illusion of a cloak of darkness. Soft music drifted into the air from hidden speakers, an effective sound screen for couples with their heads inclined toward each other in an intimate fashion.

"Your drink, ma'am."

The bartender placed a glass filled with deep amber liquid and ice cubes on the tiny square of napkin and set a glass of water next to it.

"In case you wanted a chaser." He gave her a half-grin.

She picked up the glass with both hands and took a healthy swallow. The first splash of the liquor on her tongue was a sharp bite of smoky flavor, a burning sensation she was unprepared for that brought tears to her eyes and made her cough.

"I wouldn't chug that like lemonade if I were you. Here."

The voice was so deep and rich it sent fingers of heat skittering along her spine and tiny pulses throbbing at the heart of her sex. A strong masculine hand held out a snow-white handkerchief which she grabbed without thinking. She blotted her eyes then picked up her glass of water and drained half of it. Then she looked up to see who'd come to her rescue.

Predator. That was the first word that came to mind. An unfamiliar thrill of forbidden temptation shot through her body at the sight of the man sitting at an angle to her right. Broad shoulders and hands with long, slim fingers. A face full of sharp planes and angles with a straight nose and sensuous lips but a totally unreadable look. Eyes blacker than coal under lashes thicker than hers. Black hair worn long and tied back with a thin strip of leather.

There was something feral about him. Wild. Untamed. Dangerous. Powerful energy radiated from him and battered against her body, all of it barely tamed beneath the civilized cloak of a custom-tailored suit and silk dress shirt. An unbidden image flashed in her mind of him naked, his dark hair loose, the muscles of his bronzed body rippling in the sunshine. A panther, that was what he reminded her of. And for a brief moment she wanted to lose herself in the jungle.

He raised an eyebrow. "Panther? Is that a code word?"

Oh, God, did I say that out loud? "Pay no attention to anything that comes out of my mouth tonight." Heat crept up her cheeks. "My mind isn't functioning properly."

His eyes burned into her and she shivered. Good sense told her to get as far away from this stranger as possible before she found herself in a situation beyond her control. Her lovers had been pitifully few and disappointing and none had made her blood heat and moisture pool between her legs the way one look from this stranger did. She wondered what it would be like to have hot, sweaty sex with him. Muscles deep in her body contracted.

She almost laughed. Her grandparents would turn over in their graves if they knew such a thought had even entered her mind. *Good. They deserve a little grave-spinning after what they did to me.*

Taylor knew she should finish her drink, go to her room and try not to think about how her life had been blown to little pieces. Or about today's humiliating episode. But resentment had been boiling inside her for a week and what had happened today had set a match to all that growing bitterness. The ruthless discipline she'd allowed to be imposed on her all her life had all been for nothing. *For a lie.*

When the attorney handling her grandmother's estate had handed her the letter detailing the monstrous charade she'd been living, she'd received the shock of her life. Nothing had been the way she'd thought. She wasn't even Taylor Scott, really. At this point she didn't even know just who the hell she was. But she did know who she didn't want to be.

Maybe now it was time for her to find out what life had to offer. To taste the forbidden fruit she'd always denied herself.

She handed back the fine cotton handkerchief, noticing his strong, lean fingers as she did so. The brief contact sent heat rocketing through her. "Thank you. I, um, swallowed a little more than I intended."

He nodded toward her glass. "You need to sip that stuff slowly, not throw it down. Good whiskey is meant to be savored."

"I know that." She straightened her back and tossed her hair. "You think I don't know how to drink good whiskey?"

She thought a smile ghosted across his mouth, but the hint of it disappeared at once.

"I think your drinking habits are your own business. I was just offering a little friendly advice." He nodded at the bartender and lifted his glass.

"Well, you can keep the advice but thank you for the use of your handkerchief. I'm fine now." *Liar!*

"Good. Happy to be of help."

Taylor finished the rest of her drink in small swallows and tried to ignore the man next to her. The liquor traced fire through her blood but left untouched the cold spot sitting inside her like a block of ice. She raised her hand and motioned to the bartender.

"Sure you want another one of those?" The deep voice spiked another flash of heat.

"Yes. I'm sure. And thanks for your concern, but I don't need someone to monitor my drinks."

He shrugged. "Fine by me." He lifted an eyebrow as the bartender set another full glass in front of her. "Celebrating? Or drowning your sorrows?"

"Neither. Just…" She searched for the right word but couldn't find one. "Just drinking."

"I hate to tell you, but you don't look like you're enjoying it very much."

Taylor turned to face him and found herself captured again by the darkness of his eyes.

Eyes without a soul. Now, where did that come from? "On the contrary. I'm having a wonderful time." She took a healthy swallow of her new drink and nearly choked again. She grabbed her water glass and drained it.

"Mm-hmm. That's certainly pleasure I see on your face."

He was beginning to get on her nerves. "You sure are nosy." She had to turn away from his penetrating gaze. "I'd say it's distressing to find out after thirty years that your life has been a lie and the one relative you seem to have left denies your existence. Take it from me. Fairy tales don't really exist."

He raised an eyebrow. "Sounds pretty serious."

Anger reached up through her again. *Serious* was hardly the word to describe her sense of betrayal. All those years of toeing the line. Of stifling rules and the short tether. Of a life with little pleasure, striving for approval that never came. Of her mother's deep sadness and her grandparents' autocratic grip on her and her mother's lives. She felt as if someone had stolen the past thirty years from her, years that were gone forever. Now, she wanted rebellion and payback.

"I'm scrubbing away my past and saying hello to the first day of the rest of my life. Creating the new me."

Because the old me was the product of a lie and very boring.

Taylor resisted the urge to slip her hand into her jacket pocket, pull out the sheet of paper and re-read the damning words. It didn't matter. She had them memorized.

I realize now it was a mistake to conceal this from you all these years. You must believe our intentions were nothing but the best. But you know what they say about good intentions. They certainly paved the road to hell for all of us.

The man finished his drink and signaled for a refill. "You don't look like someone with a past they need to be rid of."

"Shows you how much you know." Taylor swallowed the last drops in her glass and the tension in her body eased just a little more. The whiskey was beginning to work its magic on her. The anger still simmered, though. That wouldn't go away any time soon.

"What brings you to San Antonio?"

A bad decision. It isn't every day I get thrown out of corporate offices like some criminal or piece of street trash.

"It's personal." *So just shut up and leave me alone.* She waved at the bartender for another refill. Maybe with enough of the liquor in her system she could forget her pain altogether.

"I take it things didn't go well." He picked up his fresh drink and swallowed some of it.

"You could say that. In fact, you could say not going well is a major understatement."

"That's too bad."

"Sure. Too bad." The whiskey in the glass sloshed slightly as she picked it up and licked the drops off her hand.

"Maybe you'd better make this your last one. I'd hate to see you try to drive home after one too many."

She turned angry eyes on him. "Listen, Whoever-you-are, I'm old enough to know how much to drink. I don't need a babysitter. And I'm staying here in the hotel, so if I pass out, I don't have far to go." She stared at him, then shook her head and raked her fingers through her hair. "Sorry. That was rude of me. I'm just in a rotten mood tonight."

He reached out to lay a hand on her forearm and even through the layers of fabric his fingers felt like branding irons on her skin. A tiny jolt of electricity sparked its way through her body.

He narrowed his gaze. She saw that he felt it, too. They stared at each other for a long moment. He broke the eye contact first. "Maybe talking to someone will help."

Yes. Talk to me so I can find out what's really going on in that pretty head of yours.

He tilted his glass and took another swallow of his club soda. No alcohol for him tonight. He had a mission and he couldn't afford to have his senses dulled. If he wished for anything, it was that she'd been ugly and abrasive. Someone he could easily dislike. *Why does she have to be such an appealing package?*

He was already regretting his decision to come here. There were other ways to accomplish the same thing. He should have taken them. Women like her were dangerous to him. Too soft. Too appealing. Too easy to let in under the barriers. And therein lay disaster.

He'd already been through it once. That was enough for him. No, he needed to keep his walls securely in place and sitting here with this woman wasn't the way to make sure that happened.

Finish your drink and go away, he wanted to tell her. *Leave this bar, this hotel, this city. Hide yourself away from me and don't ever come back.*

For the first time in years, he craved a real drink.

She took another swallow of her whiskey. "You can't do anything about the years I've lost. Or make my own flesh and blood accept me."

"So, this is about family problems?"

She gave a short, bitter laugh. "It would be if I had any family." She downed the rest of her drink and signaled for yet another one. They were going down more easily now.

"I know I'm just a stranger in a bar," he went on, "and no one you should take orders from, so consider this a suggestion. I think you should make this next drink your last."

"Thanks, but I'll decide when I've had enough." *And that might be sooner rather than later.*

Taylor concentrated on finishing the drink, the letter still burning a hole in her pocket. The man just watched her with those deep black eyes. Finally, she swallowed the last of the whiskey and gestured toward the bartender for her check. She had no problem signing it, but when she tried to move off her stool she nearly dumped herself on the floor.

Strong hands caught and lifted her. "How about if I walk you to the elevator? Just to make sure you get through the lobby all right."

"I'm not drunk," she insisted. "Just a little...weak in the knees." And she wanted him to keep those hands on her, to touch her, to bring back that electric spark.

The ghost of a smile whispered over his mouth again. "Understandable if you've had a bad day. Come on. Let me prove that chivalry isn't dead."

He took her arm and led her out of the bar, his impressive height making her feel secure for some reason. They walked to the elevator with his arm around her, steadying her. Taylor leaned in to him and caught his scent, spice mixed with a maleness that somehow reminded her of jungles. Or what she thought jungles would smell like. *Panther.* She felt the taut muscles of his body through their clothing and wondered what he'd be like naked.

As fast as the thought hit her, she tried to brush it away. Taylor Scott didn't entertain images of naked men. She even had sex with all the lights out.

If you can call the few fumbling and embarrassing attempts sex.

"What floor?"

"Hmm?" She raised heavy-lidded eyes to him.

"Floor. Where your room is. I want to make sure you get inside okay."

"Five. I'm on the fifth floor." His nearness overwhelmed her, the masculine heat of his body wrapping around her like a cloak. He was everything she'd denied herself all her life. Everything she'd been taught to avoid. Protect herself from. Now that life was in shreds and she wanted what she'd missed. Wanted him.

And why not? I'll never see him again. One night. What could it possibly hurt?

On the walk to her room, he held her braced against him. At the door, she opened her purse to take out her key card and fumbled trying to slot it in the lock.

"Here. Let me." He removed it deftly from her fingers, swiped it and opened the door. Inside, he flicked the light switch and a lamp came on. "Well, you got to your room safely. I think you can take it from here."

Taylor drew in a breath and for the space of a heartbeat tried to reach for all the inhibitions the whiskey had let loose. In thirty years, she had never done one impulsive thing. Did that make her disciplined or repressed? And if she gave in now, who was there left to give a damn, anyway? Her body was shimmering with unfamiliar sensations and a need she could barely identify was clawing its way up from her core.

Tomorrow, she'd be gone, back to whatever waited for her now in her fractured life. Tonight, she wanted something for herself. Something dangerous, something wicked.

The man stood there, looking down at her, assessing her as if trying to reassure himself that it was safe to leave her. With something close to desperation, she grabbed the collar of his suit jacket and pulled him toward her.

One minute, she glimpsed his startled face. The next, she was pressing her mouth to his and wishing he would open it so she could drown herself inside.

Home of Erotic Romance

Sign up for our newsletter and find out about all our romance book releases, eBook sales and promotions, sneak peeks and FREE romance eBooks!

https://totallyentwinedgroup.us7.list-manage.com/subscribe/post

About the Author

A multi-published, award winning, Amazon and USA Today best-selling author, Desiree Holt has produced more than 200 titles and won many awards. She has received an EPIC E-Book Award, the Holt Medallion and many others including Author After Dark's Author of the Year. She has been featured on CBS Sunday Morning and in The Village Voice, The Daily Beast, USA Today, The Wall Street Journal, The London Daily Mail. She lives in Florida with her cats who insist they help her write her books, and is addicted to football.

Desiree loves to hear from readers. You can find her contact information, website details and author profile page at https://www.totallybound.com

CPSIA information can be obtained
at www.ICGtesting.com
Printed in the USA
LVHW091418120319
610364LV00001B/10/P

9 781786 863904